Grant felt gu— —g —
way Kat flinched at his words. A part of him
wanted to step closer and pull her into a
comforting embrace. But he didn't dare until
he could be sure she didn't have anything to
do with her husband's disappearance.

His mouth twisted in something like
amusement. Yeah, imagine how she'd react
if he tried to take her into his arms. It would
probably be like trying to cuddle a feral cat.
Teeth and claws would fly, and he'd bleed.

"Yes," she said, so quietly he scarcely heard
her. "The way people looked at me back
then, I knew what they were thinking." Her
eyes met his. "What you were thinking."

Grant shook his head. "I was doing my job,
staying open-minded. No more, no less."
That was a lie, of course, but she wouldn't
welcome the truth.

"And is that what you're doing now, too?"

His jaw tightened. "Yes."

"But you'll let it go if I ask you to?"

"Yes." After a pause, he added, "For now."

Dear Reader,

I've realized recently how many of my books are really about finding someone who has been missing from our lives. Never knowing what's become of a loved one would be worse, I think, than losing him or her to a tragic accident. You might be haunted even more if you hadn't said goodbye on good terms; if you're gripped by guilt as well as grief.

Bone Deep started from a newspaper article about a woman who has spent years checking with police departments every time human remains were found in hopes they'd be her brother's. But then I got to thinking... What if your loved one didn't stay missing? What if he was returned to you after a long time—piece by piece? I don't know about you, but I'm pretty sure I wouldn't be as gutsy as Kat, the heroine in *Bone Deep*. Of course, it would help if I had a man as sexy and determined and loving as Grant Haller backing me up.

But back to that theme... Funny thing, but my upcoming book is turning out to be about finding that missing person, too. And, hey! I've never lost anyone in my own life. Really.

Happy reading,

Janice Kay Johnson

Bone Deep
Janice Kay Johnson

TORONTO NEW YORK LONDON
AMSTERDAM PARIS SYDNEY HAMBURG
STOCKHOLM ATHENS TOKYO MILAN MADRID
PRAGUE WARSAW BUDAPEST AUCKLAND

Recycling programs
for this product may
not exist in your area.

ISBN-13: 978-0-373-71692-0

BONE DEEP

Copyright © 2011 by Janice Kay Johnson

ABOUT THE AUTHOR

The author of more than sixty books for children and adults, Janice Kay Johnson writes Harlequin Superromance novels about love and family—about the way generations connect and the power our earliest experiences have on us throughout life. Her 2007 novel *Snowbound* won a RITA® Award from Romance Writers of America for Best Contemporary Series Romance. A former librarian, Janice raised two daughters in a small rural town north of Seattle, Washington. She loves to read and is an active volunteer and board member for Purrfect Pals, a no-kill cat shelter.

Books by Janice Kay Johnson

HARLEQUIN SUPERROMANCE
1197—MOMMY SAID GOODBYE
1228—REVELATIONS
1273—WITH CHILD
1332—OPEN SECRET*
1351—LOST CAUSE*
1383—KIDS BY CHRISTMAS*
1405—FIRST COMES BABY
1454—SNOWBOUND
1489—THE MAN BEHIND THE COP
1558—SOMEONE LIKE HER
1602—A MOTHER'S SECRET
1620—MATCH MADE IN COURT
1644—CHARLOTTE'S HOMECOMING†
1650—THROUGH THE SHERIFF'S EYES†
1674—THE BABY AGENDA

HARLEQUIN EVERLASTING LOVE
21—CHRISTMAS PRESENTS AND PAST

SIGNATURE SELECT SAGA
DEAD WRONG

HARLEQUIN ANTHOLOGIES
A MOTHER'S LOVE
 "Daughter of the Bride"

HARLEQUIN SINGLE TITLE
WRONG TURN
 "Missing Molly"

*Lost...But Not Forgotten
†The Russell Twins

For Mom, who reads every word
before anyone else does.
Thank you, Mom,
for loving me, inspiring me...
and helping make my writing better.

CHAPTER ONE

*"THIS YEAR'S SNOHOMISH County Business Owner of
the Year is..."* Behind the podium at the front of
the ballroom, Judith Everest paused long enough
to search out the five nominees in the crowd, her
gaze pausing at each until she reached Kat. Smiling,
she concluded, *"Kathryn Riley of Sauk River Plant
Nursery!"*

The room erupted in applause. Dazed, Kat stumbled to her feet.

Four days later, she still glowed at the memory.
To think that, four years ago, the business had been
close to going under.

Too bad she couldn't actually slow down to savor
the honor the way she'd like. This was spring, for a
plant nursery the equivalent of the pre-Christmas
rush for most retailers. She was going nonstop.

In as close to a break as she could afford, she'd
escaped to one of the greenhouses to pot seedlings.
Now she gently sifted a little potting mix around a
sturdy petunia, then scooped up some compost from
a separate wheelbarrow with her trowel. Even though
she worked without pause, with hundreds of seedlings waiting to be potted, she reveled in both the

silence and the humid warmth. This was as peaceful as it would get for her until July.

And all that publicity about her being honored by the business community, reported in both the *Seattle Times* and the *Herald,* wouldn't hurt business.

She patted the new soil into place, then set the seedling onto a flat and grabbed an empty pot from a stack of them. She dumped two inches of potting mix into the pot, tucked the next seedling in, then scooped up compost to add richness for the roots.

Snohomish County Business Owner of the Year.

Unbelievable. Four years ago, left alone and facing bankruptcy, she'd clung fiercely to dreams. The nursery had been her salvation, and look what she'd done with it even though she knew no one had believed she could handle the business at all.

Smiling, she carefully tilted the trowel to pour the dark compost into the four-inch plastic pot.

Something fell with it. The seedling quivered.

"What on earth…?" she murmured.

Setting down the trowel, Kat stripped off her gloves and pulled the long, ivory-colored rock from the pot.

Wiping the dark, damp compost from it, she realized, *no, not a rock.* Porous, it didn't weigh enough, and widened at each end like a segment of bamboo. She stared down at the thing in her hand, the ball of her stomach knowing what it was before her brain caught up.

A bone. There'd been a bone in her compost.

"Kat?" The voice was loud and close.

She jerked, adrenaline shooting through her,

and lifted her head. Her newest employee, a lanky nineteen-year-old named Jason Hebert, had come all the way into the greenhouse without her noticing, probably calling her name all the way. He looked perplexed.

"Are you okay, Kat? Was I supposed to not interrupt you? I'm sorry. I'll go away…" His gaze dropped to the object in her hand. "Is that a *bone?*"

"It was in the compost." She turned it in her hand. "From some animal, I guess."

He peered more closely. "You sure? It looks like a finger bone." He held out his own hand and waggled his fingers in a 3-D demonstration. "You know, a phalange?"

No, she didn't. Although maybe she should, given that she thought about human remains way more often than the average person.

"I'm taking Anatomy this semester. We saw a real skeleton. That's what this looks like."

If this was a finger bone, it was larger than hers, Kat couldn't help thinking. Longer and thicker. A man's, maybe.

"You know, it's probably dumb," she said, giving a half laugh as if no more than mildly startled by the find, "but I'd better call the police just in case."

"Yeah. Maybe some guy got it sliced off." Jason sounded ghoulishly pleased.

They did operate heavy machinery at the compost facility not two miles away. She didn't remember hearing about anyone losing a finger—especially a finger they never found to reattach—but that did make sense.

Or it was a leg bone from something small, something dog- or cat-sized. It was silly to get alarmed because a community college student who'd once seen a real human skeleton had identified this bone. Still…the unease that made her queasy decided her. If it was a human bone…

Oh, God. Hugh.

With an effort she suppressed the sickening mix of dread and…not hope. She couldn't be feeling hope. Since Jason was still hovering, Kat asked, "What was your question? Can it wait while I make a quick call about this?"

"Huh? Oh, sure. It was just Ms. Lindstrom, about the garden club meeting. But she said something about needing a flowering plum or maybe cherry and went out that way, so she's probably forgotten."

Annika Lindstrom was one of their best customers and the owner of a spectacular garden that was the centerpiece of many a garden tour. She and Kat weren't quite friends, but close enough that she wouldn't be insulted if Kat didn't immediately appear.

"I'll find her when I'm done."

"Oh, and that guy from the *Globe*. He was here, but I think he got a phone call and left."

Mike Hedin was the editor of the local weekly newspaper. She'd been half expecting him to want to talk to her about the award.

"Okay, thanks," she said. Sending Jason back to work, she took the rear door out of the greenhouse, stepping from tropical warmth into the crisp air that still felt like winter.

The temperature in her small office at the back of the main nursery building was somewhere in between. Setting the bone in front of her, she sat at her desk and reached for the phone.

Halfway through dialing, it struck her. How many times had she called police jurisdictions throughout the state to ask about remains found buried in some backyard? What were the odds that she, of all people, had actually found a human bone? God. The local police would probably think she'd gone completely around the bend.

A giggle escaped her throat like a hiccup, and she covered her mouth, swiveling to make sure the door was still closed and nobody had heard her. Sternly, she told herself this wasn't exactly funny, just… ironic.

"Fern Bluff Police Department." She knew the bored sergeant who answered the phone.

"Martin, this is Kat Riley at the nursery. I've found a bone in the compost. It's probably from an animal, but, well, one of my employees is taking an anatomy course at the college and he thinks it looks like a human finger bone." A little ashamed of herself, she thought, *That's it, blame poor Jason.* "So I thought I'd better report it."

"Well, let me get the chief for you."

"That's not necess—"

The quality of the silence told her she was on hold. Kat muttered a word she wouldn't have said in front of a customer. He hadn't even waited for her protest!

But she guessed it made sense for him to call the

chief. Fern Bluff had grown with stunning speed these past several years, since software giant Microsoft had opened a Snohomish County campus on the outskirts of town. The police force had quadrupled in size, as had crime, but even so she suspected Chief Grant Haller was the only member of the force with any real experience with homicide.

Besides…the sergeant knew about Hugh.

Martin came back on a moment later. "The chief says to tell you he'll be out to take a look."

"Fine," she said. "Thank you." She hung up the phone, hating how short of breath she suddenly was, how dismayed. She didn't see Grant Haller often outside chamber of commerce meetings or the like. She'd armored herself against those occasions. But that moment at the banquet last week had shaken her. When her name had been announced, out of the several hundred people present, he was the only one she seemed able to focus on. He'd dipped his head in acknowledgment of her triumph, then given her an odd, wry smile, his eyes warm. Heart drumming, she'd realized he was still interested. She hadn't dreamed, hadn't thought…

But now she had, and now he was on his way here. And she wouldn't be seeing him in the midst of a crowd at a city council meeting, but rather in the close quarters of this office, her sanctuary.

Breathless, she thought, *I'm not ready*. But she had no choice. This wasn't the kind of thing she wanted to talk about in front of half a dozen customers lined up to pay for their flats of early spring bedding plants.

This. Oh, God. She'd almost forgotten. She looked

down at the bone, lying on her desk blotter, bits of dark compost still clinging to it like soil from a grave. Unable to help herself, she laid her hand next to it, comparing the length and thickness to her own finger bones. It could be a man's.

It could be Hugh's.

Kat shuddered and withdrew her hand, curling it into a fist she pressed against her belly. No! How many times had the compost been turned and bagged or loaded into trucks and replaced over at Wallinger's? At least yearly, they must get down to bare ground and start over with yard debris and Christmas trees and fallen branches from the road cleanup crews, grinding it all up, mounding it fifty or more feet high, letting it gently steam as it rotted. No part of those mounds had been there for the nearly four years since Hugh's disappearance.

Anyway, how likely was it that her husband had ended up dead in the compost pile two miles down the road? Without a single bone turning up until now?

She blew out a breath and sat back, the ancient oak office chair squeaking. Thank God for the voice of reason. She'd really worry about herself if she started seeing bits of Hugh everywhere.

I may be obsessed, she thought, *but I'm not crazy. Not yet.*

GRANT WOULD HAVE BEEN GLAD of an excuse to get out of the station and away from the spreadsheets he'd been peering at on his computer, if only the bone had turned up someplace else.

He was both surprised, and not. Every damn thing involving Kat Riley was complicated for him, even though Grant had known for a long time that he should give up any hope that whatever they'd briefly had would go anywhere, whether they were both single or not. Clearly, she wasn't going to let it, not obsessed as she was with the husband who had driven away one day in his rattletrap pickup, supposedly to check out a rhododendron wholesaler up Chuckanut way, never to be heard from again.

Downtown's half a dozen lights all turned red against him, a not uncommon occurrence as they were the old-fashioned kind that were indifferent to the presence of any real cars on the road. Like most other remnants of small-town life, they were slated to be replaced in the next year. He'd once found them annoying, but now felt almost nostalgic.

He was able to speed up once he hit the outskirts. City limits had been generously drawn, and took in a wide swath of river valley and wooded country upriver. The nursery sat on low ground, taking advantage of rich soil deposited by floodwaters, but also at risk when the water rose every couple of years.

Grant pulled his squad car into the parking lot and had to wait for someone to reverse out before he could park. The place was bustling, staff helping customers load bags of peat moss and compost into car trunks and the backs of pickups. He wasn't even out of his car before he spotted a city councilwoman and a school board member. Out of habit and since he was wearing his uniform, he nodded at folks he knew and didn't know as he crossed the lot and entered the nursery, which involved threading a strategic maze of tables bearing brightly colored pansies—even he recognized them—and pots of tulips and daffodils as well as cedar window boxes and tubs. Shrubs, set in big pots here and there, were breaking into bloom and scenting the air.

Was there any chance at all that Hugh Riley's body had been right here at the nursery all these years, missed in the intensive search he and his men had conducted?

If it had been… His jaw tightened. If this bone was her husband's, Kat Riley would have to be the principal suspect in his death.

Yeah, but then why would she have called today to report finding this bone? Why not make it quietly disappear?

Because one of her employees had seen it, Grant remembered. He'd talk. She couldn't dump it.

Damn, he hoped this bone wasn't human.

One of the employees spotted him and when he said he was looking for Kat, called to a skinny teenage boy who had an air of suppressed excitement. Grant would lay money he was the budding forensic anthropologist.

"She said she'd be in her office," the boy told him importantly.

Grant nodded. "Thanks."

In the years since she took over management of the nursery, Kat had made big changes, including the expansion of a small gift area into a spacious indoor shop that included an attached conservatory with tropical plants for the house. He bet she'd done well with Christmas shoppers, since she now stocked the work of a dozen local artisans as well as gardening tools and gadgets, a vast selection of pots and garden statuary, seeds, bulbs and fertilizers.

He had to be directed to the door to her office, which, almost hidden behind a rack of hand tools, said Employees Only. When her husband disappeared, Grant had spent plenty of time out here, but what had been her office then was now part of this expanded gift area.

He lifted his hand to knock, then hesitated. Damn it, why her? He kept thinking that eventually he'd feel only indifference when he saw her, but that hadn't happened yet. The sight of her last week at that banquet, wearing a peach-colored sheath that bared a mile of legs and the top swell of her breasts, had been like a gut punch. He'd almost bent over at the pain.

Kat Riley was tall and lush and vibrant. Some people might have called her thick, glossy hair "brown," but it had a copper gleam in sunlight and some strands as pale as dried cornstalks, others as dark as mahogany. He'd sat directly behind her once at a chamber meeting and, lost in fascination with her hair, missed ninety percent of what was said.

No loss, of course, and thank God no one had asked him a question.

She had great cheekbones, deep blue eyes and a mouth he thought would have gentle curves if she ever let it relax. He wasn't sure her face was entirely symmetrical. The details didn't seem to matter. Some combination of physical characteristics and personality and—hell, who knew?—chemistry made her irresistible to him.

Once, he'd thought she felt the same.

He took a deep breath, rolled his shoulders and knocked.

"Come in," she called.

When he opened the door, it was to find her standing behind her scarred oak behemoth of a desk as if she, too, had braced herself.

She looked at him coolly. "You didn't have to come yourself."

Stung by how obviously she wished he *hadn't* come himself, he only shrugged. "I was arguing with my budget. Any excuse."

She nodded, the movement a little jerky. "This is a waste of your time anyway. But I have a kid working here who's taking Anatomy at the college, and when he saw the bone he was just sure it was human." She rolled her eyes, as though to say, *Of course, I never thought anything that stupid.*

Not surprising she was sensitive about having to make this kind of call. She'd spent the past four years riding every law enforcement department in western Washington about any human remains that turned up, making sure they remembered that her husband had never been found, dead or alive.

He'd been peripherally aware of the bone lying there right in front of her, but now he said, "Well, let's see it," and reached across the desk.

The moment he really looked, Grant knew. Well, crap. He turned the small bone in his hand, seeing the way she stared at it as if it were a black widow spider. Oh, she knew, too, on the same gut level he did.

He didn't tell her how many bones he'd seen. Didn't like to think about the killing field in Bosnia where they'd dug up forty-eight complete skeletons. A few men, mostly women and children. Most of his nightmares involved human skeletons, whole or shattered to fragments.

"I'm no forensic scientist," he said, "but I think your kid's right. It looks human to me, too."

"Oh, no," she whispered, and sank into her chair as if her legs had lost strength. Her unblinking, shocked gaze stayed riveted on the bone in his hand. "How could it be…?"

"I don't know. I'll get it looked at to be sure, then ask some questions." He set it down on the desk and pulled a small spiral notebook from his breast pocket. "Where did you find it?"

He relaxed a little when she explained that it had been in compost she'd shoveled into a wheelbarrow that morning from the piles in back that were regularly replenished by Wallinger's. Grant's men had dug through those heaps of compost, bark and shavings after Hugh's disappearance. No body. So this bone had nothing to do with her. Cruel chance had made her the one to come across it. Hell, most people probably would have thought, *animal bone,* shrugged and tossed it out.

And maybe it was an animal bone.

He had her walk him to the greenhouse where the wheelbarrow sat, and with her permission combed through the dark, damp compost carefully to be sure the rest of the finger wasn't in it.

"Show me which bin you got this batch out of."

Back outside, shrubs in big black pots marched in rows, evergreen separated from deciduous, all carefully labeled so purchasers would know the eventual size, sun and soil needs and time of bloom. Then flowering trees, some already budding, were heeled into ridges of shavings. Half a dozen customers prowled out here on the back forty. He knew several of them, including Pete Timmons, one of his own deputies who happened to be off today. Pete returned his nod, but eyed Kat speculatively. She clearly noticed, because her cheeks flushed.

Grant was most surprised to see George Slagle, who owned the lumberyard and hardware store in town. There'd been talk that George resented Kat's nomination for Business Owner of the Year, considering his revenue was likely two or three times hers. And Grant knew his house had been landscaped by the builder and probably maintained by a yard service. George was no gardener.

Some woman Grant didn't know spotted Kat and called, "Can I ask you something?"

She smiled and held up her hand. "Give me a minute and I'll be right back. George, nice to see you."

George nodded, looking a little unhappy.

She was good, Grant mused. She must be thrumming with tension, but she'd exuded the friendliness and helpfulness that brought return customers.

Behind the last greenhouse, a row of bins, each five or six feet wide and maybe eight feet deep, had been constructed with railroad ties. Lower fronts allowed access. Kat pointed to one, with the compost getting low.

"Go help that woman," he suggested. "I'll dig through this."

She bit her lip, nodded and left him to it.

He should have asked her for gloves, but shrugged, grabbed a shovel leaning against the dark ties and stepped into the bin.

Trying to be systematic, he lifted one shovelful at a time, moving compost from the back to the front. As he poured compost from the shovel, he watched closely.

Nada.

His arms and shoulders ached by the time he was confident he'd examined every damn inch of that pile. Since he'd moved it to the front, he had to climb over it to get out, his shoes sinking into the soft, damp heap.

Damn it, despite a temperature in the high thirties, he was sweating and filthy. He'd better go home and shower before he went back to the station.

Kat appeared as soon as he leaned the shovel against the ties. Seeing the anxiety in her eyes, he didn't make her suffer.

"Nothing. May turn out I'm wrong and it's from an animal. If not…" He shrugged. "Chances are, we'll never know how that one bone ended up in there. I'll go talk to them at Wallinger's, though. They might've had an accident, or know of one at a logging site or with one of the road crews."

Relief leaped into her eyes. "I was thinking

that earlier. It would be easy to stick a hand into a shredder."

He nodded. "That's my best guess. Not something we'd necessarily hear about."

"Yes." She gave a long exhalation as tension left her body. "Okay. You'll take it, then?"

"I'll take it." He already had; he'd slipped it into an evidence bag and then his pocket.

"And you'll let me know?"

"Minute I hear anything."

"Okay." Shyness wasn't usual for her, but she was plainly feeling it. Still, she met his eyes. "Thank you."

So now she was grateful he had come, Grant realized, which meant she'd been more scared than she would want to admit.

"Coming out here's my job."

"You could have sent someone."

"I want to find Hugh as bad as you do."

Seeing the turmoil on her face, he cursed himself immediately for baiting her that way. Their history had no place here, and neither did his longing for something that wasn't going to happen. "That's the only major open case on our books," he explained. Let her think that's all he'd meant.

After a moment, she managed to suppress her reaction and give a jerky nod. "I'll walk you back." Her gaze lowered, seeing his hands. "You popped a blister."

He'd acquired several blisters. The one that was now flattened and seeping burned. "Don't worry. I'll wash it up at home."

"I should have found you some gloves." Kat sounded contrite. "I didn't think."

"Don't worry," he said again. He nodded at the nursery around them. "Business looks good."

"It's been great. Didn't even slow down this winter as much as usual, maybe because of the mild weather."

"I was surprised to see George Slagle here."

"He's planning to put in a row of trees to screen the lumberyard from Legion Park."

Beautification didn't seem George's style, but who was Grant to say?

Changing the subject, he said, "You've turned this nursery into something special."

"Hugh and I made plans years ago."

He didn't believe it. She'd probably made plans, and her husband had nodded agreeably. Hugh Riley had been known for charm but not ambition. Grant had never been one of his fans, although the fact that he coveted Riley's wife might have had something to do with that.

They'd arrived out front. "What smells so good?" Grant asked, at random.

"Daphne mezereum." She pointed out a small shrub with pink flowers just opening and no leaves.

"I wouldn't mind one of those in my yard," he said at random, wanting to hold her in conversation.

Eyebrows raised, she glanced at his blisters. "They can be fragile."

So, okay, she could tell he wasn't any kind of gardener, but, irked by her pitying tone, he said, "I'll take one."

Next thing he knew, she'd deftly turned him over to a brisk, wiry woman who lectured him on planting it right away, digging a hole bigger than the root-ball and filling it with compost and peat moss. Kat herself vanished long before he handed over his debit card and winced at the total, then drove away with bags of both peat moss and compost in his trunk and the shrub on the floor next to him, its sweet smell damn near sickening in the confines of his car.

No wonder business was booming if all the customers were as easy to manipulate as he'd been.

Putting the car into gear, Grant shook his head at his own idiocy. He didn't want to plant anything, but now he'd spent so much money, he had to take care of the shrub as though it were a baby. Planting it would have to wait until Sunday, though. If it could sit safely in a plastic pot at the nursery, it could sit a few more days at his house.

So…home to unload, shower and put on a clean uniform and at least one bandage, then up to the community hospital to find Dr. Arlene Erdahl, the pathologist, and get answers about the bone in his pocket.

He might be ninety percent sure it was human, but he was praying for the other ten percent. Despite what he'd told Kat, he had an uneasy feeling about this. No human bones had turned up in Fern Bluff since he signed on as police chief. Now, assuming one had, it was at the nursery owned by Hugh Riley.

Who so happened to be the only person who had gone missing locally in Grant's tenure.

He never had believed in coincidences.

CHAPTER TWO

"Oh, DEFINITELY HUMAN." Sitting behind her desk, Dr. Arlene Erdahl turned the single bone over in her hand. "Likely male, because not many women have hands the size this suggests." She held out her own as a comparison.

Grant nodded. He'd guessed as much.

Dr. Erdahl was a brisk woman with a stocky build and close-cropped graying hair. Grant put her at about fifty. Murder victims went to the county coroner, not the pathologist at the hospital in Fern Bluff, but she was always willing to answer questions when he called or stopped by. Her husband was an E.R. doc, an interesting pairing. One fought to keep people alive, the other explored them once they were dead.

She took a magnifying glass from a drawer and scrutinized the bone. "No sign of trauma. If this finger was cut off, it happened below the knuckle. Age…? Not juvenile, no obvious osteoarthritis… Twenties to possibly mid-forties, tops. More likely this came from an individual in his twenties or thirties."

He didn't want to push his luck, but asked, "I don't suppose you can tell which finger it is?"

She set down the magnifying glass with a decisive

movement and handed the bone to him. "Gut feeling, not the pinkie. Likely the second or third digit."

"Ah...middle fingers?"

"No," she said patiently. "Your first digit is your thumb. Index finger is second."

"Oh." Grant contemplated his own hand. So. Someone had lost either the finger he pointed with, or the one he used to give people the bird.

Unless, of course, that person was dead, and this bone had become separated only after death.

"Given the lack of tissue, whoever this came from—" she nodded at it "—either lost the finger at least a couple of years ago, or has been dead that long. But I'll tell you what. That bone hasn't been in a compost pile for two years."

Jolted, he asked, "What makes you say that?"

"Look at it. The most interesting thing about it is the lack of any stains or discoloration. It's more likely to have been kept in a drawer than buried unprotected in the ground."

Grant stared at the single finger bone lying in his hand. He should have noticed how pure the ivory color was. "What the hell...?" he muttered.

"I've heard of instances where someone's cut a finger off accidentally and kept it."

"Yeah, so have I. But then how did it end up in the compost at the nursery?"

"A joke?"

His gut tightened. Remembering the shocked expression on Kat Riley's face and the tremble in her voice, he said grimly, "If it's a joke, it's a nasty one."

He thought about that as he walked to his car. A

joke—if you could call it that—meant the bone had been planted there for her to find. But from what she'd said, it hadn't been lying on top of the compost in her wheelbarrow, or on the worktable. In theory, she could have dumped it in a plant pot without ever spotting it. Which would have meant a nice surprise for someone else.

An innocent explanation would violate his rule regarding coincidences, but shit did happen, right?

He took the bone to Wallinger's the way he'd planned. It got in that damn compost somehow, and Grant would be a lot happier to find that had happened here rather than at the nursery.

Fred Wallinger himself came out of the office. A backhoe was turning one steaming pile of compost behind them, while a couple of guys were feeding yard debris into a shredder that crunched up its meal, choked occasionally, and spewed digested bits in a plume.

They had to raise their voices to be heard over the din. A middle-aged, bulky man wearing quilted coveralls over a red buffalo plaid wool shirt, Wallinger shook his head at Grant's question about stray fingers. "Haven't heard of any such thing in a long time." He grunted. "Well, 'cept over at Northland. Guy lost four fingers to a saw. Maybe six months back? Didn't you hear at the time? You could ask over there. Seems they might have reattached 'em, though. Doubt they lost any."

The sawmill, the only one left in Fern Bluff despite the town's logging past, was less than a quarter of a mile down the road.

A logging truck rumbled past as Grant parked and got out, breathing in the tangy smell of sawdust. The piles of logs went on and on and on, a giant's version of pick-up sticks.

He stepped into the office and found the receptionist, a busty blonde, happy to talk to him. She abandoned her headphones and computer and leaned against the short counter, arms crossed on it.

"Oh, that was Wally Camp." Her eyes widened in remembered distress. "It was awful! I guess he just got distracted, and that saw sliced clean through. He's on disability right now." She lowered her voice. "From what I hear, he's not going to be able to come back."

"Were they able to reattach his fingers?"

"Only two of them." She wrinkled her nose. "The other two were practically ground up, is what I heard." Her tone brightened. "But at least he didn't cut off his thumb, too."

"Do you have an address for him?"

She did, and shared it.

Wally lived a good fifteen minutes outside of town, deeper in the Cascade foothills. The two-lane, yellow-striped road wound along the river by new developments of outsize, suburban houses that looked misplaced in this rural setting even if they did sit on five-acre lots, dairy farms held on to by stubborn old-timers and second-growth forest. Not far above, snow clung to the trees, defying the promises of spring at the nursery.

He found the address scrawled in white paint on the side of a dented mailbox and turned onto a rutted dirt driveway that led to a run-down, single-wide mobile home and rusting metal shop or garage. A couple of enormous mixed-breed dogs came howling from a hole beneath the porch to circle his car, froth splattering the window and claws scratching the paint job as he slowed.

Since their tails wagged furiously as they waited for him to get out, Grant took a chance and opened the door. Apparently he was the high point of their day. He petted, told them they were good dogs, and they happily bounded ahead of him across the frozen yard to the trailer.

He'd have thought the pandemonium would bring someone out, but when he knocked a voice yelled over the din of a television, "Leave it on the porch!"

"Mr. Camp?" He knocked again.

After a long pause, the door opened. Grant's first thought was to wonder why this kid of Wally Camp's wasn't in school. He'd seen the traffic near the high school as he went by and knew this wasn't a holiday or in-service day.

But then he saw the hand, dangling at the kid's side as if he no longer knew quite what to do with it.

Wally, a scrawny redhead, had to be older than he looked.

He'd better be, Grant thought with quick pity. *Otherwise, who the hell had let him operate a saw?*

Though it was now late afternoon, Camp looked as if he'd barely rolled out of bed. He hadn't shaved in days, leaving patchy growth on his gaunt jaw.

From the odor wafting out, he hadn't remembered to shower, either.

"I thought you was the UPS guy," Wally said. "Sorry."

"It's okay. Wally Camp?"

"That's me. Dad's not here, if'n it's him you want."

Huh. He had arrested a Camp one time, after a bar brawl, if his memory served him. Robert? Ray? Grant could see the family resemblance. Apparently Wally was used to cops coming calling.

"No, I'm here about your hand," he said.

"My hand?" Wally echoed, forehead creased. Then his voice quickened with hope. "You mean, you think the mill committed some kind of crime?"

Grant shook his head, pity seizing him again. Along with it came uneasiness that made him want to back away. He should have phoned, not come in person. He didn't want to see this kid's misery.

"No. Sorry. We've had a finger bone show up where it shouldn't be, and I understand you're the only person in town who has lost any fingers in the recent past."

Wally Camp gave a bitter laugh. "So I'm famous now, huh? Too bad that don't pay the bills."

Grant regretted having raised the subject at all. He could see that the kid's hands weren't big enough to have bones the size of the one in Grant's pocket.

Obligated to say something, he asked, "You getting physical therapy for that hand?"

Wally gave a dispirited shrug. "Yeah, but what's

the use? Doctors say the nerves ain't growing the way they was supposed to. And it's my right hand."

Grant wanted to be gone so bad, keeping his feet rooted to the porch required a physical effort. "You're getting disability, aren't you?"

"I'm twenty-three. What am I gonna do for the rest of my life?"

What decent answer could he give? It wasn't any help to say, "one of these days that mill's going out of business, too, and then you'd be starting over anyway."

Because at least he would have been starting over with two good hands.

"Did they even try to attach your other two fingers?" he asked.

Wally shook his head. "They was chewed up pretty good. I heard 'em say there wasn't nothin' left to save."

Grant thanked him for his help and left, accompanied to the main road by the two dogs, who cheerfully pretended to be chasing him off their property.

He felt lousy about the visit and kept thinking, *Bet I made his day.*

Since he'd failed to find the owner of a missing finger, his speculation inevitably circled back to Kat.

Grant made himself be analytical. Did Kat know damned well where that bone had come from this morning? Would it have vanished immediately if her employee hadn't unexpectedly walked in on her?

If so, she was an amazing actress. Grant would swear she'd been shaken to her core.

Hugh Riley had disappeared from the face of the earth that morning four years ago, after driving away from the nursery just before 10 a.m. He didn't get pulled over by the highway patrol or cross the Canadian border, he didn't use his ATM card, he didn't show up at any nursery or plant farm, including the one he'd supposedly planned to visit. Not one single witness had reported seeing his truck. He pulled out of the nursery, turned west toward I-5, and apparently crossed into some other dimension.

A single tear had slipped down her cheek that day as her voice sank to a whisper. "He didn't signal. That's one of my pet peeves, when other drivers don't. I watched him go, and was irritated because he didn't signal." Her teeth sank into her lip so hard, Grant had expected to see blood. "And there was hardly any traffic. He didn't even have to wait, so no one else would have seen his blinker anyway. It was just..." A shudder racked her, and she didn't finish.

Just his usual carelessness? Just a slap in my face, because he knew I was watching and liked to piss me off?

It hadn't seemed to matter, what she didn't say.

And still didn't.

Grant's problem was, he hated not being able to figure out where this damn bone had come from. But like it or not, that was police work. Hell, that was life. Not all mysteries got solved.

Live with it, he told himself.

"THE PATHOLOGIST AT THE hospital says the bone is human," Kat told Jason Hebert. "Right now, Chief

Haller is leaning toward thinking someone lost a finger accidentally."

"Whoa." Her young employee curled his hands into fists, as if making sure none of his fingers were hanging out there in danger. "That would really suck, wouldn't it?"

"Yes, it would. Fortunately, we don't use many power tools here. Now, hadn't you better get back to work?" She nodded at the handcart loaded with forsythia that he had been hauling to the front. With their early, cheerful yellow bloom, they sold as fast as they could be put at the entrance to draw attention.

"Oh." He blushed and bent to pick up the handle. "Yeah. Sure. I just wondered. You know."

"I don't blame you," she said, smiling. "It was a weird thing to find."

"Yeah." He grinned. "Too bad it wasn't in the bonemeal!"

She pretended to laugh, and he must have been convinced, because he chuckled as he pulled the heavy cart away.

God. She wished Grant would discover some county road worker had lost a finger accidentally, as he'd suggested when he was out here. She wanted to know where the damn thing had come from, so she could put it out of her mind. She wanted, with a passion that startled her, for that bone *not* to be her husband's.

Kat picked up a sign that had fallen from beside a bare-root rose and thrust it firmly back into the shavings. *And I thought I wanted to find Hugh.*

Had the search become habit more than a real need

to know what had happened to him? Maybe when people disappeared from your life, you should just let them go. Maybe her mother had been right after all, not even trying to find Daddy.

With a sick knot in her belly, Kat knew that if Hugh had been murdered and his bones turned up somewhere in a shallow grave, she'd have to relive the original investigation and the suspicion that had, inevitably, focused on her. Back then, it had made her furious and kept her from sleeping at night, even though she knew she had nothing to do with Hugh's disappearance and nothing to feel guilty about except maybe not having a better marriage. She'd gotten so she hated Grant Haller, constantly showing up with a few more questions.

If that finger bone was Hugh's... But it couldn't be. That made no sense at all. Finding it in her compost was cruel mischance, that's all.

But the queasy feeling stayed in her stomach as she waited to hear from Grant.

George Slagle was back at the nursery today. It seemed he'd wanted her personal advice on what tree to choose.

"That kid who was trying to help me probably knows more about rock bands than he does plants," George said dismissively. "They're going to cost a pretty penny if I put in a whole row of the damn trees, and I don't want something I'm going to have to tear out five years from now."

"That's smart of you," she said. "I do teach all my employees about the plants I sell, but I'm glad to help you, George."

"You have problems yesterday?" His eyes had an avid glint, as if he wanted to be the first one in town to know her troubles. Was he back today to be nosy and not because he wanted to buy those damn trees? "I saw Chief Haller's car out front."

"Nothing big. You know how it is." She shook her head, hoping he'd assume she was talking about shoplifting. "He bought a nice daphne yesterday for his own yard while he was here."

Apparently her suspicions were unfounded, because she was able to turn his attention to ornamental trees. She wasn't surprised to find that he had his mind set on the typical spring flowering cherry or pear; he wasn't interested in foliage or fall color. He liked pink. She steered him to a prunus cultivar with a columnar shape and semidwarf stature that wouldn't outgrow the narrow strip or make passage on the sidewalk impossible, and promised delivery of eight trees as soon as he had the holes dug. He hinted that she might give him a price break, as a fellow chamber of commerce member, and she deftly sidestepped.

After he left, having paid full price but still smiling, Kat's oldest—in both senses of the word—employee murmured, "I think he was flirting with you."

They were having a momentary lull at the cash registers, although through the open double doors Kat could see several customers filling flats with annuals.

Flirting? "Is *that* what he was doing? Oh, ew." She frowned at Joan. "You didn't hear me say that."

"Deaf as a post," her friend and right-hand woman promised with unfailing cheer. "I'm just saying."

"He's got to be sixty!"

Batted eyelashes were incongruous on Joan's round face. "May-December relationships can work, you know."

"Am I May?"

"You just turned thirty-three. You might even be June. And, hey, at sixty, he's not December, either. Maybe October."

"God."

Joan leaned an ample hip against the counter. "Were you planning to tell me about that finger bone?"

"Didn't I…? No," she said, remembering, "you weren't here yesterday. Well, I gather Jason has beaten me to it."

"And it really is human?"

"So Chief Haller says."

"You're okay?" Joan asked, tone tentative. "You're not thinking—?"

"I'm fine. And no, I'm not thinking. Shoot," Kat added. "I never connected with Annika yesterday. I'd better give her a call."

"She was by half an hour ago when you were with George. She left flyers for the garden club meeting." Joan gestured toward the table that held reference books, business cards for other nurseries and informational bulletins.

Kat glanced that way, then said, "I'm going to be in the office for a few minutes, then in greenhouse four if you need me."

Kat hadn't been back in the greenhouse since yesterday, her taste for potting seedlings having evaporated. But the work had to be done, business was slower today, and as long as she was brooding she might as well occupy her hands with something useful.

Once she made it there, she discovered that nobody else had taken up where she'd left off. Kat put on her gloves and resumed work.

It had to be the uneasiness she couldn't shake that made her so conscious of how alone she was in the big greenhouse filled with long, plank tables covered with tiny, potted seedlings and seed trays. The quiet that yesterday had seemed peaceful today felt... thick, as if her ears were stuffed with cotton. She strained to hear anything at all and began to wonder if she shouldn't get her iPod out of her car to keep her company. But she knew she wouldn't use it; with earbuds in, she really wouldn't hear anyone coming. As it was, she remembered her start of near-terror yesterday when Jason had gotten so close without her even hearing the creak of the old door swinging open and closed.

Sitting so that she could see the doors at both ends of the greenhouse, at least peripherally, she reached for another seedling, another empty plastic pot, and kept working.

The rhythm freed her mind to begin circling old doubts, as if on a looped tape.

She knew what people had said, out of her hearing, when Hugh disappeared. They speculated about their marriage and why a man as expansive and outgoing as Hugh had married someone so cold. Maybe running away was the only way he could escape her, they'd said.

Kat hadn't let herself do this in a long time. Mostly, she tried not to think about Hugh, beyond the inchoate desire to know what had happened, where he was. She believed he was dead. He'd had his flaws, but he wasn't the man to leave her in endless purgatory like this, not on purpose.

Only sometimes did her stomach clutch up and she wondered whether their marriage could have been bad enough that he'd wanted to escape and would take any way to do it. He'd always warmed and cooled toward her, going two or three months without turning to her in bed at all, then suddenly becoming the passionate man who'd wooed her in the first place. She couldn't call it moodiness because he stayed cheerful. It even seemed to her that she was still his best friend. Just…not his lover.

That had made her wonder, but she'd never had any proof, and he'd denied it the one time she confronted him and insisted he must be seeing another woman. So she let it drop because mostly she was happy. Not rapturously so, but she had a husband and a home and a business and somewhere to belong. Was any marriage perfect?

No, she would swear Hugh wasn't unhappy enough to run away. He had to be dead, not to have ever come home.

But then, where was his body?

Her trowel, dipped in the potting mix, seemed to grind on something.

Kat froze.

No. It couldn't be. The bone had been in the *compost,* not the potting mix.

Nonetheless, her breath came fast as she adjusted the angle of the trowel and scooped whatever it was up. She turned the trowelful over on top of the garden cart full of potting mix.

Another bone lay, half-exposed. Another…what had they called it? Phalange?

No, no, no.

Heart lurching, she stared at it.

Then, in a frenzy of fear, she set it on the table and began scrabbling in the potting mix with her gloved hands, flinging soil aside, not caring that she scattered it over the floor. Within seconds, she found yet another bone, smaller. Only when she reached the wooden bottom of the cart did she stop, panting, realizing that now she had a whole finger.

The creak of the door brought her spinning around, a gasp escaping her. The heavy door bounced slightly, as it always did when the spring pulled it shut, but nobody was there.

CHAPTER THREE

"PROBABLY SOMEBODY STARTED to open the door and then noticed the Employees Only sign." As close to hysteria as she'd ever been, Kat perched on the old kitchen stool in the greenhouse, her arms wrapped herself. Despite the warmth in here, she shivered. "Or the wind. I noticed how breezy it was earlier."

Grant didn't bother commenting. He didn't need to. The damp breeze couldn't have stirred the heavy door.

Her teeth wanted to chatter. She clamped them shut until she regained control, then said, "Or one of my employees was looking for me but got distracted."

He watched her stolidly. She couldn't tell what he was thinking, which bothered her more than she should have let it.

Today he wasn't in uniform. Wearing jeans, running shoes and a flannel shirt under a quilted vest, he leaned a hip against one of the potting tables, the same small spiral notebook he'd used yesterday flipped open. Kat couldn't see that he was making many notes, even though he held a pencil in one hand.

As always, his presence produced a flood of conflicting emotions in her. As scared as she'd been, his big, powerful body was a comfort, as was his very intensity and intelligence. She felt safe because he was here.

She was also unnerved, physically conscious of him in a way she didn't want to be, reminded that he'd evoked the same, unwelcome response in her when Hugh had still been around.

"You're afraid someone was watching you," Grant said.

This shudder shook her whole body. She tightened her arms around herself, as if she could keep from disintegrating.

"Yes." Her voice came out rusty, shaking. "Or—" and this was the more appalling fear "—someone was in here already and I heard the door when he was slipping out. I'd never have seen him if he was sitting under one of the tables."

"Waiting for you to find the bones."

"Yes."

He'd come the minute she called. Thank God she'd had her cell phone with her. She'd been so terrified, she hated to think what she'd have looked like if anyone had seen her burst out of here. As it was, she'd also called the front desk, and Joan had come tearing in to the greenhouse. She'd stayed protectively at Kat's side, and now glared at Grant as if he were at fault for upsetting Kat.

"We'll find out if an employee started to open the door," he said. "That's easy. If it was a customer...we may never know."

Kat gave a stiff nod.

For the first time, his tone softened. "I think it's

unlikely someone was waiting in here. Think about it. If you'd been a little busier, you might never have come to this greenhouse today at all."

That was logical. More logical than she'd been, in her fear. Of course no one had crouched in here waiting all day. She was letting paranoia get the best of her. Some of the tension leached from her body. "That's true."

"But you told me you were heading back to this greenhouse," Joan said unexpectedly. "Remember? We were out front. Somebody might have heard you. There were several customers in there, and I didn't look to see if anyone was behind us."

Grant's eyes narrowed. "Did you come straight here after you told Ms. Stover your intentions?"

Kat shook her head. "I stopped by my office. It was maybe…ten minutes before I got here."

His gaze, intense to the point of being fierce, pinpointed first Kat and then Joan. "You'll make me a list of anyone you've seen at the nursery today. And a separate one of anyone here yesterday."

"So you think someone was in here?" she whispered.

"Not while you were. But it's pretty clear these bones were planted."

She couldn't help looking at them, lying on the splintery worktable, hard to connect with a real-life human being, and yet…gruesome. She wanted to wipe the bits of compost from the bones. Like yesterday, she was unpleasantly reminded of the dark, dank soil from a grave.

"They might have all been there yesterday."

"They might." His jaw flexed. "I wish like hell I'd poked through this potting mix, too. But I'll tell you what. I'm betting they were added today."

"Why?" Joan asked.

"If this was meant to be one surprise, why not plant all three together? Why separate them this way?"

Kat thought about his point, and didn't like the implications. "To…up the ante." She wished her voice didn't sound so thin.

"And to give you two scares, not just one."

"Does this person…um, have *more* bones?"

He shut his small spiral notebook and shoved it in a breast pocket. "That's the question, isn't it?"

Kat swallowed. "Is there any way to check those bones for DNA?"

"I don't know." When he'd disappeared, the police had taken hair from Hugh's comb, so they'd have it as a reference if needed. "The thing is, even if we can, it often takes months. I can't demand a rush job. This is upsetting for you, but it's not as if we have a serial killer operating here. On the scale of crimes, this is about a one."

Months? she thought, aghast. And then she took in his dismissive *one.* Her spine stiffened. "If those are Hugh's bones, and somebody kept them, then the chances are he was murdered. That's a *one,* in your opinion?"

"Only in terms of urgency."

"Well, I'll tell you what." Mad now, she slid from the stool and faced him with her chin thrust out. "I'm feeling a little urgent here. Whether those are Hugh's bones or not, this feels a lot like a threat to me. I'm taking it seriously, even if you aren't!"

"Oh, I'm taking it seriously." His eyes still glittered with what she suddenly realized was major temper. "Can you sit down and make me those lists right away? In the meantime, I'm going to go talk to anyone who is working today, find out if they were back here and if they saw anyone else nearby. We'll get lists of names from them, too."

With his anger both comforting her and ratcheting up her fear again, Kat nodded. "We'll be at the cash registers."

He went out ahead of them, pausing to examine the door with its rusting, wrought-iron handles, then shook his head as if in frustration. Kat guessed he was thinking of fingerprints, and realizing the pockmarked handle was unlikely to provide a good surface for lifting a print. Besides…how many people had grabbed it? Even on a glossy surface, could one print be lifted from atop thousands?

She and Joan walked to the main nursery building, heads ducked as if that would keep them from getting wet. The earlier mist had become a steady, cold rain, one that wasn't more than five degrees Fahrenheit from turning into snow. *Ah, spring,* Kat thought wryly.

The few customers had evaporated, and who could blame them?

"Ugh," Joan said, when they hurried inside. She, at least, wore a vest. Anticipating the near-tropical warmth in the greenhouse, Kat had left her jean jacket in her office earlier despite the bite to the air outside.

They shook off the rain. Kat grabbed a notebook and they both sat on stools behind the counter. "Let's start with today," she said.

"George Slagle." Joan rolled her eyes.

"He was here today *and* yesterday," Kat said, explaining.

She started two sheets, labeled the top of each Wednesday and Thursday, then wrote George's name on both. "Annika. You said she was in today."

"Right."

"Yesterday, too," Kat said, and wrote her down. "Uh…I waited on Becca Montgomery. Her teenage boy was with her."

"Billy. He's a good kid."

Despite the hair dyed goth-black and the tattoos spreading like a skin fungus on his lower arms. Kat had seen the way he dragged after his mother, every line of his body resisting the necessity of being at a nursery with her. He was probably petrified that one of his buddies would see him. But he hadn't argued when his mom asked him to heft five gallon pots, so maybe he was okay.

"Jason said Mike Hedin came by yesterday," she remembered.

"He was here today, too." Widening, Joan's eyes met hers. "Just after you called. I was ready to sprint back to you, but he stopped me and asked for you. I lied and said you were gone for the day."

Mike Hedin was an odd duck, but he'd been nice to Kat. She detested this, having to suspect everyone.

"Did you see what direction he came from?" she asked.

Joan shook her head. "He just…appeared. You sounded so freaked, I wasn't noticing anything else."

Carefully, Kat wrote *Mike Hedin*.

"Lisa Llewellyn was here today, remember? She bought a bunch of annuals."

Their lists grew. Carol Scammell, a school board member, had bought a Japanese maple to replace a tree in her yard damaged by a February storm. Greg Buckmeier, one of the few male members of the garden club, trolling for the unusual perennials that were a specialty of the nursery. People neither knew.

"I didn't take the receipts to the bank yesterday," Kat admitted. "Which is lucky. I'll look at the checks and credit-card slips. I'll bet I can add more names."

By the time they were done, they had over thirty people listed for Wednesday, eighteen…no, nineteen for today even though business had been slower. And those were only the people either she or Joan had personally waited on or noticed. Kat had had at least two other employees working both days.

Worse yet, the nursery wasn't fully fenced. Somebody on staff would probably spot a customer who parked in the lot and came in the front entrance, but Hazeltine Road ran north-south alongside the nursery, and who'd notice a car parked on the shoulder for a brief time? A dirt lane behind the nursery led to the Schultz farm, once a going concern and now more of a hobby for Will and Martha Schultz, who Kat happened to know were still in Arizona where they wintered.

Oh, yes, it would be all too easy for someone to slip entirely unnoticed onto the nursery grounds, keeping the greenhouses between him and the main grounds of the nursery.

Only…how would someone like that know that she was the one working in greenhouse four? Didn't whoever left those bones almost have to have seen her go in there yesterday morning and then leave her work undone when the nursery got busier?

Confused and frightened, she said, "I'll leave this here for now. We can add to it if we remember anyone else."

Joan nodded. "Is that rain turning to snow, or am I imagining things?"

Kat followed her gaze and grimaced. "Boy, that's great for business."

Even worse, she thought, would be the story coming out of human bones being found here at the nursery. People would be reminded about Hugh's disappearance. The whispers would start again, maybe even worse because everyone would see how well she'd done without him. No, the taint of murder would *not* be good for business.

Which might be the whole point of this, except she couldn't for the life of her imagine who would benefit from hurting her business. She didn't have any real competitors, only a couple of specialty nurseries that benefited, if anything, from the success of hers. For goodness sake, she bought her rhododendrons from Mountain Rhodies and her bearded iris from A Rainbow of Iris, and happily gave both a plug in case a customer wanted more variety than she could offer. And she couldn't imagine the garden manager at Lowe's Home and Garden Center sabotaging her.

No, dumb idea. Something else was behind this grisly plot. Someone playing a mean game, and Kat was pretty sure she was meant to lose.

She sucked in a ragged breath. Right now, what she wanted most was to know whether those bones were Hugh's.

HE HAD NO OBJECTIVITY whatsoever where Kat Riley was concerned, which made him a dangerous man to be conducting this investigation. Trouble was, he didn't trust anyone else to conduct it, either.

Grant dug out the binder that held police reports and notes on Hugh's disappearance, in case he'd forgotten anything. He hadn't. But now, reading again the original missing persons report, he had to ask himself: *Could she have made all that up?*

Sure she could have. They had only Kat's word for it that Hugh was at the nursery at all the morning of his disappearance, that he'd intended to visit the rhododendron wholesaler, that he'd driven away. Only one other person had been scheduled to work that day—the nursery had been considerably smaller four years ago—and he hadn't yet arrived at work. Only Kat had seen her husband off.

Her story might all be so much fiction.

Grant kept coming back to the problem of where the bones had been to stay so clean. If she had her husband's body stashed…where? In an outbuilding the police had somehow missed? Then how did that bone end up in her wheelbarrow? And why?

Just for size, he tried on the concept that she had killed Hugh in a fit of rage, say, because she'd discovered his latest affair. Okay, then why were bones appearing now? Grant would swear she was genuinely rattled. Did someone else know she'd killed him? Was it possible she was resisting blackmail, and these bones were a form of pressure on her to pay? Someone might be saying, *I know what you did. I know where the body is.*

He wanted to believe in her. He'd always wanted to, since the first time he met her and had been stunned speechless. Police Chief for less than three months, he was being introduced at a city council meeting when he saw Kat in the audience. He'd never thought, *She's the most beautiful woman I've ever seen,* because she wasn't. Rachel, his wife, was conventionally prettier. But Kat had something. Some magic that had captured him from that moment.

He'd felt sick when he found out she was married, not letting himself think about the fact that he was married, too. That he'd moved out to Washington State to please Rachel, whose family was in Seattle.

What he had to face now was that he didn't really know Kat. She was an intensely private woman who had held herself together better than he would have expected when her husband vanished. At the time, he'd told himself she knew or at least guessed that Hugh was running around on her, and, while perplexed and shocked, wasn't exactly grieving.

But he'd been wrong. She hadn't let go of her cheating husband's memory for one minute, not in the almost four years. She clung to it with a fervor that bordered on obsession. She must pore over the damn newspaper every single morning looking for snippets about human remains found down in the Auburn Valley or up toward Blaine. Dissatisfied with police performance, she'd hired a private detective to find her husband and spent God knows how much before the investigator confessed to having found exactly nothing.

Had it all been more elaborate fiction, embroidery intended to convince police and townsfolk alike that she truly was the baffled, grieving wife? Or—damn it—was it possible she'd never known that Hugh screwed around on her? Maybe she'd genuinely loved the guy, and the flicker of attraction she'd felt for Grant had been one of those things, unimportant except as a source of shame for her.

His pride alone made that an unwelcome thought. Grant was thirty-seven years old, and had never in his life felt anything like this for another woman, not even the one he'd married. It was bad enough that Kat clung to the belief she was still a married woman, but he hated like hell to think she didn't feel anything special for him at all.

But he knew it was possible. She might be uncomfortable with him only because he'd kissed her once, because she'd responded. Or, even more likely, because he'd had to consider her a suspect in Hugh's disappearance.

Just as he had to now.

Brooding, he faced the fact that there was a limit to how much time he could give to this. No crime had actually been committed; it all might still turn out to be nothing but somebody's nasty idea of a joke. It wasn't impossible to acquire bones. He'd heard that there were still whispers about Kat and her missing husband, about how much more successful the nursery had become without him. She kept to herself, too, which meant she wasn't universally liked. And she'd gotten a lot of attention with that award. Could it have triggered enough temper that someone had decided to give her a scare?

Man, he wished that explanation would turn out to hold water. It was unpleasant as hell; finding out you were so disliked would be a shock—but not near as big a shock as some of the alternatives.

He made another trip out to the nursery, knowing it would be useless. He was right. None of the staff admitted to having been out to the greenhouse in which Kat had been working. Presumably it was a customer who'd tried the door yesterday, maybe belatedly noticed the Employees Only sign. Or she was right, and the person who'd put the bones in the potting mix had stayed to see her reaction…or had come close to being caught in the act and had hidden beneath one of the long plank tables, waiting for a chance to slip unseen out of the greenhouse.

Grant found Kat out front of the main building, rearranging a display of spring blooming shrubs designed to trap the unwary into buying something they hadn't intended, like the sweet-smelling whatever-the-hell-it-was-called that was sitting in his driveway at home waiting to be planted. As he watched, she hefted the five- and ten-gallon pots with ease, despite her slender frame. She was filling holes, he realized, replacing plants that had sold.

He stepped forward, and when she saw him apprehension immediately deepened the color of Kat's blue eyes.

"Are you leaving?"

"Nothing else I can do out here. I could talk to the customers you know were at the nursery both days, but if I do it will start a storm of gossip."

Yesterday's snow had been a mere skiff, but the temperature hadn't risen since much above freezing. Today Kat wore faded jeans and a sacky sweatshirt as well as work gloves, not enough to maintain her body heat unless she kept moving. Even so, Grant was pretty sure her shudder was just that, not a shiver from the cold even though she also wrapped her arms around herself as she'd done yesterday when she was scared.

"The fact that you've been out here three days in a row already has people giving me funny looks."

"Tell me what you want," he said. "Do I push it now, and the hell with gossip? Or do we wait for the other shoe to drop?"

"It will, won't it?" She hugged herself tighter.

"I'd say so. Unless someone just wanted to give you a little scare."

She gave him a look. *"Little?"*

"It could get worse."

He felt guilty immediately, seeing the way she flinched. A part of him wanted to step closer and pull her into a comforting embrace. But he didn't dare until he could be sure she didn't have anything to do with her husband's disappearance.

His mouth twisted in something like amusement. Yeah, just imagine how she'd react if he tried to take her into his arms. The result would probably be something like trying to cuddle a feral cat. Teeth and claws would fly, and he'd bleed.

"Yes," she said, so quietly he scarcely heard her. "The way people looked at me back then, I knew what they were thinking." Her eyes met his. "What you were thinking."

Grant shook his head. "I was doing my job, staying open-minded. No more, no less." That was a lie, of course, but she wouldn't welcome the truth.

"And is that what you're doing now, too?"

His jaw tightened. "Yes."

"But you'll let it go if I ask you to?"

"Yes." After a pause, he added, "For now."

After a moment Kat nodded. "Let's wait and see what happens."

"Have you been working in any of the greenhouses?"

"No." He saw the helplessness on her face and how much she hated feeling it. "Every time I dip a trowel into potting mix or compost, I'm going to expect—" She didn't have to tell him what she expected. Her eyes searched his. "You don't think he could be alive, do you?"

Surprised, Grant rocked back on his heels. "Do you mean, *he's* the one doing this?"

"I had a dream last night." More softly, she corrected herself. "A nightmare. Hugh was reaching for me, only he was missing a finger."

"I didn't know your husband well. You did. Was he capable of coming back and doing something like this just to get at you?" He'd spoken mildly, but he'd tensed at her question.

"No." Her voice became stronger, more definite. Some of the rigidity left her body. "No. Of course not. Hugh was a nice man. He'd be horrified to think an idea like that had ever crossed my mind. It was just a nightmare." She sighed. "Not Hugh, but *somebody* wants to see me upset."

"Kat."

Along with the sound of her name, footsteps crunched on the gravel behind Grant, and he turned to see the editor of the weekly newspaper coming toward them. Mike Hedin was thin and intense. He'd been a reporter at the *Seattle P-I* before getting caught in a round of layoffs that preceded the eventual demise of the city's second major newspaper. The Fern Bluff weekly, Grant couldn't help thinking, had to be one hell of a comedown. Hedin would never get a Pulitzer nomination from here.

"Chief Haller." His gaze darted between them. "I'm glad I caught you. I picked up the list of this week's police calls, and the nursery isn't on it."

Grant had made damn sure it wasn't. Kat's mystery was not going to appear in the newspaper, not if Grant could prevent it.

"No, it isn't," he said. "You're out here on a cold day." And wasn't it interesting that he, too, had visited the nursery three days in a row.

Kat had gone very still, a small creature hoping to go unnoticed.

Hedin flushed. He was prematurely balding, and the red swept up over his bare pate. "Yes, well, I was hoping to interview Kat about the award. Just a follow-up. What strategies she thinks have increased business, any changes she envisions making this year, that kind of thing."

Well, hell, Grant thought in stunned realization; Hedin had a thing for Kat. Face facts: he and Mike Hedin probably weren't alone. No, she wasn't beautiful, not exactly, but she was sexy, even on the days when she wore shapeless overalls or, like today, a man's sweatshirt with the sleeves rolled up four or five times. And, while she was very good at being friendly, she also had that touch-me-not air that could seem like a challenge.

His eyes narrowed. The sweatshirt was Hugh's. He'd be willing to bet on it. She still wore her husband's clothes.

Question was, why? Because they were there, and comfortable? Or as another way to hold on to his memory?

He was suddenly, deeply offended by the sight of that faded blue sweatshirt long enough to hang halfway down her thighs. Hugh Riley hadn't deserved her devotion.

Although he *had* left behind a house in town and the nursery out here on the flood plain. Kat no longer had a cheating husband, but she hadn't lost her home or her livelihood along with the husband.

She had motivation to have killed him, no question. But, damn, Grant did *not* want to believe she had it in her.

"I'd better run," he said, hoping his disturbing thoughts didn't show on his face.

She looked briefly dismayed, or maybe that was in his imagination. Then her mouth curved into a smile, presumably because Mike still waited, hopeful for her attention. "Thanks for coming." She bent to reach for a pot on a flatbed cart, but instead straightened. "Oh. Did you get that daphne in the ground?"

That was what the shrub was called. *Daphne.* "It'll have to wait until Sunday."

"If it gets too cold before then, you might want to stick it in the garage. They can be delicate before they're established."

So she'd said. Or maybe it was the other nursery worker who'd told him that, he didn't remember. Grant was beginning to see the damn plant as a challenge all its own, as if Kat and her employee both doubted his ability to make the sweet-smelling shrub happy.

"I'll be careful," he promised, although how you could be careful when you stuck a bush in the ground, he didn't know. As far as he was concerned, things he planted either grew or they didn't. If they didn't, something else would. But this daphne he'd coddle with infant formula if he had to. If it died, he wouldn't admit it. He'd go buy an identical one somewhere else and plant *it*.

As if, he thought bleakly, getting in his car, there was any chance at all that Kat Riley would ever stroll in his yard wondering where that shrub he'd bought at her nursery was.

There was one upside to the appearance of those bones. If it turned out Hugh really had been dead all these years and Kat accepted that she was a widow and not a wife… Well, then, things might be different.

Assuming, of course, that she hadn't killed him and already knew full well she was a widow.

CHAPTER FOUR

"You know all about her husband, right?"

Kat froze where she was, with the corner of a toolshed between her and the speaker. She knew the voice, and she knew who Melinda Simmons was talking about.

"Well, sure." That was Jason Hebert, sounding puzzled. "I mean, someone told me he, like, disappeared."

"Lots of people still think Kat killed him."

Kat closed her eyes. Melinda had worked for her for two years now. Kat had given her ten rosebushes when Melinda got married and she and her new husband bought a house that hadn't yet been landscaped. They weren't friends, Kat hadn't kidded herself about that, but she'd thought Melinda liked her job and liked Kat.

Guess not, Kat realized. There was too much malice in that voice to allow her even to pretend that Melinda was only idly gossiping.

"Do *you?*" Jason asked.

"I'm not saying that." Melinda must have heard his surprise and maybe indignation, because she was cautious enough to backpedal. "Just that plenty of people do. Like Ron Barrett. You know, the assistant city manager. He won't buy from Kat. Bobby says he heard Mr. Barrett say the plants here were fertilized with blood."

"Couldn't he get in trouble for saying that, when he doesn't have any proof?" Jason's father was an attorney.

"It's not like he announced it in front of a city council meeting," Melinda snapped. "Bobby's dad and Mr. Barrett are friends. It was at a barbecue at my parents-in-law's. When Mr. Barrett heard I work here."

"Well, I don't believe it," Jason declared stoutly. "I like Kat. And I saw her face when she found that bone."

His voice had receded. They were walking away. Melinda said something back, but Kat couldn't make it out. She was glad.

She heard herself panting. *God,* she thought. Knowing people were talking was one thing, hearing it was another. Especially from someone she'd liked. What had she ever done to Melinda to deserve that vicious tone?

It was all she could do not to walk after them right now, take Melinda into her office and let her go. But…what if other employees thought the same? Could she fire all of them?

Except Jason. Bless him.

Ron Barrett. She'd known vaguely that he had never shopped here at the nursery, but Kat had seen his house and yard and knew he wasn't really a gardener, so she hadn't thought much of it. She'd only met him a couple of times. Why was he convinced she was a murderer?

Of course, there'd been talk. It was natural, when a man disappeared. Spouses were the first suspects for a reason. But nobody even knew for sure that Hugh was dead. *She* hadn't believed it, not at first. And yes, she'd been left the house and business Hugh had owned before their marriage, but the house had had—and still did have—a hefty mortgage and the nursery had barely made a profit. Kat doubted she could have sold it then. Hugh had run up large credit-card bills. The equity in the house wouldn't have done more than give her a down payment on one somewhere else, if that, once she paid off those credit cards. Hugh hadn't had any life insurance—that required more planning for the future than he could ever be stirred to do. He hadn't left her rich, or even semi-well off. What he *had* left her was the seeds of a business she'd nurtured into what it was now.

She'd done it, and on her own. Anger rose in Kat, choking her. Why would people who didn't even know her well assume the worst about her? She didn't understand.

Carrying the rake in one gloved hand, she strode out from behind the shed. Jason was no longer in sight, but Melinda was talking to a couple over by the lilacs. Her expression was earnest as she gestured at one in a five-gallon pot.

Firing her would only make of her a worse enemy. Gritting her teeth, Kat turned away. Raking up scattered shavings suited her mood just fine. She needed the physical exertion, the chance to sweat.

There were other, more important things she ought to be doing, but she still hadn't worked up the nerve to dip another trowel into a wheelbarrow of potting soil or compost.

She'd had a week now without a visit from Grant Haller. Almost seven full days that felt like the sickly quiet before a tornado back in Kansas, where she'd grown up. That week, for the first time ever, Kat had dreaded opening the nursery, talking to customers who'd likely heard the whispers. She'd found herself looking at every single person differently than she had before. Wondering. It wasn't pleasant, to find herself speculating about who might have planted those bones as a joke…or worse. About who knew exactly what had happened to Hugh and had kept his remains for some unimaginably horrific reason.

But she kept stumbling over the fact that she would have sworn everyone liked Hugh. He wasn't perfect; she'd gotten so frustrated with him sometimes *she* wanted to bash him, although not lethally. His refusal to listen to ideas for changes at the nursery that might have required a little more effort on his part, or a modest outlay of money, had made her crazy. He liked plants, he liked people, but he had no business sense at all. And no ambition. He didn't *care* if they made more money. He didn't care if Sauk River Plant Nursery drew gardeners from beyond their small community. If she got mad when he blew off some suggestion of hers, he'd look at her in bemusement and wander away.

"Honey, bigger isn't always better," was one of his favorite lines.

No. It wasn't. But *better* was better. It undoubtedly said something about her, that she couldn't bear mediocrity, but Kat craved the success Hugh couldn't be bothered to strive for. She even knew why. She'd been eight years old when her mother left her at a neighbor's house and never came back. She wasn't abused in the succession of foster homes that followed, but she wasn't loved, either. She'd sometimes felt like a ghost. Foster parents and the other foster kids in each of the homes had known she was there, but, as though she were semitransparent, they never saw her, not really.

School was different, though. Teachers noticed when she excelled. And later, when she held after-school and summer jobs, employers noticed. If she did an assignment or a job right, better than right, they saw her and they smiled. Once she married Hugh, Kat threw herself heart and soul into the nursery business. There might be times he seemed to forget they were married, but if she could become indispensable at the nursery, she would matter.

Only, she hadn't mattered very much, or he wouldn't have left her.

It had bothered her terribly back then that she'd almost hoped he was dead, so she could believe he hadn't abandoned her, not on purpose.

She worked until her muscles ached, until strands of hair stuck to her sweat-dampened face, until she felt a blister forming even though her hands were calloused and she wore heavy gloves.

The same thoughts circled maddeningly in her head. Why? Why kill Hugh, kind and disinclined to offend anyone? But if he'd died accidentally and someone had found his body… Why keep silent? Why taunt Kat now with bones?

None of it made any sense.

She saw Joan coming, stomping her way along the rows in her sturdy boots.

"Enough already," Kat's friend snapped. "What are you doing, trying to make it clean enough for somebody to eat off the ground?"

Kat glanced around. The shavings mounded in rows now had ruler-sharp edges. There were a few perfect circles protecting the roots of specimen trees. Not a wood chip was left on hard-packed paths. She had the sudden, fanciful thought that she was looking at one of the mysterious designs known as crop circles. Her own motivation in caring so fiercely that the nursery grounds be utterly pristine would be as unknowable to someone else as those crop circles were to the bewildered farmers who found them in their cornfields.

There was so much she couldn't control, but the nursery was hers now. She could shape it to a vision only she saw.

She let out a shuddery breath. "I guess I'm done, anyway."

"What set you off?" Joan asked.

"Gossip. Nasty gossip."

Joan's eyes narrowed. "Anyone I know?"

"Yes. And no, I won't tell you who. Not until I decide what to do about it." She turned and walked to the shed, her friend behind her. After hanging the rake on its hook, she said, "I guess I'm naive, but I didn't realize there was still so much talk."

"Things are changing with all the new people in town. But for the old guard…well, there hasn't been that much to talk about. Hugh's disappearance was too juicy to let go."

"Does everybody assume I killed him?" Kat hated the helplessness that underlay her rage, but couldn't entirely quell it.

Joan reached out and gripped her hand. Her expression was both kind and worried. "You know better than that."

"I'm not sure I do anymore." Kat shook herself. "Don't listen to me. I'm in a mood. It's like seeing the flash of lightning and now waiting for the boom of thunder."

"But it's been a week."

"Think how much fun it is to draw out the suspense."

A sound escaped Joan. "Is that what you think?"

"I don't know what to think!"

"Has Chief Haller—"

"I haven't heard from him. Unless something else happens, I probably won't."

"Isn't he talking to the people on our lists?"

Kat shook her head. "We agreed that wouldn't accomplish anything but cause more talk and damage business. It's not like someone was going to admit to planting those bones." She snorted. "Planted. Get it? A pun?"

"Very funny." Joan wasn't amused. "But what if we never find out who did it?"

"Then…" Kat found herself voiceless for a long moment as she tried to imagine this week replaying over and over and over again, the tension stretching thin but never disappearing entirely. "Then," she whispered, "I live with it." She knew she could; after all, she'd had plenty of practice after Hugh's disappearance.

"Ms. Riley?" It was another of her employees, a beefy young man named Chad Harris who wasn't awfully bright but who could lift anything and worked uncomplainingly from the minute he arrived in the morning. "I've got those rhododendrons you ordered. Where shall I put them?"

"Excuse me," she said to Joan, and went with Chad.

The day didn't improve, either, because this was the every-other-week Thursday when she had to do payroll. There was no putting it off. Friday was payday, and everyone expected their checks. She'd added a time clock a couple of years ago, which should have made calculating hours a breeze but didn't. Employees forgot to clock in, or clock out. Sometimes they clocked in and out for lunch, sometimes they didn't. Now she had to figure pay down to the minutes they worked, not just the hours. The whole thing was a giant headache.

Kat reluctantly collected the time cards from the small employee room that had space for a bank of metal lockers salvaged from the old middle school, a microwave on a cart, a dorm room-size refrigerator and a plastic table with chairs that allowed people to sit to eat lunch. Then, after signaling to Joan, she closeted herself in her office.

It took her an hour and a half with paper, pen and calculator to figure out how much to write the checks for. After swearing for about the tenth time, she thought as she did every other week about how maybe it was time to consider computerizing. How hard could it be to learn QuickBooks or some similar program? Let *it* do the calculating, and she could even print the checks instead of writing them out by hand. Or maybe she was getting to the point where she could afford a part-time bookkeeper, although she didn't really have office space to spare.

She opened the left hand drawer in her ancient desk where she kept the checkbook and was reaching in with barely a glance when her brain caught up with what her eyes were telling her.

A skeletal hand lay there. Not just a bone, or even a couple, or a jumble. An entire hand, laid out as carefully as her paths on the nursery grounds. A few of the ivory bones, she saw with horror, were strung together with dried gristle.

And—oh God—the hand wore a man's plain gold wedding ring.

"YOU CALLED IN TO SAY you were taking a break at 10:32." Grant glowered at one of the two young officers standing stiffly in front of his desk. "You, Erickson, never called in at all."

Blond and skinny, the kid had an enormous Adam's apple. It bobbed a couple of times. "I guess I forgot. Sir."

Grant transferred his gaze to Dennis Porter. "I drove past the Starbucks at 11:18. There were then two patrol cars parked out in front. Your break had extended to forty-six minutes. We had only three officers patrolling this morning." He let his voice rise. "Two of you were sitting on your asses sipping cappuccinos for damn near an hour this morning."

Erickson was stupid enough to say, "Sir, I wasn't there that long. I was only—"

Porter gave him a dirty look before turning his flushed face forward again.

"At least dispatch knew where Porter was. You, now—" The cell phone at his waist vibrated. Grant looked down and saw a number that he'd programmed in, just in case.

Shit.

"I have to take this call," he said. "Consider yourselves warned. Now get out of here."

They scuttled so fast, they had to wrestle briefly to decide who was getting out the door first. Grant swung away to look out the window at the parking lot.

"Haller."

"Grant, this is Kat. Um, Kat Riley, from the nursery."

"I know who you are."

"I have more bones." She sounded eerily calm, which meant she was scared to death.

"Where this time?"

"My desk drawer." She paused. "It's a whole hand this time. And…and I think it's wearing Hugh's wedding ring."

"Oh, damn," he said, his eyes closing briefly. "Kat...you haven't touched anything, have you?"

"No." There was a tremor in her voice now. "I can't think of anything I less want to do than touch those."

"Okay. Stay where you are. Don't tell anyone else. I'm on my way."

"Thank you," she whispered.

He didn't run any of the red lights downtown, but it was a close call. He sure as hell wanted to. He kept picturing her sitting behind that desk in her dim little hole of an office, staring fixedly at the skeletal remains of her dead husband's hand. God almighty.

We still don't know that these bones are Hugh Riley's.

The hell they didn't, he thought. He'd reached a point where he'd be willing to bet a year's pay that Kat's husband was being returned to her piece by piece. Nothing else made sense.

Was she being blackmailed? Was that what this was about? If someone had retrieved Hugh from wherever she'd stashed him—say, in a storage locker—this was a dandy way to scare her into paying up, and continuing to pay.

Except, she clearly wasn't. And that begged the question of why she was calling him every time a bone appeared.

Thwarted by the last traffic light on the main street, he drummed his fingers on the steering wheel and stared, willing it to turn green. As if to piss him off, it stayed red for an eternity.

When he finally got there, the parking lot in front

of the nursery was almost empty. They were only an hour from closing, he realized, and rain clouds darkened the sky although they hadn't opened up yet. It had been the wettest damned spring so far that he could remember since he moved to the Northwest. It was a good thing no one was around to notice his fourth visit in not much over a week.

He entered the main nursery building, greeted the woman behind the counter—Joan Stover—and went directly to Kat's office. When he knocked, she called, "Come in."

"You should have locked," he said brusquely as he entered. "And asked who I was before you invited me in."

Kat wasn't behind her desk. She stood in the corner, almost pressed against the wall, as if she'd been trying to get as far from her discovery as she could while staying in the office. Her face was skim milk pale. He'd noticed before that she didn't tan well, even working outside year-round as she did. She was more likely to have a constantly peeling nose during the summer. Her pallor today, though, had more to do with her shock than it did with naturally pale skin.

"I'm sorry," Grant said more gently. "I shouldn't yell at you."

"No, you shouldn't. Nobody's tried to attack me. It's ridiculous to think—" She swallowed. Remembering, he suspected, the heavy door to the greenhouse bouncing on its hinges after she discovered the second bone.

"You don't think this is an attack?" He nodded to her desk.

She shuddered and stayed where she was, her gaze on the desk rather than him.

He circled it and saw the drawer half-open, as she must have left it. And, damn, all the bones in a hand laid out. Or, he amended, enough of the bones to make an effective tableau. A human hand had twenty-seven bones, some tiny, and he wouldn't swear there were that many here. Grant leaned closer.

"I'm going to get some pictures," he said, opening the case of the camera he'd carried in. "We can try for fingerprints on the drawer handle—"

"Why bother?" Kat said dully. "Do you really think whoever did this is that dumb?"

"Criminals can be remarkably stupid." He began snapping pictures. "That's why most of them get caught. Haven't you read about bank robbers who use one of their own deposit slips to write the holdup note on?"

She was staring fixedly at the contents of the drawer and didn't respond.

God, he hated seeing her like this. Once again he did battle with the desire to take her in his arms and promise to keep her safe. He'd be an idiot not to realize that this didn't look good for her. Someone was tormenting her, and there was a reason. He couldn't think of a logical one if Kat had nothing to do with her husband's disappearance.

When he had enough photos to be satisfied, he pulled on thin latex gloves and gingerly edged the proximal phalange apart from the metacarpal on the ring finger—yes, he'd done his research on human bones since the first one had appeared in the compost—and picked up the simple gold band.

Inside, in delicate script, was incised *Hugh and Kathryn* and a date that he presumed was their wedding day.

"You saw the inscription?"

She nodded jerkily. "Just a bit of it. Kath. But that was enough. What were the odds it really said *Kathleen,* or *Katherine,* or—" Another shudder silenced her.

"Not good," he admitted, his jaw tensing. "I'm going to need something stiff to move the bones onto, then I'll get a fingerprint technician in here."

"I'm sure I have some cardboard somewhere." She looked around vaguely, as if an appropriate piece would materialize. Then seemed to pull herself together. "A plant flat. We have piles of them."

"That'll do," he agreed.

He let her go and used the time until she returned with the shallow-rimmed cardboard box to call for a fingerprint technician. Then he said, "Kat, I need to ask you some questions."

She waited, having stepped back until she'd bumped into a bookcase stuffed full of horticultural books and what looked like plant and tool catalogs. Her eyes were huge, the usual rich blue as dark as ocean waters scarcely touched by the sun.

"When did you last open this drawer?"

"Days," she said. "Let me think. I don't keep much in there but the checkbook. I don't remember. If you want to look in it, you can see when I wrote the last check."

"All right. Let me get the bones out first."

She stayed by the door while he carefully shifted the entire assemblage onto the flat, trying not to separate bones that were still linked by cartilage or whatever the hell the gristle was. It might tell Arlene Erdahl something. Then he nudged open the checkbook, avoiding the flat surface of the cover in case their suspect had been careless enough to pick it up when moving it out of the way, and riffled the carbon copies until he reached the last one. It was made out to Northwest Wholesale Perennials and was dated four days before. Sunday?

Kat frowned. "That delivery came Monday. We were closed on Sunday. I guess I got the date wrong. So three days ago."

"That's going to make it a lot harder to pinpoint when someone could have put this in here."

"Yes." Her teeth worried her lip. "To think it was lying here for *days*."

"Or was left here five minutes before you walked in the office."

"Oh, God," she said again. "I was working outside most of the day. I came in here a couple of hours ago to do payroll." The calculator, pile of time cards and notepaper with scribbled calculations all told of her labor. "I was ready to write the checks."

"You still have to. Do you have another book of them? I'd like to fingerprint this one."

"Yes. I can do that. This is…a nightmare. Oh, Hugh." Softer now, seeming to ache, her voice told

Grant that the reality of her husband's death was crashing down on her.

Yes, goddamn it, he's dead. At the same time as a part of him rejoiced, pity tore at Grant. Had she really believed Hugh lived, or was it only difficult to mourn without having seen the corpse, his face empty of life?

Or was she an Oscar-worthy actress?

"You're losing weight," he said, studying her.

She flushed and wrapped her arms around herself. She'd peeled off whatever sweatshirt or jacket she must have worn earlier, and had on only a thin, crew-necked T-shirt over jeans that, unlike her more usual overalls, were only a little loose. The unfamiliar gauntness was in her face, and her upper arms were too skinny, stick thin. He could see the sharp outline of her collarbone through the knit fabric. Damn it, had she quit eating the minute she found that first bone?

Purplish bruises beneath her eyes suggested she wasn't sleeping, either. She was being haunted, although whether by guilt or innocent grief, Grant couldn't yet guess.

He wanted her to be innocent more than he'd ever wanted anything in his life, except her. God help him.

"I've been thinking and thinking," she said. "Why would anyone want to kill Hugh? He was nice to everyone. Do you know, he wouldn't even send bad checks to collections? He just, um, avoided unpleasantness rather than ever confronting it. I never saw anybody mad at him." But her gaze slid away from

Grant's at the end, as if she'd realized suddenly that she was lying.

"What about you?" he asked softly. "You lived with him. Did you ever get mad at him?"

Her eyes met his again, and he felt drenched in the resurgence of color. "Yes! Yes, he made me mad. Is that what you want me to say?"

"Damn straight." He heard the harshness in his voice. "Everyone knew the son of a bitch cheated on you. You should have been mad then, and you should still be mad."

She blanched, and he hadn't thought her skin could get any paler. She seemed to shrink, too, and he knew suddenly that he was the son of a bitch, as much or more than Hugh Riley. Oh, hell. She *hadn't* known. Until he'd told her, bluntly and cruelly.

"What?" she whispered.

"I'm sorry. So sorry, Kat. Don't listen to me." He came around the desk toward her, and she flinched even more from him. Grant stopped, hating his sense of helplessness.

She looked at him. "Is it true?"

He hesitated. "Did I ever see him with another woman? No. I was told it was common knowledge."

"Oh, Lord." She seemed not to be breathing. "That's why…"

"Why what?"

"Everyone thought I must have killed him." Kat focused on him. "Why you suspected me."

"I would have been obligated to take a hard look at you in any case."

"What about the other women, if there really were any?"

"You don't believe it?"

She was silent, her gaze inward. It was a long time before she said, "Maybe. I...wondered."

"Did you ever ask him?"

"Once." Her mouth twisted into a sad excuse for a smile. "It seemed like the kind of thing there's no going back from. You know? If he was faithful to me, he'd feel betrayed that I suspected him. Trust goes both ways, and I think it must be hard to regain once it's lost."

Grant nodded. He suspected he'd lost her trust when he kissed her that night four years ago—kissed her although he was married and knew damn well she was, too. She must have thought he wanted to have an affair with her, both of them cheating on their respective spouses. He doubted she'd ever believe he wouldn't have taken it that far, that he'd acted on an irresistible impulse that had shocked him as much as it had her. She'd never given him a chance to explain.

"But...he used to lose interest in me for a few weeks, or even a few months at a time. You know." Spots of color burned bright on her cheeks. "And so I did finally ask. He said, 'Don't be ridiculous.'"

Grant looked at her incredulously. "That's all? Was he angry?"

"No." Her lashes shielded her eyes. "Just...vaguely surprised at such a silly question. And then he changed the subject like I'd asked whether he needed anything at the grocery store. Although…that was like Hugh. He didn't *get* mad."

"So you believed him."

"I suppose I did." She bowed her head and seemed to be staring fixedly at the hands she'd knotted together. "There wasn't even a flash of guilt."

"Amoral people don't feel guilt."

"Hugh was a good man."

"Perhaps not sexually." Grant didn't even know why he was arguing. Maybe the rumors were wrong. If not…Grant was going to have to find out the truth, now that it was clear Hugh Riley had died under suspicious circumstances, but it didn't follow that Kat ever had to learn the truth about her husband. She might be better off holding on to illusions.

But Grant didn't want her to. He hated the idea of her continuing to hug the memory of her lazy, charming, faithless husband to her as if she intended to take it to the grave when her time came. Frustration chafed at Grant. Damn it, Kat had been attracted to him. He knew she was. Why couldn't she let herself *see* him now?

"Rumors sometimes lie," Kat said quietly, lifting her chin proudly. "Cops don't always believe everything they hear, do they?"

"No," he admitted.

"Then?"

"I'm going to find out," he warned her. He gestured toward the plant flat containing the bones. "I have to now."

After a moment she pressed her lips tightly together and nodded.

"Kat," he heard himself say roughly.

She didn't seem to want to look at him anymore. When he hesitated, a knock came on the door.

Scowling, Grant called, "Come in," and Jen Wisniewski, his fingerprint tech, entered.

"If I can grab a checkbook out of the file cabinet," Kat said, "I'll get out of your way."

Grant had no choice but to let her go. "I'll be in touch," he said brusquely, just before she left the office. Kat barely paused, then kept going.

CHAPTER FIVE

KAT GENERALLY ENJOYED the garden club meetings. Members varied from the few with glorious gardens they'd created themselves to some who put out rows of bedding plants every year and merely enjoyed the camaraderie—and had some desire to improve the appeal of their hometown. Her own participation was good for business, but after marrying Hugh she'd developed a genuine passion for plants and their artful placement, and it was also fun to spend time with other people who felt the same.

But this month, it was all she could do not to plead sickness and miss the meeting. If talk was spreading at all, everyone here would have heard it.

They met this month in the community room at the library. She slipped in at seven on the nose, so she didn't have to make conversation beforehand. Annika Lindstrom was already at the front of the room, clapping her hands to call for silence. She smiled upon seeing Kat, then swept her gaze over the group.

"Good to see you all here tonight. We have some minor business to discuss, and then as you all know the principal item on our agenda is to make decisions about the flower baskets for downtown and the island planters that will greet visitors to Fern Bluff."

Annika was somewhat older than Kat, perhaps forty, only the fine lines beside her eyes giving away the years. Kat had heard secondhand that her husband was considerably older than her and had died of an unexpected heart attack a good ten years ago. Annika had never remarried.

Except when working in her yard, she always wore her Scandinavian pale hair in a classic chignon. She was tall for a woman, nearly six feet, Kat guessed, model slim but stronger than she looked. Kat had once helped her dig out a new flowerbed by city hall, and they'd both worked hard for eight hours, shoveling, dumping the wheelbarrow, hauling heavy plant pots. Annika hadn't flagged any more than Kat had. Kat wasn't surprised; Annika had a glorious, English cottage-style garden that had been featured in the *Herald* garden section in September, and she did all the work herself. She wasn't exactly pretty—her face was too long for that. *Elegant* might be a better word for her appearance. Kat liked her and appreciated her patronage at the nursery, but their relationship had never moved toward real friendship. Kat always figured it was her fault; she didn't make friends easily or often.

The approval of the minutes and the usual discussion of budget and upcoming elections went quickly under Annika's deft guidance. Kat glanced around to see who else was here tonight. Everyone, she realized immediately. Which was maybe natural, because the projects to be decided on were the garden club's raison d'être. Debate was likely to be spirited, with the bedding plant advocates on one side and the fans of perennial and shrub beds on the other.

The mother of sixteen-year-old Billy with the tattoos and—most recently—an eyebrow piercing, Becca Montgomery caught Kat's eye and gave her a friendly smile. Lisa Llewellyn was here, and Greg Buckmeier, sitting as always at an end of one row with his chair deliberately scooted a few feet from the next, so as to set himself apart from the group. Carol Scammell, school board member and mother of four. Mike Hedin, scribbling notes for the newspaper. Amanda Hinds, whose husband owned the pharmacy, met Kat's gaze and then turned her face away with no expression whatsoever. Kat felt a chill; she couldn't remember the last time she'd seen Amanda, formerly a good customer, at the nursery.

Something like fear rose in her. She scanned the rows quickly. There was Dorothy Glenn, plump, sixtyish, and famous for her massed tulips in the spring and the dozen or more spectacular flower baskets that would hang from the eaves of the Glenns' faux Tudor home. Jim and Tracy Baldwin—Jim was the vice principal at the middle school, and his wife worked with homeschool parents. None of them had been to the nursery lately, either. Neither had Fay Cabot, or Nancy McKee or Bridget Moretti.

Panic made it hard for Kat to draw a full breath. She forced herself to stare straight ahead and keep her hands quiet on her lap as if she were entirely caught up in the discussion that had begun. She didn't hear a word.

Receipts had been down these past two weeks.

She had assumed it was the weather, insofar as she'd thought about it at all. But now…now she couldn't help thinking about how these were her core customers. Some spent thousands of dollars a year at Sauk River Nursery, others at least a few hundred. If they abandoned her…

She'd dismissed the idea earlier, but…*was* someone trying to destroy her business? Was Hugh's death not personal at all, but rather intended to put the nursery out of business? Maybe no one had thought she'd want, or be able, to keep it going, much less make a success of it once Hugh was gone.

But if that was so…why wait so long to make the next move?

And who would benefit from the nursery going under? She'd speculated already, and had no better answer this time. There was no other general nursery in Fern Bluff; there used to be an excellent nursery in nearby Marysville, but the owner had passed away and it had closed a few years ago. The nurseries in Lake Stevens and Everett were each a half hour drive away. They weren't competitors. And the closer nurseries were all specialty ones, from A Rainbow of Iris and Mountain Rhodies to Old Thyme Roses. Her business benefited theirs, and theirs hers.

She tuned in to hear Amanda arguing that perennial beds took virtually year-around maintenance without the return of displays of annuals that could be replaced to offer spectacular color nonstop until late in the fall.

Rather mildly, Annika said, "Planting, deadheading and replacing annuals is hardly low maintenance."

"Roses—" somebody began, to be interrupted by someone else who thought they ought to fill the space with low-growing, nearly maintenance-free shrubs.

"There are plenty of them that flower, if we have to have blooms."

"Kat?" Annika said eventually, after argument had raged for another fifteen minutes.

"There are advantages and disadvantages to all the alternatives," she said. "Shrubs often outgrow their space. If they aren't skillfully pruned, they can become leggy and unkempt. We'd either need to use landscape fabric and bark beneath—and replace it yearly—or plan on regular weeding parties. In some ways, a selection of old roses—perhaps rugosas or musk roses—would be the easiest to care for, but we wouldn't have a long bloom season."

"The hips give fall color," Lisa Llewellyn chimed in.

"That's true," Kat agreed. "But let's keep in mind that a massing of shrubs could block visibility for drivers on the roundabouts. We could have full season color with a mixed bed—a couple of spring blooming shrubs in the very center with leaves that are spectacular in the fall, summer and fall blooming perennials, perhaps annuals mixed in. And there's no denying the beauty of a profusion of annuals. We do," she pointed out, "have two roundabouts and two center dividers to fill. We could compromise by doing perennials, mixed bed or roses in the round-abouts, which are larger anyway, and annuals in the dividers."

While she swept her gaze over the group as she

talked, she met no one's eyes. She dreaded the idea of seeing open contempt or dislike on the face of someone she'd known for years. Liked.

Talk immediately broke out again. Eventually, to her surprise, her suggestion was followed. A committee was assigned to choose the planting for the roundabouts, another one for the dividers. A third committee would plan the flower baskets.

Kat wondered how many of the plants would be purchased at Sauk River this year.

She fled as soon as she could after the meeting, glad she'd been able to sit near the door. Annika raised her eyebrows as if in question when she saw Kat going, and Kat mouthed, "I'll call you tomorrow."

A nod, and she slipped out, hurrying to the parking lot, the first to reach her car. She felt sick. What if Grant couldn't figure out what was going on? What if the next bones were presented to her publicly? Leg bones in one of the ceramic pots for sale inside? A pelvis hung over the rack of seeds? The possibilities were many and so awful, she had to close her eyes and rest her forehead against the steering wheel. The police would have to make a statement. The whole story would be revived in not only the local paper, but the *Herald* and even the *Seattle Times*. The way the bones were being presented was macabre enough to potentially appeal even to national news organizations.

Kat didn't know if she could bear it.

She straightened and in her sideview mirror saw a cluster of people exiting the library and spreading through the parking lot. Her hands were shaking, but she put the car in gear anyway and drove home, grateful that the roads were mostly empty.

The house was dark. She should have left lights on. For the first time it occurred to her that her home was no more inviolate than the nursery. She'd been glad enough since Hugh's disappearance that she had near neighbors instead of living out at the nursery. The houses to each side of hers were dark, too, though, and she thought uneasily about how the back door had only a push-button lock. She wouldn't swear all the windows were locked at all. If *she* was the object of this campaign of terror and not just her business, home might not be a refuge.

Feeling like such a coward, she sat in the car for a good three minutes before working up the nerve to get out and go up the front steps. She heard only silence when she unlocked the door and stepped cautiously inside. She turned on a light in every room and left them on behind her. She wouldn't feel comfortable until she was sure she was alone in the house.

Downstairs she checked the windows, the coat closet, the pantry. Upstairs, she looked under beds and in closets. She propped a chair under her bedroom doorknob and, even so, couldn't sleep.

Which meant she looked like hell the next morning, with huge dark circles under her eyes, a lovely contrast to pasty skin. Kat groaned, peering at herself in the mirror. With a sigh, she scraped her hair back in a ponytail. The nice, brisk air outside would give her cheeks color.

She dressed in faded overalls, long-sleeved T and thick socks to keep her feet warm inside rubber boots, then added a fleece jacket since the forecast on Yahoo! called for temperatures in the forties.

Spring, where art thou? Her attempt to be whimsical fell flat in her own mind.

She knew—*knew*—that Grant would show up at some point during the day. For once, she wanted to see him, even if another visit from the Fern Bluff police chief would only add fuel to the gossip. Had he learned anything?

This would all be easier if his presence alone wasn't enough to put her on edge. She had so many conflicting emotions where he was concerned, it was like…like putting fried oysters, jalapeno peppers and chocolate chips all on a pizza. Nothing went together. Result: upset stomach.

It was the push-pull between her attraction to him and her knowledge that he could hurt her as she'd never been hurt before that caused most of this inner turmoil. Well, that along with the fact that she saw him look at her sometimes with that flat cop stare and knew he expected to be arresting her for murder one of these days. Not what you'd call reassuring. And yet…when she was scared, it was Grant she wanted.

Which made no sense at all.

Midmorning she called Annika and lied, telling her she'd been battling a migraine last night. Annika thanked her for helping to reconcile the warring factions, and they exchanged a few words about the unseasonably wretched weather. Going out in it, Kat thought ruefully about how only two weeks ago she'd been glorying in the validation of being chosen for the award. Hadn't the sun been shining, too? Business had already been picking up for spring, she did remember that, and she'd assumed the publicity would boost it even more. Instead, today was all but dead... Poor choice of words, she thought, hastily correcting herself. Business was *slow*.

She'd made herself go to work in the far greenhouse, sans iPod and wishing she could lock the doors at each end. But she gradually relaxed, the rhythm of repotting settling her nerves, the humid warmth welcome after the chill outside. Nonetheless, her head came up sharply when the heavy door opened. Her pulse leaped.

The sight of Grant in his uniform didn't do anything to settle her heartbeat.

Their eyes met briefly, then he glanced around the greenhouse, taking in the rows of potted seedlings laid out on long tables. He strolled toward her, peeling off the parka with a police department patch on the chest as he came. Kat suffered from the usual ache she felt whenever she first saw him. He looked too good, even though he wasn't exactly handsome. Nowhere near as handsome as Hugh had been. His features were blunt, his nose a little crooked, his mouth...hard. He didn't seem to smile all that often, and too frequently his dark eyebrows were drawn together in a frown. Something about the lines to each side of his mouth and the crow's-feet beside his eyes made him look world-weary and older than she suspected he was.

But he was also big and broad-shouldered and he had a way of moving that twisted her up inside. He was lighter on his feet than he should be, and she knew without ever seeing him in action that he could respond with lightning speed and violence when he had to.

"Waiting for a bone to pop up?" he asked, nodding to the trowel in her hand.

"I've reached the point where I'm numb. It'll take more than another small bone to faze me."

His eyes searched her face, seeing more than she'd like, Kat guessed. "How are you?" he asked, his voice a low rumble that felt like his big, calloused hand did when he touched her.

The very few times he'd touched her.

Kat's throat closed. She, who hated admitting to any vulnerability, heard herself say after a minute, "Shaky."

"I don't know how you could help but be." He pulled up another stool and sat facing her, close enough his knee would have bumped hers if she moved at all.

"At the garden club meeting last night, some people wouldn't meet my eyes. Another one or two gave me the cold shoulder."

"You might be seeing what you're afraid you'll see, not what's really there," he said with surprising gentleness.

Kat laid down the trowel and bent her head to look at her hands, which suddenly wanted to tremble. "Yes. I suppose that's possible."

"Did anyone actually say anything?"

"No." She paused. "I overheard one of my own employees talking about me the other day, though. I wanted to fire her, but..."

When she didn't finish, Grant did for her. "You'd make an enemy out of her."

"Apparently, she's next best to one already." She lifted her head, hoping she didn't look too beseeching. "I don't understand why."

He surprised her again, laying a big hand over one of hers. *Oh, yes,* sighed a voice in her head that had to be hers even if the satisfaction in it did shock her.

"You lived through it last time," he said quietly.

She tried really hard to smile. "I know I did. But this…is different."

"No. It's just part two of whatever happened then."

That jibed with what she'd thought last night at the garden club meeting, but… "Why now?" she asked. "Why wait so long?"

"I don't know. If we can figure that out, we can probably figure out the rest."

Kat nodded after a moment. "Business is down. It's going to be down even more if I wasn't imagining all those snubs last night. Those are my best customers. If they quit shopping here—"

"Gossip can have the opposite effect, you know. People don't want to miss out on anything. They may shop here in droves in hopes they'll be the eyewitness to something exciting. You'll gain new customers."

She shuddered. "It occurred to me to wonder how the ante can be upped. If you know what I mean."

"I know." His expression had abruptly become unreadable. He was all cop again, watching for her to betray herself in some way.

Kat quit feeling safe because he was there and switched seamlessly over to feeling threatened. With a small movement she withdrew her hand from under his.

His gaze flicked down, then focused on her face. "What are you bracing yourself for, Kat?"

"A stray bone or two won't have much impact. What occurred to me is that a public presentation would be hideous."

"You mean, let one of your customers find the next bone?"

She couldn't help this shudder any more than she'd been able to the last. "Can you imagine?"

"Unfortunately, yes. The thought's crossed my mind, too."

"What do I do, come early every morning and search the nursery before we open?"

"Might not hurt."

"Dear God."

"Kat…"

There was something in his tone. Kat stiffened.

"Do you know anything you haven't told me?"

She withdrew, infinitestimally enough she hoped he didn't notice. Flippancy seemed her only defense. "You mean, did I bash in Hugh's head and forget to mention where I hid his body?"

Grant's expression hardened. "Have you gotten any notes? Any phone calls?" He paused. "Is someone trying to blackmail you?"

It took her a moment to suppress the wash of anguish. "Oh, didn't I tell you? Sadly, I can't afford the million bucks." She shrugged. "Apparently somebody doesn't like 'gee, no' as an answer."

Muscles flexed in his jaw. He waited.

"No!" It burst out of her, a detonation that left her raw. "No! I don't know anything." She was trembling as she stood and backed away from him. Why had she ever imagined he was on her side? She knew better.

"Kat." Grant stood, too, slowly, as if he was being careful not to spook her. "I'm sorry. I had to ask."

"And you thought if I'd killed him, I would tell you?" she said incredulously.

"I thought if it was an accident, you might be getting scared enough that you would."

"He drove away. I never saw him again." Maybe she managed the monotone because she'd said this so many times before.

"All right." There was that damn gentleness again. He was placating her, thinking he'd soothe her into forgetting that he had accused her of murder. "Then we're still at square one."

"There's no *we*. You're investigating a murder." She stared at him. "I'm facing the fact that somebody hates my guts."

"I want to believe in you."

"But you don't," Kat said flatly. "Don't bother pretending." She crossed her arms. "Are you testing the bones for DNA?"

Somehow he'd closed the distance between them. Kat couldn't go much farther without bumping into one of the big tables.

"No." He held up a hand before she could say

anything. "I will if I have to, but I think the wedding ring is a pretty clear indication that the bones are Hugh's. Unless there's any chance he wasn't wearing the ring when he disappeared?"

Was that a question, or not? Kat tried to decide. "He was wearing it," she said. "He never took it off. Never fiddled with it. I'm not sure he even remembered he was wearing it. It was just…there."

"Would you have noticed if he wasn't?"

She momentarily closed her eyes. "Yes. He'd been…affectionate the day or two before. When I woke up that morning, his arm was lying over me. I remember studying his hand when I woke up. I won't absolutely swear he didn't take it off and put it in the glove compartment as he drove away, but why would he?"

She saw something on Grant's face. She couldn't decide what.

"All right," he said again. "If nothing else shows up in the next week or two, I'll request a DNA test. Results are slow coming, though. The crime lab gets pretty backed up."

"But you don't think you'll have to."

Eyes watchful, he said, "Dental X-rays would tell us the same thing, easier and cheaper."

Her breath huffed hard from her. It was a moment before Kat could speak. "You mean, if…if his skull shows up."

He made a quick movement toward her. She made as quick a one back, until the rough edge of the table pressed into her lower back. Very, very calmly, she said, "I always enjoy talking to you, Grant. But now, if you don't mind, I'd better get back to work."

"You've never wanted anything to do with me, have you?" His voice was hoarse, his eyes dark and searching.

The first truly personal words he'd spoken to her in four years, these felt like another body blow.

"Not if I can help it."

"Why?"

"You shouldn't have kissed me."

"No. I shouldn't have." He sounded angry. "You shouldn't have kissed me back."

Her arms tightened around herself. "No. You're right." She was mad at her own thin wisp of a voice.

"I was divorced and you were widowed not that much later."

Her chin snapped up. "I didn't know I was widowed."

"In all these years, you never suspected the son of a bitch was dead."

"Of course I suspected it!" She swung away, presenting her back to him. "But I didn't know. How could I?"

"You couldn't let yourself feel anything for me because you still thought you were married."

Oh, damn, damn. Why now?

"I didn't know he was screwing around on me. If he was. But you did. So you figured I should do it, too, is that it?"

His hand closed on her shoulder. Squeezed, just a flex of his fingers. "I never thought that, Kat. I didn't mean to kiss you. I wouldn't have cheated on Rachel."

"Then what?" Kat whispered. "What?"

"I went deaf and dumb. Not blind. I could see you. But…I couldn't stop myself. I don't know how else to explain. I couldn't *not* take you in my arms." He was still kneading her shoulder; with him so close, his ragged breath ruffled the tiny hairs at her nape. "I was sorry. Kissing you once made it worse. I hated myself for doing it."

Her eyes were glazed with tears, and she never cried. Never. "I hated you for doing it, too. I felt like a slut."

"Some things," he said in that gruff but heartstoppingly tender voice, "can't be denied. What I felt from the first time I saw you is one of them."

"And that makes it fine?"

"No." He heaved a deeper breath. "It doesn't. It didn't then. But I've been hoping like hell ever since that someday you'd forgive me."

It wasn't him she hadn't been able to forgive. It was herself. But telling him that would bare something she didn't dare let see the light of day. The best she could do was lie.

"I didn't give it as much thought as you seem to think I did. I was mad, and I was upset with myself. What we'd done…it made it worse when Hugh disappeared. And when you were the one investigating his disappearance."

"I know it did." His hand left her. "I wanted to find him dead in a way that made it plain you had nothing to do with his death. I wanted you to be a widow. You think that hasn't haunted me?"

The pain she heard made her turn so that she could see his face. "Your divorce wasn't even final."

"No, it wasn't." That betraying muscle jerked in his cheek. "I felt like scum, but I wanted you too much not to think it was meant to be."

"I...didn't know."

His gray eyes were turbulent. "Didn't you?"

Oh, Lord. She *had* known. Maybe not then. Then she'd been consumed with bewilderment and grief. She'd been frantically trying to keep the business afloat, and it was all she could do to hold her head high despite the sudden pools of silence that were louder than whispers. But in the years since, Kat couldn't deny she'd seen the way Grant looked at her sometimes. And although he'd never said a word, never made a move toward her, she'd known that if she had ever quit turning away when he approached, he would have made that move. And she'd been afraid of what she'd feel if he did.

"Not then," she whispered. "Later, I wondered."

"Every time you rebuffed me, it sliced me to the bone."

"I don't understand." She'd already said that, hadn't she? She didn't understand anything anymore. Why people did what they did, why they felt what they did.

Why *she* felt what she did.

"This is no time to be having this conversation," Grant said roughly.

"No."

"But we are. Kat…" His Adam's apple bobbed. "You did kiss me back, didn't you? You felt it, too."

God help her. "Yes."

With a groan, he gripped her upper arms and pulled her close. Even before their bodies collided, she was reaching for him. Her mouth claimed his as much as his did hers. The kiss was deep and hungry and desperate, just as the one four years ago had been.

Kat hadn't let herself think about that kiss, and she'd wanted another one more than she'd ever wanted anything in her life.

Teeth, tongue and lips. The slam of his heartbeat and the moan that escaped her. The hard length of his body against hers. The hand he'd plunged into her hair to cradle her head and tilt the angle to suit him. She was all sensation, all longing and urgency and *need*.

But he did raise his head eventually. Panting, they stared at each other, and Kat remembered. Only three days ago, her dead husband's skeletal hand had been given back to her. And this man, the one holding her, still harbored more than a niggling doubt about her innocence in Hugh's disappearance.

She let her hands drop from Grant's chest and scooted sideways out of his reach. He took a step after her.

"That wasn't a good idea," Kat told him.

He stopped. The heat in his eyes cooled even as she watched. "No," he finally said. "I guess it wasn't. It was inevitable, though, Kat. And it will happen again."

"No."

"Yes," he said softly. "I've given you time. Too goddamn much time. But I'll leave now." He backed away, grabbed his parka without his gaze once leaving hers. "I'll be back, though, Kat."

She still stood in exactly the same place when the greenhouse door bounced closed, leaving her alone once again.

CHAPTER SIX

WHAT KIND OF IDIOT WAS HE? Berating himself, Grant went straight to his car. Once he got in, he realized he'd all but brushed past several people without acknowledging them. Worse yet, he had no idea who they were. And he was a cop! Cops were never blind to their surroundings. They couldn't afford to be.

Every muscle rigid, he sat behind the wheel and tried to figure out what it was Kat did to him. But there weren't going to be any answers. She sure as hell wasn't trying to get to him. She couldn't have made that any plainer. She didn't *want* to be attracted to him.

But for the first time ever, she'd admitted that she was. And he hadn't been able to stop himself from kissing her, any more than he'd been able to all those years ago. Even though this time it was just as wrong, just as stupid, if for a different reason.

He had no business touching her until he could be absolutely, one hundred percent sure she had nothing to do with Hugh's death. And face it: right now, he couldn't with honesty say that he was.

There was too much emotion storming in her eyes for him to believe she was trying to manipulate him with this unholy hunger he felt for her. No. Not prickly, independent Kat.

What he did fear was that she had responded to him today only because, in her terror, she needed closeness with somebody, anybody, and he'd been there. While they held each other, she had to know she wasn't alone, not the way she'd been ever since Hugh drove away. The temptation must have been enormous.

Making a harsh sound, Grant rubbed a hand over his face. He hated knowing she hadn't kissed him because she was deeply, desperately in love with him the way he was with her. That made him pathetic, didn't it? Especially coupled with his reaction to the inference that she and that cheating scum named Hugh had been doing it like rabbits a couple of days before he disappeared. It had been all Grant could do not to flinch.

Figure this out, he thought. If he could do that, free Kat from her obsession with her long-dead husband, then they'd see. Because, whatever her reasons, she *had* kissed him back.

All right. *Think.*

Why now? she'd asked. It wasn't as if he hadn't already been wondering that himself.

One possibility was that whoever had had Hugh's bones stashed had been out of the area, and had only recently come home. If this were a different kind of crime, Grant would look for someone who'd recently been sprung from prison. Thing was, this was a small town. He'd know if there was someone like that, the kind of someone who might have had contact with Hugh and Kathryn Riley.

Okay, someone who'd moved away and now returned. Worth considering. He'd ask some questions. Grant didn't believe that was the answer, though. He thought there was another kind of trigger altogether. Whoever this was—and he now believed that that someone was a killer—had been satisfied by Hugh's death. Content to let Kat run the nursery and live her life.

Or, to look at it a different way, maybe he or she had been content, rather, to watch Kat suffer, caught as she was in limbo. She hadn't known whether she was abandoned wife or widow, whether the business was really hers or she was only a caretaker for it. Even though police interest and gossip both eventually waned, the taint of suspicion stayed with her.

So maybe *that* was the point. Maybe the killer had really, really enjoyed watching her suffer, and had recently come to the conclusion that she wasn't anymore. Not enough, anyway.

Oh, hell. That made no sense. Why would someone who was enraged enough by Hugh to kill him give a good goddamn about his wife? If they'd been in on something together, why not punish her then? Why wait?

Say that Hugh's death/murder and the reappearance of the bones were separate, connected only by the fact that the person taunting Kat now had somehow discovered Hugh's body. And that *this* somebody maybe didn't care about Hugh one way or another, but hated Kat.

He didn't like the sense in that, because it suggested again that she was the likeliest person to have knocked off her husband.

No, damn it! Assume there were two perps, and she wasn't one of them. Okay, then. Back to the calculated appearance of the bones. What had she done to earn this kind of malevolence? So far as he could tell, she kept to herself. He'd never heard any rumor that she even dated, far less played around with other women's husbands, say. She worked sixty-plus hour weeks, if he was any judge, she was a member of the chamber of commerce, she grocery shopped, gardened at home and had reputedly been refinishing kitchen cabinets and stripping and replacing wallpaper in that crap of an old house her husband had left her. Still…something could have happened.

Sure. She could have been rude to someone. Snubbed them. Sent a bounced check to collections. He could think of a million small offenses, none of which seemed in any imaginable way to explain why that somebody would be mad and hateful enough to start a campaign of terror. Not to mention risk getting caught planting a missing man's bones at the nursery.

He wanted to tear his hair out. No, logic said Hugh's death and his current, bizarre reappearance—so to speak—*were* related. Were, in fact, parts one and two of the same thing, whatever that was, as Grant had said to Kat earlier.

Which took him to her desperate, whispered question: *Why now?* Had the killer been happy, only something had recently happened that was a trigger, that set him or her off again?

But, once again, that suggested the original grudge had been against both Hugh and Kat. And if so, why not take action against her at the time?

Grant circled to the simple answer: because she was suffering. And now she wasn't deemed to be suffering enough.

Had the killer kept the body handy with this in mind from the beginning, rather than disposing of it?

Keeping a corpse "handy" was problematic. Decomposition was messy and smelly. Ask any homicide detective. Some of them would claim they got used to the stench, but for most, it would be a lie. There was nothing quite like that smell.

Buried then, in a coffin or well wrapped in some other way? No animal had gotten to the bones that had shown up so far. Grant grunted. Hell, he guessed someone could have stashed the body in their basement, if they didn't mind living with the stench for a few weeks as it seeped up through the floorboards. Or they had rural property and a secure outbuilding. God knows there were plenty of places like that around here. About two-thirds the kids in the school district were bused from outside the city limits. Farming was still a way of life here, and the rest of the rural landscape had been carved up into two-and-a-half acre and five acre lots. People hereabouts liked their slice of rural Americana. Detached workshops, RV garages and small barns were a dime a dozen. A long-unused, concrete-lined well might work, or an empty septic tank.

Yep. Lots of places to stash a body.

Sitting there, Grant made up his mind. Whether the city would pay for it or not, he was going to have security cameras installed. If he had to foot the bill himself, he would. Covering the whole damn nursery probably wasn't feasible, but half a dozen would give them a good shot at catching a glimpse of someone who wasn't where they belonged. He'd need to get Kat's permission…but not right now. He'd call her later, when the tension between them cooled down a little.

Grant drove to the station mulling over how and when the cameras could be installed the least conspicuously. Normally a business wanted security cameras to be visible and therefore deter crime. This was an exception. By God, he *wanted* this sicko to creep into the greenhouse or Kat's office with bones. He wanted that face captured on digital imagery.

He wanted this to be over.

KAT HAD BARELY WALKED in the door at home when her cell phone rang. Damn. She'd hoped to avoid talking to a single soul all evening. Worse yet, when she glanced at the number on the screen, she recognized it as Grant's cell phone.

Although tempted to mute the ring and ignore the call, she groaned on the fourth ring and flipped the phone open. "Hello."

"Kat, this is Grant."

She couldn't read his voice. Surely this wasn't personal. Hadn't they said everything this afternoon?

"Yes?"

He started talking about installing cameras, and she relaxed.

"That's actually a good idea," she admitted.

"Thank you," he said drily.

"I've been thinking of putting a couple in the main building, anyway. Shoplifting has become more of a problem than it used to be." Which was true, but she was thinking more that cameras would make her feel safer.

"You haven't called us out there that often. I didn't realize you had much shoplifting." He sounded mildly surprised at her comment.

"No, we hardly ever catch anyone. Stuff is just gone. Maybe smaller plants, too, we don't know. I mean, it would be easy for someone to pop an extra perennial or annual or two in a flat of plants they'd already paid for. But I'm talking garden art, tools, some of the pricier stuff. And it's hard to prevent, because on a busy day we're all distracted so often. Plus, it's not like a pharmacy or department store where clerks know to keep an eye on teenagers. We don't get that many, and they're mostly with parents. And what fifteen-year-old would want a concrete garden gnome?"

"Unless they intended it as a murder weapon."

She laughed, something she would have sworn when she walked in the door was beyond her capability. Who knew murder could be funny? "Or a practical joke."

"Mother's Day present."

"That's true." She sighed. "No matter what, it's hard on the bottom line."

"I'm thinking at least half a dozen cameras," he said. "Maybe more. A couple inside. I'd like one that catches the door to your office. Maybe motion-activated ones in the greenhouses."

They talked over possibilities for a few minutes, and agreed that Sunday would work to get them quietly installed. Hiding them entirely wouldn't be possible, but some of them could be screened, the outdoor ones peeking through lattice, for example.

"Sunday is, um, still a few days away," she said finally.

"I know." He sounded grim. "I've made a few calls, though, and getting anyone out sooner would be tough. Plus…working at night would be likelier to draw attention, wouldn't it?"

"Maybe." Kat thought about it. "Although there are grow lights in the conservatory for the indoor plants and orchids, and I do have some outdoor lighting. Plus I sometimes stay late. So it's not like the place is pitch-dark at night."

"Quit staying late," he said flatly.

Another time, Kat would have bristled, but with the things that had been happening, there was no way she'd have stayed alone at the nursery anyway. She was nervous enough home alone, and at least here she could lock up.

"Yes," she agreed.

"I'll see if I can persuade this guy to come sooner. Friday or Saturday night, maybe."

"Just let me know."

"All right." He paused. "Don't let what happened this afternoon keep you from calling if you need me, Kat."

The softness of his voice made a lump form in her throat. It was a moment before she could speak.

"No." She swallowed. "I have you on speed dial."

"Good. I'll be talking to you."

Silence suggested he was gone. Slowly Kat closed her phone. He could shake her up so easily. He was the only person she'd ever known who could. Even Hugh…

No. She wouldn't compare the two men. She wouldn't.

Kat settled on a salad for dinner. She tried to watch TV and didn't care about a show she'd always found at least mildly gripping. TV-land drama wasn't all that compelling compared to her own, real-life version.

She slept poorly, as she had ever since the first bone appeared in the compost, and woke tired. She had a cup of coffee before she even looked out the window, atypical given how weather-dependent her business was. The sun was out, Kat saw with mild surprise.

She'd have put on makeup to try to cover the purple smudges under her eyes, except she was bound to sweat once she got to work, which was hell on foundation. And who would even notice what she looked like, anyway?

Lots of people, she discovered, as the morning

progressed. The nursery was busy, and plenty of the customers had come to gape.

At her.

At first she thought she was imagining it, but no. People she'd barely met made excuses to talk to her, or stared at her over rows of bare-root roses. The good part, she concluded grimly as the day went on, was that most of them bought something. Grant was right. Scandal was good for business.

Joan wasn't supposed to work today, but she appeared after lunch and said, "I guessed we'd be busy," and dove in. Moments later, she'd led a woman who had been waiting for help to the hanging flower baskets.

Annika got out of her SUV, met a couple of other garden club members in front and smiled when Kat stopped to say hi.

"We're browsing for roundabout plants, no need to bother with us. We're still at the discussion stage. Looks like everyone is taking advantage of the sun."

At least the perennial/shrubbery contingent of the garden club apparently intended to buy at her nursery, Kat was grateful to see. Who knew about the bedding plant group? She hadn't noticed any of them yet today, but then, she wouldn't necessarily.

She was loading a lilac for a customer when she felt a tug on her sleeve.

"Uh, Kat?" It was Jason, and his eyes were wild. "I need you."

Not, Kat thought with a sinking heart, to explain

the soil and exposure needs of a *Choisya ternata* to a potential customer.

"Give me a second," she murmured, then made nice to the one who'd already written a sizable check for two lilac bushes and a mountain laurel. Only when the station wagon was backing out did she turn to Jason.

"What?"

"You know we put that *Viburnum carlesii* by the shed? I looked over there, and right behind it—" A shudder rattled his skinny length. "There's a skull, Kat. It's…wow. It's hanging on the wall like…like some kind of garden art."

"You're sure it's…?" *Real,* she was going to say, *human,* but he was already nodding.

"Pretty sure."

"Did you cover it?"

"Well, it's sort of behind the viburnum."

"Oh, God," she said. "All right." Without even looking to see if he was following, she started through the nursery grounds. She couldn't run. She even had to smile and pause briefly to talk to a couple of people. Ahead she could see the red-painted toolshed with a barn-style door. To one side of the door, a trellis held a clematis that would burst into salad-plate-size, sky-blue blooms in June. To the left was the potted viburnum, which would have gloriously fragrant clusters of white blooms soon.

Apparently no one had wandered close until Jason had, because even from some distance away she could see the ivory *something* against the red clapboard siding. It was barely veiled by the new spring leaves of the viburnum.

She turned abruptly. Her teenage employee was all but stepping on her heels.

"Jason, keep customers away. Don't let anyone—*anyone*—near. Got it?"

His head bobbed. "I won't. I promise."

"And don't tell anyone else. Not even co-workers."

"Okay." Wide-eyed, he kept nodding.

She spun away. *I'll take it down, hide it in the shed.*

Grant wouldn't like that. He'd want to photograph it in place, check for fingerprints. Like there'd be any. Mind working frantically, Kat thought, *To hell with him.*

But then it occurred to her that there were gunnysacks in the shed. She could cover the skull until Grant could get here. No. She didn't want him here until after closing. He'd understand, wouldn't he?

Leaving Jason to stand guard, Kat stepped close enough to the shed to see the awful grin through the newly unfurling leaves. The skull was so pale, almost unreal, like a plastic decoration for Halloween, except she knew it wasn't. The texture wasn't plastic. It was granular, like the other bones had been. The eye sockets were horrible, gaping pits, as was the nose, and it seemed to be grinning with those two awful rows of protubcrant teeth.

She was shaking all over when she reached for the door to open it. A glimpse of color made her pause, take another look. The lower jaw was wired in place, she saw, with green-wrapped garden ties. Perfect for the purpose. She sold them herself.

Kat shivered at the idea of touching the skull. Covering it was a much better idea. *Hugh.* She slipped through the open door, snatched up a gunnysack and hurried out. A glance told her that Jason had stood firm and was talking expansively to a couple of women. His body blocked her from recognizing them.

Bile rising in her throat, its sour taste in her mouth, she managed to drape the roughly woven sack over the skull. Then, despite unsteady hands, she unclipped her cell phone from her belt and, grateful for the fact that she *had* set Grant's number up on speed dial, pushed number one and Send.

It rang only once. "Kat?" he said.

"Grant. Thank God." She closed her eyes. "I need you, but I don't want any customers to see you. We're…really busy."

"More bones?"

"Skull. It's…" Even her voice shook. "Hanging on the shed wall."

He swore inventively. "Okay, Kat. Is it in plain sight?"

She told him what she'd done.

"All right. That's good. When do you close?"

"Five."

"I'll be there then. Just don't let anyone get near."

"No. I'll…find something to do near here."

If it hadn't been midafternoon already, she didn't think she could have survived. As it was, she pretended to rearrange shrubs, hurrying to talk to the few customers who ventured her way. The one time she was called away to answer questions, she caught Jason's eye and he took her place. By five, Kat felt wrung out, almost worse than she had in the days following Hugh's disappearance.

At her request, Jason walked through the nursery with her, making sure no strays were left in greenhouses. Kat hated feeling so vulnerable she needed a skinny kid as a guard. When they returned to the main building, Joan was closing out the till.

"Good day," she said.

"Everyone gone?" Kat asked.

"Um…" Joan looked up distractedly. "I think so."

Jason went over and peered in the break room. "All clear."

"Dear God." Kat sank onto a stool behind the counter. "The skull is hanging on the shed. Jason spotted it." She focused on him. "You've been a lifesaver today. I can't thank you enough. This is such a nightmare, but it would have been worse if someone else had spotted it."

"Yeah. Jeez." He still looked jittery, but also a little bit excited. "Who could have put it there?"

"I don't know."

He told Joan when he'd noticed it, and they talked about whether it could have been there all day without reaching any conclusions. The sound of car tires crunching on gravel outside brought Kat's head around, so she wasn't surprised when Grant walked in a moment later. Jason once again told his story, and they recapped their conversation to that point.

"I can call the other employees who worked today and find out if anyone had reason to go in the shed," Kat offered.

Joan said gently, "Why don't I do that? You look a little rattled. Besides, it will sound less threatening coming from me. I can pretend we're trying to track down a missing tool or something."

"Do it," Grant agreed. "As soon as you think they'd be home."

Having agreed to keep this quiet for the moment, Jason finally left. Kat could tell he hated to go.

"He's a good kid," Joan said, while dialing.

She reached one of the day's other two employees, James Cheung, spoke briefly, then reported, "He says he wasn't near the shed today."

Tess Miller answered her cell phone. Nope, she hadn't been in the vicinity, either. She'd spent most of the day helping people out front, or with perennials and annuals. Out of five people working today, not one of them could narrow down when the skull appeared.

"All right." Grant pushed himself away from the counter. "Let's take a look."

"Do you want me to stay?" Joan asked, but Kat shook her head and managed a semiconvincing smile.

"I'll be okay. Bless you for coming in today. I don't know what we'd have done without you."

"It was like the Indianapolis 500," Joan muttered.

"And we're the car heading into the wall."

"But thanks to Jason, we're not in flames."

"Yet," Kat said, following Grant.

When they got out there, he asked questions. Had the viburnum already been tucked right up against the shed like that? *Yes.* Was the nail the skull was suspended from already there, or did it have to be hammered in? *Already there.* What was kept in the shed? Kat showed him, then watched him prowl inside and around the exterior before he finally removed the gunnysack.

She looked away, peripherally aware of him snapping pictures. Finally he put the camera in its case and reached for the skull, his big hands cradling it as he lifted it from the nail and contemplated it.

"You know anything about this kind of wire?"

"They're garden ties," she told him stiffly. "We sell them."

"Hmm."

"How soon before you can tell me…" She couldn't finish.

"Whether this is Hugh?"

"Yes."

"I'll have Dr. Espinosa take a look."

Dr. Espinosa had been Hugh's dentist, and was hers, as well.

"But I can tell you now, I'm ninety-nine percent sure, Kat." Grant's voice was low, gruff; like Joan, he was clearly trying to be gentle for her sake. "I have a copy of the dental records in my file. I took a look at them before I came out here. See that tooth missing? Hugh had a bridge there. Did you know that? And there's a couple of fairly distinctive fillings on those back molars." He paused. "I'm sorry, Kat. Sorrier than I can say."

Just like that, her stomach revolted. With a strangled sound, she bolted around the shed and fell to her knees, heaving. She retched over and over, grateful she'd skipped lunch and there wasn't much to come up. At some point she became aware that Grant had followed her and crouched to one side, his big hand laid lightly on her back.

Finally—finally—she was done, and sank backward onto her butt, head hanging between her knees. Her mouth tasted vile, her throat burned and her stomach hurt.

Better than her heart hurting, she thought blearily.

"Honey, I'm sorry." Still squatting on his haunches so he'd be at her level, Grant watched her with compassion.

"I could have put it there." She wouldn't have known her own voice.

"You could have." His hand had slid up to her nape and kneaded. "Did you?"

"No!"

"Then why did you say that?"

Something like hysteria gripped her. And why not? She was entitled, wasn't she?

"You think I killed him, don't you? Let's not pretend."

The hand on her neck went still. After a moment he said levelly, "Don't goad me, Kat. You know damn well I want to believe you didn't have anything to do with it. I'm hanging on to some semblance of impartiality by my fingertips. If I can't do my job, I'll have to ask someone else to take it over. Is that what you want?"

She sagged and whispered, "No. I'm being a bitch, and I don't even know why."

"Sure you do. Get mad at me if that's what you have to do to survive."

There he went again, so tender and *nice* she could hardly bear it. Kat squeezed her eyes shut on the terrible longing to throw herself in his arms and beg him never to let go. She couldn't. *He* couldn't.

"No," she said at last, dully. "I don't have to do that. I'm okay now. I let it get to me for a minute."

"Stomach better?"

"Yes." Feeling as steady as a newborn calf, Kat got to her feet, resenting the ease with which Grant rose, his muscles fluid. "Are you going to dust for fingerprints or anything?"

"No. The shed side is too rough to hold one, and it's unlikely whoever hung this up there touched anything else. I'll use that gunnysack to carry it in," he told her.

"Fine." Thankful he'd already wrapped the skull so she didn't have to see it again, she stopped long enough for him to pick up the bundle. He waited in turn while she grabbed her purse and locked buildings. His official car and her pickup were the only two vehicles left.

Stopping with her driver's side door open, Kat said, "It's probably not worth putting in the security cameras now, is it?"

"There are still plenty of body parts left."

She shuddered. "This feels like the finale."

"I doubt it," Grant said. "Especially since I'd guess the plan was for a customer to see the skull. Keeping it quiet the way you did, that may be real frustrating."

How could she come to work tomorrow, and the next day, and the next, knowing what kind of surprise still could be sprung on her?

"At least I know…" She couldn't finish.

"That Hugh is dead? Let me get confirmation from Espinosa."

Kat just looked at him over the roof of his car.

"I can't let this go anymore," he said quietly. "You know that, don't you?"

"Yes." She wanted him to leave, let her drive home before she fell apart.

Grant's forehead creased. "Kat…"

"Not now. Please."

His expression didn't ease, but he said, "All right. We'll talk tomorrow."

Kat got in, started the truck and backed out, leaving Grant standing beside his car, watching her go. When she turned onto the highway, she saw in her rearview mirror that he still hadn't moved.

CHAPTER SEVEN

CONFIRMATION THAT THE BONES were Hugh Riley's came quickly; Dr. Espinosa hung the dental X-rays on the light box on the wall in his office, glanced from the skull he held to the X-rays and said, "No question." He gingerly handed the skull back to Grant. "Do you, er, have the rest of his skeletonized remains?"

"Some of the other bones," Grant said evasively. "This at least answers the question of whether Riley is dead."

"Tough on his wife."

Grant remembered her on her knees puking in the weeds and thought, *You have no idea.* He didn't see how she could have faked that demonstration of shock. Her skin had been bleached white, her eyes wild, the tremor in her hands impossible to hide. She'd been shaken to her core, both by the gruesome appearance of the skull and by Grant's certainty that it was Hugh's.

If it was the last thing he did, Grant vowed, he was going to find out who was doing this to Kat.

"You ever shop at the nursery?" he asked casually.

The middle-aged dentist grinned. "I mow the

lawn. Under duress. Any flowers that get planted, my wife puts in. She came home with a few flats a week or so ago. Pretty sure that's where she bought them."

"Good selection."

"Good service, is what she says. She's strictly a weekend gardener, and she likes having someone tell her what she should buy and how to take care of it."

"That's their reputation," Grant agreed. "Kat Riley has built quite a business there."

"So I hear." There was some reserve in Espinosa's voice.

"Yeah, she's done wonders at the nursery since Hugh disappeared." Grant paused. "I suspect some people think she's better off without him."

The dentist gave him a quick, sharp glance. "I'm one of those people. I believe he was seeing one of my dental technicians at one time." His mouth was tight with disapproval. "She and her husband were having problems."

"Hugh had something of a reputation," Grant said carefully. "Tell me, is the technician still with you?"

"No. She became unreliable. I believe she's divorced now, but one of the girls mentioned her the other day. If you want to track her down…?"

"Yes."

He walked Grant out, where one of the office workers said that yes, Corinna had moved to Stanwood and worked for Dr. Tuller there now.

"She went back to her maiden name. Pantley…

no. Pankey." She smiled in satisfaction. "That was it. Stuck in my mind because her married name was Jones, you know. From never having to spell her name to always having to."

In his car, Grant called Dr. Tuller's office and, without needing to identify himself, found that, indeed, Corinna Pankey worked there and was in today. He made the twenty-minute drive, presented his badge to the receptionist, and a minute later a visibly nervous young woman in a white lab coat came to the waiting room.

"Chief Haller? I understand you wanted to see me?"

"Is there someplace private we can talk for a minute?"

The whites of her eyes flashed. "I…yes. I'm between appointments. Um…we can go out in back. There's a bench there where we take breaks sometimes."

She led him through the office, down a short hall and outside, where the bench sat against the stucco wall and looked out at a vacant lot of tall, brown grass.

After they'd sat, Grant said, "I understand you once had a relationship with Hugh Riley."

She stiffened. "Who told you that? It was years ago. Does this have something to do with him going missing? I hadn't seen him for, like, a year before that."

"I'll be blunt," Grant said. "I'd heard rumors that Hugh had a number of affairs, and I'm look-ing for confirmation that it's true. And perhaps a better sense of his personality, if you're willing to talk to me about him."

"Why do you want to know?" She gazed at him in obvious perplexity. "I don't understand."

Damn. He couldn't wrap his mind around the idea that a man married to Kat would cheat on her with this woman. Corinna was pretty enough, he guessed, but ordinary. Late twenties, maybe, buxom but plump, her hair an obviously dyed blond, starting to look a little strawlike. Faint traces of acne scars peeked from beneath her makeup.

"We believe that he's dead," Grant said, "and are trying to get a better handle on who he was spending time with."

"Well, it wasn't me." Despite the heavy foundation, color stood out on her cheeks as if painted there with a heavy hand. "We—I thought we were in love." She stared at the vacant lot. "Eli—he was my husband—and I weren't getting on so good. He was drinking too much, and Hugh—" Her shoulders moved. "He was really sweet to me. I knew he was married, but he said it was like my marriage. Lots of yelling and not much good left. You know?"

"Yeah." That pretty much summed up the last months of his own marriage.

"We had coffee a couple of times, and then he showed me around the nursery. It was a Sunday, so it was closed. In one of the greenhouses we…" She stole a look at Grant.

It would sicken Kat to know that her husband had brought women to the nursery to screw them. Goddamn it. He was even more of a scumbag than Grant had thought.

"After that?" he asked, keeping his voice neutral.

"A couple of times we went away for a Friday night or something. By that time Eli and I were about done. He thought I was going to Mom's. Hugh kept saying Kathryn and he were arguing about the nursery and whether he was going to have to pay alimony. Stuff like that. But after, like, six weeks, I started to wonder."

Grant nodded encouragement.

The vivid color in Corinna's cheeks hadn't dimmed any. "I left Eli, and when I told Hugh I didn't like knowing he was still living with his wife, he said to be fair he had to give his marriage a chance, and he realized he *hadn't* been fair, seeing me the way he was. And he loved me, so this was really hard, but—" She shrugged. "Me, I figured out he was another creep. Except—" a wistful note crept into her voice "—he was nice and funny and, just, sweet. So I didn't know for sure. Except I ran into him at Safeway, like, a couple months later, and he acted as if he didn't even recognize me. That's when I knew for sure I'd been really dumb." She straightened, looking at Grant with a dignity that made him sorry he'd put her through this. "Is that all you wanted to know?"

"Unless you saw him with any other women later…?"

She shook her head. "Eli and I were done, like I said, and I went to stay with my mom in Lynnwood for a while. The only other time I ever saw Hugh was that time at the store. Except on the news about him disappearing, and I thought maybe his wife had caught him with another woman. And you know what? If I wasn't the only one, he deserved whatever she did to him." She rose to her feet. "I need to go back to work."

Grant stood, too. "Thank you. You've been very helpful."

Corinna gave a shamed nod and hurried into the clinic. Grant walked around the outside of the building to the parking lot and his car.

So now he knew. Gossip had it right. Hugh Riley hadn't just had trouble keeping his pants zipped, he'd been a predator. He'd seen the vulnerability in Corinna Jones and used it, feeding her what she needed to hear until she got suspicious and became too much trouble. He'd ditched her, then, with a story that sounded well used.

Grant muttered a couple of vicious words that fit the son of a bitch well, then mulled over his next steps.

Find Hugh Riley's other women. In particular the ones who came after Corinna Jones née Pankey.

How many would there be? Kat had said she'd wondered, because he would lose interest in her for a few weeks to a few months at a time. So there was a pattern; probably that was how long it took most women to see through his lies. Or maybe how long it took him to tire of each new conquest. What Kat hadn't said was how far apart those periods of disinterest in her were.

He could ask her.

Grant grunted. No. Not happening.

All right. Assume it also took that shit weeks to months to find and seduce another woman. So… maybe two or three affairs the last year.

If he'd kept up that pace, there were a hell of a lot of women out there who might have reason to hate Hugh's guts. Kat wasn't alone in having a motive, not when Hugh had likely left other women's marriages strewn like so much garbage under his feet.

How could Kat not have *known,* rather than merely suspected? Grant knew he was going to have to ask that question. He wouldn't be doing his job if he didn't.

He knew where to start his inquiries. Shelly Gill, a dispatcher, was married to the one and only mortician in West Fork. Somehow, she always seemed to know everything about everybody. Grant respected the fact that she was also remarkably closemouthed about what she knew, perhaps because much of it came from Bert, her husband. But when Grant had needed to know something before, she'd been a gold mine.

He asked her into his office as soon as he arrived at the station. A petite, freckled redhead in her forties, she raised carefully plucked eyebrows and asked if she could bring her coffee.

"Yeah, let me pour a cup, too," he agreed.

Once she was settled across the desk from him, he said, "Bert's storing some bones for me. They're Hugh Riley's."

"I heard rumors."

He shook his head in amazement. "We didn't know for sure until today."

"A couple of Mrs. Riley's employees aren't real discreet. Everyone knows some bones have turned up out at the nursery."

"Good God," he muttered, and she grinned at his naivety.

"Small town."

"I'm reminded every day." He sat back in his chair and studied her. "Shelly, I'm told Hugh couldn't keep it zipped. I want to find out who he was seeing before he disappeared."

After a moment, she said, "I can tell you what I've heard, but I don't know how true most of it is."

He nodded his understanding.

"You know Belinda Foster, don't you? She's a loan officer down at County Mortgage. It's pretty well-known he had an affair with her."

"Before or after her divorce?" Grant asked grimly. Belinda had been married to John Foster, who headed the city's Department of Public Works.

"After." Shelly hesitated. "Maybe during."

She had a better memory about such things than he did, and they were able to pin down the timing to a year and a half or more before Hugh drove away never to be seen again. Still worth talking to her, he guessed.

"All right. Anyone else?"

She came up with a couple of other names. Julia Bailey, a clerk at the library and not married, then or now.

"Although that might have been longer ago," she said thoughtfully. "She'd probably tell you."

He added the name to his notes.

"And there was an aide at the school. I knew her a little because she worked in Aidan's classroom." Aidan was her son, now eleven or twelve, Grant thought. At that stage where he was starting to trip over his own feet. Frowning, Shelly gazed into space. "Pretty. And young. I actually saw them together. So this one isn't rumor. I saw them coming out of La Hacienda in Marysville. They kissed before she got in her car. Angie," she said suddenly. "Angie Hewitt or Hiatt or something like that."

"Is she still around?"

Shelley shook her head. "I think she moved away. I know she wasn't back the next fall, anyway. I remember wondering if it might have something to do with him."

She wasn't sure when she'd seen the two of them together, except the weather had been warm because Angie had been wearing a tank top, cropped pants and flip-flops. "If she was more than twenty-two or -three, I'll work an extra shift at the next full moon without pay." Her mouth was tight. She had a daughter, too, at the high school. One not that much younger now than Angie Hewitt or Hiatt had been back then.

"Damn," Grant muttered.

"Bert may have a hard time handling his remains with respect," Shelly said, voice hard.

Their eyes met. "As long as he treats Kat Riley with respect, I'm okay with that," Grant said softly.

"If I asked around, I could probably dredge up a couple more names from longer ago, but those are the ones that come to mind from nearer the time when he went missing."

She went back to work, and Grant back to brooding. He'd like to know which of Kat's employees had spread the gossip about the bones. The kid who'd been so sure that first one was human? Had any of the others even seen a bone? Joan Stover knew about all the discoveries, but he had a hard time picturing her rushing to call all her friends with the latest. She'd struck him as fiercely loyal.

That said, if there was one thing he'd learned in his years in law enforcement, it was that you couldn't judge by appearances. He'd seen a pierced, tattooed drug addict rescue a kitten from the river, and had personally arrested a handsome, well-liked banker with a beautiful family for raping his eight-year-old daughter. Joan Stover could conceivably be harboring resentment of her employer.

A teenager, though, would be more prone to texting his friends the minute he left work. Who might tell their parents. And Kat had eight employees, full- and part-time.

He glanced at his watch and decided he could catch Belinda before lunch. She was an easy one to talk to.

Since he and her ex-husband were both city employees, he'd met Belinda a few times when Grant had first taken the job here. He'd liked them both, and would have been more surprised when he heard she and John were getting a divorce if his own marriage hadn't been rocky. He and Rachel put a good face on it in public. Those kinds of troubles didn't always show to casual acquaintances or even close friends.

He got lucky and spotted her coming out the rear door of the mortgage office as he pulled up.

When Grant told her what he wanted to talk about, she looked more resigned than upset, and agreed she could spare a few minutes.

In the car with him, Belinda sat with her back so straight it barely touched the seat, purse gripped on her lap, and stared straight ahead through the windshield during most of their conversation.

"The bastard dumped me," she said. "I fell in love with him. It was stupid, when I knew he was married. I'd even met her—his wife—a couple of times, but I had myself convinced she must be some kind of bitch or he wouldn't have been so unhappy with her. John and I had just split up, you know, and I guess I was…" She hesitated.

Vulnerable. Just like Corinna.

"Primed," was the word Belinda chose at last. "He came into the office to talk about refinancing his house. He said he wanted some capital for the nursery."

"Did he go ahead with the refinance?"

She shook her head. "He said his wife didn't like the idea. He dropped it after that. But he took me out to lunch a couple of times. Dropped by, and it seemed casual at first. Friendly. You know."

"How long did the affair last?"

She shrugged, her expression bitter. "Four or five weeks. He was romantic. Bringing me flowers, taking me to out-of-the-way, candlelit restaurants. And then I guess he could tell I was getting serious about him, and next thing I know I'm getting this spiel about how he needs to give his marriage another chance. It was the first time I could look at him and see plain as day that he didn't mean a word he was saying. I felt like such an idiot."

She knew exactly when she'd started seeing Hugh, because she knew when she and John had separated and when their divorce was final. September and early October.

Hugh had disappeared in May of the following year.

The very young teacher's aide must have been his last affair, Grant realized. She sounded like an unlikely murderess, but he very much wanted to find and talk to her.

Grant couldn't help wondering, though, whether there might have been another woman in between Corinna and the teacher's aide. Unless Shelly's memory was off—and he didn't believe that—there would have been eight or ten months, minimum, between the end of one affair and the start of the next. Had Hugh and Kat had a good stretch for some reason?

Another question Grant hated to ask her but would anyway.

He phoned the school district office and a woman in Personnel promised to do some research. She was prompt; not half an hour later, her call was put through to him.

"It was Hiatt," she told him. "Angela Jo Hiatt. She

wasn't even with us a full school year. The last day I show her working was May 16. She let us know she had a family emergency. It was an email. I have it in her file."

The day after Hugh Riley disappeared. That couldn't be a coincidence. But what did it mean?

"She quit?" he asked.

"She wouldn't have been automatically rehired anyway. Para-eds have to reapply annually. They put in for the school they want, the number of hours, whether they'd like to do special ed or work at certain grade levels. No guarantees. She didn't reapply."

Armed with the address and phone number she had in her records for Angela Hiatt, Grant thanked her. When he tried the number, he reached a perky voice mail message for Loretta and Pete Ringstad. He didn't leave a message. The phone company reassigned numbers after six months.

He knew the apartment building where Angie had lived, and called the manager, who, regrettably, Grant also knew. Joe Grier was a cranky old bastard who had a habit of letting himself into apartments and browsing whenever he was inclined. The out-of-state owner cared only that he maintained the building adequately and kept the units rented. Tenants hadn't been able to prove Grier had been in their apartments, but Grant knew damn well he had, although whether he was actually stealing or merely rifling through drawers and who knew what else wasn't clear.

Grier wasn't pleased to hear from Grant. He grunted and said, "You expect me to remember some woman from five years ago?"

"You do keep records, I assume."

"Yeah, yeah."

Grant heard heavy breathing and the scraping sound of a file cabinet drawer being opened, followed by the thud of it closing and a second one opening.

"Unit 203? That what you said?"

Grant agreed that it was.

"Angela Hiatt. She paid through May."

"Did she give notice?"

"Key and a note were dropped through my slot. Place was empty by the time I checked it out. I don't know whether she stayed the whole month or not."

"Did you reimburse any of her cleaning deposit?" Grant asked. "Do you have an address?"

"Doesn't look like she ever applied. Lotta people don't."

Lotta people probably knew Grier would find some excuse not to give them their deposits back, Grant suspected. Tenants talked to each other.

He checked Department of Motor Vehicle records next and found Angela Jo Hiatt's driver's license had expired the following year and she had never renewed it, which presumably meant she'd moved out of state. *Damn it,* he thought in frustration. He'd have really liked to talk to her. He was pissed at himself for not digging deep enough then to find out about her. Then he would have suspected the two of them ran off together. Now, he knew that hadn't happened. But what in hell had?

Finding Angie Hiatt had become a priority.

It was time now to go out to the nursery and have a long talk with Kat.

"THEN HUGH'S BEEN DEAD all this time." Kat knew she sounded too calm. She had gone numb sometime during the night. The confirmation from Dr. Espinosa that the dental records were a match couldn't penetrate this weird, puffy insulation that seemed to muffle her emotions.

"We don't know that for sure," Grant corrected her. He sat across the desk from her in her office. He'd requested an interview with her in a voice she had recognized from those days. He was all cop. And she was a suspect. "Did he die that day? Probably, but not necessarily. It could have been a day later, a week later, months later. A long time ago, sure. The condition of the bones tells us that. But all we're certain of is that he drove away. Where did he go that day? Who did he see?"

She went very still. "What is it you suspect?"

His gray eyes were watchful. "I believe he was having an affair at the time with a young woman named Angie Hiatt. She quit her job, citing a family emergency, the day after Hugh disappeared. I haven't yet been able to locate her."

That hurt did penetrate, slipping lethally through her ribs. *Angie Hiatt*. For all her wondering, Kat had never had a name. Never been sure.

She kept her chin high, not letting him see the wound he'd dealt. "Who was she?"

"A teacher's aide at the elementary school. Not quite twenty-three years old. That's about all I've learned so far."

After a moment she nodded.

"You say you didn't know. Kat, I've verified two

other affairs. The women confirmed having them with him. He took them away for weekends, out to candlelit dinners. He brought one to the nursery on a Sunday." He leaned forward, so large he loomed, his intent obviously to intimidate. "How is it possible you didn't know?"

It took everything she had not to move, to shrink away from him. "You think I did," she whispered. "You think he told me that he and this Angie Hiatt were going away together."

"That seems a likely scenario," he said in a hard voice.

She carefully removed her hands from the desk and laid them on her lap to hide the tremor from Grant. "I suppose it does," she said, around the huge ball of *something* caught in her throat.

He waited, his face as hard as his voice. Yesterday, he'd been kind. He'd changed his mind about her since.

"But you're wrong." She made herself return his gaze. "It's true I'd been afraid he was seeing someone, but I didn't know for sure. I never did. He... just wasn't that different when he was from when he wasn't. Mostly, I'd notice stretches when he wanted sex more or less often."

"The weekends away?"

"There weren't very many. Supposedly he was visiting wholesale or specialty nurseries." She moved her shoulders, hating the helplessness of the gesture. "We deal with ones down in Oregon and even northern California, so that wasn't unusual. Once there was a high school reunion. He convinced me I had to keep the nursery open, and I'd be bored anyway. I didn't mind."

His stare had become incredulous. "You must have had a real loving relationship."

Humiliation made her cheeks burn. "I…suppose we didn't. I didn't have anything to judge by. I thought we were mostly happy."

"Happy."

Anger lit a pilot light beneath her breastbone. "Is that so impossible?"

"The guy was screwing half the women in town, and you thought he was happy with you."

"He was!" Shocked, Kat realized she'd half risen to her feet and was shouting. "He didn't want anything more from me! Don't you get it? He *liked* having me as a partner in the nursery and someone to put dinner on the table at night and laugh at his jokes and not… not challenge him too much. I think…" Oh, this was even more humiliating, but she had to say it. "I think maybe he turned to someone else when I pushed too hard. When I'd get mad because he wouldn't do what he should have to make the nursery more successful, or work on the house, or talk to me about something that mattered. *That's* when he'd drift away."

"And find someone who'd admire him."

"Yes," she said dully. It had been her fault. She supposed she *had* known. She'd simply…protected herself, by pretending she didn't.

Grant said a crude word. Suddenly he wasn't just a cop. "Why in hell did you put up with it, Kat? Tell me that."

She was still standing, she realized. Her knees

gave out and she dropped into her squeaky chair. She didn't know how to begin to explain. This big, domineering man would never understand.

"Maybe I didn't care enough." That wasn't quite it, though, was it? Because she had. It hurt, losing the illusions she'd clutched when she first married Hugh and imagined them deeply, forever in love. "It was gradual," she said. Whispered. She cleared her throat, pushed herself to speak louder, stronger. "I liked working at the nursery. Having a home. Hugh was easy to live with. I never really knew anyone with a marriage any better."

Oh, that sounded pathetic, and was. She'd been so damned grateful for what Hugh had given her, she'd resigned herself to not having the more he'd promised. Love and passion and genuine friendship, the kind that accepted vulnerability to each other. Except for the occasional sex, she and Hugh had ended up like roommates who'd found each other on Craigslist, ones who got along fine and liked each other but were unlikely to stay in touch very long once either moved on. Only…to all appearances he'd been content; he was satisfied with his life the way it was.

And she'd so lacked in pride and confidence, she'd been grateful to be his partner and wife even if both relationships had been so shallow she'd had to be very, very careful not to look beneath the surface.

"If you'd caught him in bed with another woman, would you have left him?"

The heat in her cheeks slid throughout her body, burning as it went. "Yes." Then, more softly, she said, "I think so."

He shook his head in bafflement. "Why would you have hesitated?"

"Because then I wouldn't have had anything." She made herself meet his eyes. "I shouldn't have said that, should I? Now you know how much I didn't want to lose what little I had."

Grant flattened his hands on the desk. Something roughened his voice; rage, maybe. "Did you catch him with Angie Hiatt, Kat? Was he going to leave you for her? Did you kill the son of a bitch so you could keep your home and the business?"

She stared back at him. "Why bother asking, when you already seem to know the answer?" Kat pushed herself to her feet. "Unless you have any more questions, I'd appreciate it if you'd leave."

CHAPTER EIGHT

ON HER COMPUTER MONITOR, video feed from one of the new security cameras played. In the week and a half since they'd been installed, Kat had tried to get in the habit of letting video run as she worked at her desk, although she'd have had to admit she barely kept half an eye on it. Like right now, when most of her concentration was on an order for fall-blooming perennials. She hadn't managed to watch more than an hour here or there of footage from any of the cameras. There didn't seem to be any great urgency, since no more bones had been left at the nursery.

What she was seeing now, she realized, was closing time yesterday. The camera had a good, wide-angle view of the interior of the main building—the counter with the cash register, the door to the employee break room, the exit to the parking lot.

Melinda Simmons was behind the counter, counting money. Kat saw herself walk by, on her way to her office, if she remembered right. Jason disappeared into the break room, reappeared with a backpack slung over his shoulder and, after a wave, went out the front. It was like a mime show, oddly unreal. Tess Miller came out of the break room a minute or two later, carrying a big tote bag. The way she glanced around caught Kat's attention; order form momentarily forgotten, she watched as Tess brushed against a table that held hand-sculpted clay figurines and paused as if checking to be sure she hadn't knocked anything over. Her next movement was smooth, practiced. She snatched one of the figures off the table, slipped it into the tote and walked out.

Maybe it was stupid to be shocked, but… Kat rewound the feed and watched again as a trusted employee stole from her.

Tess always carried a big tote instead of a purse. She brought her lunch in it, sometimes had a crochet project to work on at lunchtime. Other days she'd pull a magazine out to skim as she ate or sipped a diet cola. Like all the employees, Tess had her strengths and weaknesses. She was good with customers, did really well behind the cash register and in the gift area, knew her annuals. She could fake it with the other plants, but didn't seem to retain what she learned about the difference between one hydrangea and another, never mind the hybrid Japanese maples or the huge sedum family. She was reliable, though, which was a plus.

Kat wondered if she helped herself to something most days. She'd done that so damned professionally, Kat bet she did, or close enough. Everyone knew she did some selling on eBay; she grumbled when she had to work Fridays or Saturdays, because those were the fruitful days for her to hit the garage sales.

Or so she'd always said. Maybe her entire online business was based on items lifted from Sauk River Plant Nursery.

"Damn, damn, *damn,*" Kat exclaimed. Firing Tess wasn't going to bother her at all, not after what she'd seen, but it sucked to have to hire and train someone new now, in one of the busiest months. And how much inventory had Tess helped herself to?

The bigger question, Kat asked herself, was whether she called Grant to have him arrest an employee she'd trusted for almost two years. Was the tape definitive enough evidence? What if Tess claimed she'd grabbed the figurine for a gift and intended to pay the next day?

After a minute Kat started the feed again and watched herself walk across the camera's eye and take the money bag from Melinda. The two of them had left together, turning out the lights when they went. The room was now shadowy and still; eventually the camera shut itself off with no movement to activate it.

Kat realized she had a headache. No wonder. Lord knows she was operating under a teeny bit of stress right now. She'd learned through the grapevine that George Slagle had been not-so-quietly talking about her, about how bones had been found at the nursery, hinting that her arrest was imminent. She'd known George resented her winning the award when he never had, but she wouldn't have guessed he'd be petty and mean. She'd never done anything to make him dislike her.

There were a lot of people, she was discovering, who disliked her. More and more this past week she'd left the customers to her employees and hid out in the office or one of the greenhouses. She'd endured enough rumors and innuendo when Hugh first disappeared, and pretended she didn't notice the way people murmured something quickly to a companion before gazes slid from hers. But she'd thought she was past all that. And this time…this time it was different, because what if George was right? What if her arrest *was* imminent? It wouldn't be all that hard to set her up. She kept expecting Grant to get a tip that the rest of Hugh's bones were in her basement, and find that they were indeed there.

Where did reasonable fear cross over into paranoia? Did it matter? She felt most of the time as if hysteria was crowding her chest, pressing her lungs, constricting the passage into her throat. She was scared.

Mad, too, she'd discovered. Mad, mostly, at Hugh. And herself, too, for being so willfully blind. Grant's incredulity made her ashamed that she'd managed to convince herself that she was happy. Had she *ever* really been happy? She didn't know.

Yes. The night of the banquet, when she heard her name.

"This year's Snohomish County Business Owner of the Year is…Kathryn Riley of Sauk River Plant Nursery!" That might have been the happiest moment of her life. She'd made something of herself. She was *somebody.*

And there had been that instant when her eyes met Grant's, and she saw in them pride in her, and yearning that told her he still wanted her. And the rueful tilt of an eyebrow that said, *If you don't want me, why was it me you looked for first?*

They both knew the answer, but he wouldn't let it stop him from arresting her if he decided she had something to do with Hugh's death.

She had always thought she would genuinely grieve if she found out Hugh had been dead all this time, that he hadn't run out on her. But Grant's revelations had made her so angry, she thought maybe she hated Hugh. Hated him for telling her so many lies, for making her feel dirty now at the memory of sex with him. For knowing that he'd never loved her at all, not really. To him, she'd been…a convenience. The fun and excitement in his life had come from the pursuit of other women. Apparently, lots of other women.

Had he intended to leave her for Angie Hiatt? Kat couldn't remember him seeming any different than ever, those last days. If anything, he'd suddenly noticed *her* again, in that way he had. Maybe…maybe Angie had quit her job and moved away because Hugh had broken up with her.

Kat was surprised to find herself thinking viciously, *That woman* deserved *to get hurt. She deserved whatever she suffered. They* all *did.*

Kat wouldn't have understood why any woman would so much as look at a married man, except for Grant's kiss. What she'd felt, and had no right to feel. What she'd done and, more, might have done if they hadn't been interrupted.

Clearly Hugh had been good at deluding women. It could be so seductive, seeing what you wanted to see. Who knew better than her?

But no, she thought wearily, she *hadn't* been

altogether deluded. She'd known something was missing in their marriage, and even in their partnership at the nursery. A whole lot of something. The trouble was, she had convinced herself that she was being foolish to yearn for some kind of ideal passion and intimacy and meeting of minds. Probably real life wasn't like that. If it existed at all, she'd never seen it.

Except… Her throat still clogged at the memory of the first time she saw the newly hired police chief, Grant Haller. She'd been attending a city council meeting because the city was on the verge of annexing the part of the river valley that included the nursery. Hugh couldn't be bothered going.

"We'll be fine either way," he had said, with one of his who-cares shrugs. He'd given her that crooked, sweet smile. "You can represent us."

Now she wondered if he'd been glad to have the evening to himself so he could slip out to meet whoever his latest lover was while his wife sat through endless, droning speeches pro and con regarding an annexation that was, by then, probably a done deal.

But toward the end, Grant had been introduced and strolled to the front of the room. She remembered losing her ability to breathe. Her heart had contracted, squeezed like a fist, and she didn't even understand why. He wasn't that handsome, just tough and solid and *male*. Broad shoulders. Deep grooves from nose to mouth. Brown hair cut short enough to subdue what she suspected was a tendency to curl. Gray eyes that scanned the audience with a certain cynicism.

Eyes that had stopped at her, stared. There had been a stunning moment that stretched long enough to make her dizzy, a moment during which she felt things she never had before. Then he'd blinked, turned toward somebody in the audience who had been asking a question, and she'd done her best to become invisible. If he looked at her again that night, she hadn't been aware of it.

But every time she saw him after that, her pulse became erratic, her breath either stopped or came too fast. And every time, he looked at her a little too long, and she saw in his eyes the same reluctant attraction she felt.

Until the night when she'd slipped out of a chamber of commerce meeting a little early, and encountered him in the parking lot. By then they knew each other to speak to; he'd been out to the nursery a couple of times in response to problems, and they had heard each other voice opinions in various meetings. Kat had even met his wife, Rachel, a beautiful, petite blonde with bright blue eyes and a smile that sparkled. Rachel was the kind of woman who, entirely unintentionally, stole Kat's limited confidence and made her feel awkward. And yet, Grant looked at Kat, even when he stayed at his wife's side.

Until that night, when he'd spoken quietly to Kat and walked her to her car. No one else had followed them out of the grange hall. The night was particularly dark, she remembered, the few sodium lamps not casting light to the far reach of the lot where she'd had to park. She had unlocked the driver door and opened it, then turned to face Grant. He was closer than she'd expected.

"You make me wish, Kat." His voice was rough. "I do the same to you, don't I?"

She still didn't know if she'd ever answered. His hands had framed her face, tilted her chin up, and his mouth covered hers. From the beginning, the kiss had had a quality of desperation. It wasn't tentative at all. Most shocking was the feeling of *rightness,* as if in him she'd found something missing from her life. It was like coming home to a barely remembered place. She had never, never wanted him to let her go.

Later, ashamed, she wasn't sure even the sound of voices spilling out as the grange doors opened would have recalled her to any sense of who and where they were. He was the one to stiffen, his fingers momentarily tightening. He'd groaned against her mouth, whispered, "Kat…" and taken a step back. The cool night air was between them, the sound of other car doors opening and slamming, voices calling across the parking lot.

All she remembered now was scrambling into her car, yanking the door shut, shoving the key into the ignition. Driving away without looking back, hot and cold pouring in turn through her body. When she got home Hugh had barely glanced away from the TV and she'd gone to bed, pretending to be asleep when he came up later.

Grant had stopped by the nursery a few days later, but she'd dodged him. She knew he saw her escaping and didn't care. Did he think she'd sleep with him?

She wasn't like that. Honestly, she wasn't that crazy about sex, anyway.

Except, of course, she'd known from the first touch of his large, calloused hands on her face that it would be different with him.

She had tried very, very hard not to think about that. It wasn't many weeks later when Hugh disappeared, which made not thinking about Grant that way a whole lot easier. He had looked at her differently after that: as a cop.

Except, even then, there'd been an odd moment here or there when she saw in his eyes that he was remembering, or feeling the same unwanted attraction that had been there between them from the beginning.

Until these past weeks, she would have said it was not only water under the bridge, but water that had long since reached the sea and dispersed. She had wanted so much to believe what they'd felt had been no more than momentary temptation. Because otherwise she'd have had to accept that she had betrayed her husband in a way that wasn't just physical.

Only, now she knew. He'd been betraying her all along.

The niggling fear crept over her that it was her fault. Maybe she was cold. She hadn't gotten a lot of satisfaction out of sex. Hugh's laziness and ability to slide out of hard work or responsibility had increasingly begun to irritate her. Maybe if she'd loved him more...

"Don't do this!" she said aloud, startling herself in her quiet office. Hugh had been gone—dead—for four years now. It was too late for regrets. And, damn it, there was plenty of blame on his side. In fact, right this minute she felt entitled to throw most of it his way. He could have talked to her if he thought something was lacking in their relationship. He didn't have to start sneaking around looking for it elsewhere. He didn't have to act as if he liked his life fine, if that wasn't how he felt.

Kat was astonished to realize she was crying. She hardly ever did. It couldn't be this crap with Tess that had set her off. Not Hugh's death, either; she was too mad at him for that and it was too long ago, anyway. Was she shedding tears for what she and Grant could have had and lost? Maybe.

Or maybe she was just scared. Scared to find that Hugh's lies weren't the only ones, that people she'd liked secretly detested her or stole from her or talked about her behind her back. What she'd wanted most from life and had thought she'd found was a place to belong. Security. A home, a chance to prove she was capable, to see respect in the eyes of other people.

And now she was finding how easily her business could be undermined, that the respect she thought she saw might have been something else altogether. And Grant had been able to look her in the eye and ask if she'd killed Hugh. He had believed she might have done it, and that hurt more than she wanted to admit.

But I'm good at something. I have proved that much. She'd turned a marginal business into a thriving one. That was something to be proud of, wasn't it?

She did have friends, too, not many, but some. Joan, for one. And she inspired loyalty from some of her employees, like Jason, who she was uncomfortably aware might have a crush on her. She had good customers, too, like Becca Montgomery and Carol Scammell who'd been back today and Annika Lindstrom, who'd been in to buy half a dozen old roses on Tuesday rather than having ordered them from one of the heirloom rose nurseries. Nobody was universally popular. Most employers sooner or later caught an employee stealing from them. Of course she hadn't been immune.

Most people, though, weren't in danger of being arrested for murder.

Now she *was* being paranoid, she thought wryly. All this brooding because she'd caught an employee stealing. She'd fire Tess tomorrow... No, Friday, if she wanted to do it face-to-face. Tess was off until then.

Okay, Friday.

Kat gathered her purse and hurried to her truck, wishing she hadn't lingered until night had fallen. Grant was right; she shouldn't be here alone, especially with dark gathering.

But then, she'd be alone at home, too. She'd taken to leaving lights on in case she was late getting in. Kat had even considered, lately, buying a handgun and learning to use it. She carried a marble rolling pin with her when she checked window and door locks. Tonight she would take it with her into the basement, when she went down to be very, very sure the rest of Hugh hadn't been left for Grant to find.

"CAN YOU TAKE A BREAK?" Feeling awkward as a schoolboy, Grant stood in front of Kat. Since that last, ugly confrontration, they hadn't been alone. "I brought lunch." He held up the pair of white paper bags.

Her gaze flicked to the employee behind the counter. Chad somebody. She had three guys working for her: this Chad, young and buff, the community college kid and James Cheung, at least mid-twenties, quiet, reserved.

She'd been arranging potted pansies on a multilevel plant stand near the front doors when Grant walked in. He'd seen her go very still when she saw him, like a rabbit caught in the open. Now, after a brief hesitation, she nodded. "Sure."

"Your office?"

"It's a nice day. Why don't we eat outside?"

She led the way out the rear door and through the nursery grounds, greeting at a few people on the way. With Grant in uniform, it was a given that pretty much everyone turned to stare. They were probably wondering when he was going to whip out the handcuffs. Kat didn't ask why he'd come, or anything else. With her walking ahead of him, he got lost in the way even the weak spring sunshine shimmered in her hair. That was when he could lift his gaze from her long-legged stride and the subtle sway of her hips.

Whether it made sense or not, he had it bad for her. Grant didn't think that would be changing.

He'd noticed before that there was a small patio behind one of the greenhouses, accessible only to staff. It was nice: white-painted metal table and set of four chairs on what was more like a courtyard paved with bricks in a herringbone pattern. Pale leaves were unfurling on thorny shoots of roses in the surrounding beds, and it looked as though a bunch of daffodils or tulips were going to burst into bloom soon.

He set the bags down on the table and pulled out a chair. Kat chose the one opposite Grant rather than the one beside him.

She looked straight at him for the first time. "What's this? A condemned woman's last meal?"

"More like an apology," he admitted. "I don't believe for a minute you killed anyone." He shouldn't be saying this to her at all, but the past week had killed him, seeing the wariness and even fear in her eyes when she saw him.

Now her lashes fluttered, the only way she gave away her surprise. "Have you shared that opinion with anyone?"

He opened one of the bags and took out the two bowls with spicy black bean soup. "Mortensen."

Jeffrey Mortensen was the city manager, which made him Grant's boss. He was a humorless stick lacking, in Grant's opinion, any human empathy. If it couldn't be put down on a spreadsheet, it didn't exist.

Kat knew him well enough. Her eyes narrowed. "What did he say?"

"Not a lot."

Do your effing job had about summed it up. Which Grant had every intention of doing. But his gut told him Kat was another victim, not the perpetrator.

After a moment she reached for one of the bowls,

peeled off the lid and sniffed appreciatively. "I forgot to pack a lunch today."

"You're still losing weight."

"Some people eat when they're stressed. I don't."

He handed her one of the plastic spoons and dipped the second one in his own soup. "Sandwiches and drinks in the other bag."

Not having any idea whether she was a meat eater or not, he'd bought croissants heaped with cream cheese and veggies. She unwrapped hers, lifted the top and peered at it, then said, "This looks good."

They ate in silence for a moment. He was tempted to tip his face back, close his eyes and let the sun soak in. He didn't have the excuse Kat did to be feeling stress, but she wasn't alone in it.

Maybe because her stress had become his.

"Why?" she asked finally. "Why did you change your mind?"

"I didn't change it. I've never believed you had it in you to kill a man."

"What?" Looking pissed, she set down her spoon. "How can you say that? You've accused me at least twice. Last time—"

"I asked you a question. I didn't say, 'Kathryn Riley, I know damned well you murdered your husband and one of these days I'll prove it.' Did I?"

"The way you looked at me." Furious color slashed across her cheeks.

"You saw frustration." He couldn't tell her how many shades of frustration she'd really seen. "The truth is, I'm getting nowhere. And you, you keep throwing stuff at me. Sometimes, I think you *want* me and everyone else to hold you responsible."

"Sometimes I wonder if I am," she said, so softly he had to lean forward to hear.

His heart pumped hard once, like the bellows in an old-time blacksmith shop. *"What?"*

Her eyes shied from his. "Not that way. Just…marriages are two-sided. If I wasn't enough for him—"

"Son of a bitch. Don't you ever say that. I've spent four long years wishing I had what Hugh did, and you can damn well bet it never would have crossed my mind to think you weren't enough for me."

She stunned him with stark, cold words. "You were married. And you still tried to have what was Hugh's."

She might as well have kicked him in the belly. Was that what she'd thought all this time?

"No," he said. "I wanted you like I've never wanted anything. You know that. I gave into temptation once. Once. And that's as far as it ever would have gone."

Her stare didn't retreat at all. "Did you tell Rachel you'd kissed another woman?"

"No, I didn't." His jaw tightened. "Did you tell Hugh?"

He hated seeing the shame that made her look down. "You know I didn't."

"We kissed. I wasn't asking you to meet me at some cheap motel in Everett. I was married and I knew damn well I was." More quietly, he added, "I knew you were, too."

"What was it you were going to say to me when you came out to the nursery a couple days later?"

"Why do you want to know now, when you wouldn't listen then?"

She didn't say anything. She crumbled a bit of croissant with her fingers.

"I was going to say I was sorry. That I shouldn't have touched you." He didn't want to be honest, but had to. "I was going to tell you that Rachel and I were talking divorce."

Her gaze lifted again to his, the blue bottomless. Shocked?

"I suppose I was hoping you'd start thinking about your own marriage," he admitted reluctantly.

"Your divorce was over me?" She sounded horrified.

"No." He paused. Honesty. They had to have it, if there was to be any hope. "We moved out here partly because things weren't so good. Rachel wasn't happy. Being married to a cop is never easy, and we both thought it would help if she was closer to her family. My hours would be more regular with small town law enforcement." He shrugged. "Turns out there was more wrong between us than that. It didn't help when I met you, Kat, but I don't think Rachel ever knew how I felt. I…tried to ignore it. Those feelings, though, let me know Rachel and I should never have gotten married in the first place. I never felt anything like that for her, and I doubt she did for me."

Shc was still crumbling the sandwich. The birds would have a feast.

"Tell me," he said roughly. "Just once."

He saw the reluctance in the way her eyes met his,

but she said, "That I wished, too? Isn't that how you put it?"

His head jerked in acknowledgment.

"Yes. I did. I wished. And that made me feel a thousand times guiltier when Hugh disappeared. It made me…"

Suddenly angry, Grant said, "Fixate on him? Decide you were going to stay eternally devoted? Eternally faithful, whether the SOB deserved it or not?"

Face flaming, she pushed back her chair. "I didn't know he didn't. If I'd known—" Halfway to her feet, she stopped, closed her eyes.

Grant didn't move. "If you'd known?"

She opened her eyes and said fiercely, "I would have begged you to take me to that cheap motel. All right?"

"So you could get back at Hugh."

"Yes! And because—" She took several ragged breaths. "Because I wanted you. I've never—" Her lips pressed together.

She'd never felt the way she did about him for anyone else, either. That's what she was confessing. His chest swelled with the knowledge, but ached, too.

"You wouldn't have," he said gently. "No matter what. Neither of us would have taken it that far."

Kat seemed to sag, and sank into her chair. "No. I've never had it in me to…lash out at someone like that, I guess. To rebel."

He found himself smiling. "If you couldn't sleep

with another man to pay back your cheating husband, it's hard to see you killing him, even in a rage."

"I didn't. I think, if I'd had incontrovertible proof he was screwing around on me, I'd have left him. And that would have been the scariest thing I'd ever done, because I'd have had to start all over."

He'd been hungry when he ordered lunch and hungrier when he had to breathe in the spicy aroma all the way over to the nursery, but food was the last thing on his mind now. Kat was all he could think about. The secrets and sorrows in her deep blue eyes.

"Why, Kat? Why did you doubt your ability to start over?"

He knew some of it. That she didn't seem to have any family. Hugh and she had had that in common. Maybe that had been part of the appeal, at least to her; the two of them allied against the world. Except, it hadn't been that way.

"I didn't know my father," she said after a minute. "My mother…um, she used to leave me with friends or neighbors. You know, anyone she could foist me on. For a night, sometimes for days. Finally, she didn't come back. I guess she was using drugs. I don't really know. Anyway—" she shrugged, as if to say it didn't matter anymore "—I grew up in foster homes. Mostly people who did it for the money. Knowing they had to be paid to take me…it keeps you at a distance. I never had anything that was *mine*." Instead of grief, her eyes held that fierceness again. "I wanted…I wanted what I thought Hugh was giving me. Sharing everything made it even better than if we'd each gone off to different jobs every day. You know? Except as it turned out, none of it was mine. If I'd had a job or business of my own…" She tried to smile and failed. "As it is, I'd have walked away with nothing, not even a means of support."

No, he thought. *You'd have had me.* But she hadn't known that, and he couldn't have told her. Not then, not until he and Rachel exhausted the counseling sessions and the talks that got both franker and more strident as they went. Sex and a whole lot of misconceptions about each other had brought him and Rachel together, and with those misconceptions punctured like helium balloons—poof!—the sex didn't work anymore, either. He didn't think they'd even tried more than a handful of times after he met Kat and knew what and who he really wanted. He had done his damnedest to see his wife and not Kat when he got in bed with Rachel, but the truth was he hadn't much wanted her. The coals hadn't only burned down, they'd gone cold. Probably for both of them, although he couldn't be sure. He wasn't proud of the fact that he'd fallen in love with another woman while he was still married, whether that marriage was troubled or not.

"So you see," Kat said, after an interval, "I guess I did have all the motive in the world. Because I ended up with everything."

"It doesn't matter. I'm going to find out who's doing this to you, Kat. I promise I will."

"He was murdered, wasn't he?"

"There's nothing in the bones that have shown up so far to indicate how, but he had to be. Hard to imagine, if he keeled over from a heart attack, say, someone taking his body home and tucking it away as a keepsake. Hiding a body after you kill someone, that makes more sense."

Kat nodded. She had to have reasoned all that out, too.

"If only his body had been found then..." she murmured.

Their eyes met. It wasn't so different than the way they'd looked at each other that very first time.

If she had known she was a widow, if Grant had been able to arrest Hugh's killer...would she have turned to him? Thinking about the lonely years since was like taking a long swallow of wine that had gone to vinegar.

He still couldn't say, "I love you." Not yet. And not just because of the investigation. Kat wasn't ready. He could tell.

Waiting...waiting might not be so hard now, not when he could hear her soft admission, replay it as often as he wanted.

I did. I wished. I wanted you.

CHAPTER NINE

KAT'S FAVORITE PART OF THE DAY was the beginning, the half hour or forty-five minutes she gave herself at the nursery before the first employee arrived. The nursery was hers then, in a way it wouldn't be once staff and customers started showing up. She loved unlocking and rolling back the chain-link gate and pulling up in front, admiring the effect of the skillfully arranged profusion of foliage and bloom, trellises and necessities. She'd spent these past years a little bit ashamed of the way she gloated.

I built this.

To hell with Hugh, she thought this morning. *It is mine. I deserve it.* Maybe it was the lunch with Grant yesterday that made her feel stronger, more sure of herself.

Kat wished it wasn't Friday, when the first thing on her agenda was firing Tess.

She parked her pickup in the usual spot, farthest from the building. She'd been thinking that, one of these days, she should add employee parking off Hazeltine Road. On busy days, it was getting so that this parking lot was full to bursting.

Hugh had always parked in this same place. Once in a while, she thought about things like that, the ways she clung to his example, to habits, when she'd long since discarded others. As she unlocked the front door, she glanced back, half expecting for a second to see Hugh's battered old red pickup in place of her slightly newer, black one. She didn't like having him so much on her mind, haunting her as he hadn't since the first months after his disappearance.

Joan would be working today, thank goodness. Kat had called her yesterday and told her about Tess. One good thing was that the two day delay meant Kat had had a chance to post the job listing on the *Herald* website and on Craigslist. Responses poured in immediately. She'd brought half a dozen résumés with her this morning, and would start making calls a little later. Two of the applicants actually, wonder of wonders, had some plant nursery background, one so much Kat was suspicious. But she could get lucky, couldn't she?

The figurines Tess had been stealing weren't doing all that well, Kat mused, pausing by the table. She hated to tell the artist she wouldn't carry them anymore, because they were clever and appealing. This wasn't the right place to sell them. eBay, she thought with some irony, was probably a better venue. Maybe she'd start by cutting back. Instead of giving over a whole table, she could have a smaller selection on one shelf by the wind chimes and sun catchers. She could use this table for something else—a rotating display of perennials mixed with garden art, perhaps.

She was heading for her office when she heard an engine and then tires crunching gravel. Somebody was early. Way early. Surprised, she turned to see a black pickup pulling *out* of the parking lot, not in.

That was *her* truck being driven away. Had she left the keys in it? Her purse was still slung over her shoulder, and with one quick glance she saw her ring of keys clipped where they should be. Jolted, she thought, *Of course I didn't leave them in the truck. I had to unlock the door.*

She dropped the purse and ran out into the parking lot. The truck was accelerating the quarter of a mile to the highway, going too fast, raising dust on the gravel road. She stopped, stunned, to see it turn right onto the highway, heading toward the freeway rather than toward town.

The same way Hugh had gone, that long ago morning.

Kat tore back into the nursery and yanked her cell phone from her purse. That speed dial was coming in handy all too often.

It rang three times, four. She'd end up with voice mail. Grant probably wasn't at work yet, she realized. She should have called 911.

"Kat?"

"Somebody just stole my truck," she said. "Right from in front of the nursery."

"How long ago?"

"It turned onto the highway going west not one minute ago."

He cursed. "If we're lucky there'll be a patrol car in the right place, for once. I'll call you back or be out there." And he was gone.

She closed her phone and stood with it in her hand,

picturing the truck accelerating away, skidding once on the gravel.

Not signalling before making the turn.

Her heart was thudding, fast, hard.

There hadn't been any other traffic that she'd seen. Any more than there had been when Hugh made the same turn.

Did other people know that she'd been mad because he hadn't signalled? Grant did, but anyone else? She couldn't remember who she'd told.

Somebody stealing a car wasn't likely to use turn signals, anyway. It didn't have to mean anything, that this thief hadn't.

Or that it was near the same time of day that Hugh had left. Early, like this. He'd dropped her at the nursery, not even kissed her goodbye, merely waved and driven away.

The echo was coincidence. It had to be. She wouldn't believe anything else.

"I DON'T BELIEVE IN coincidences," Grant said flatly. "If you'd been careless enough to leave your keys in your truck and it had been taken from the grocery store parking lot, that would be one thing. This is something else."

"But…" She felt more shell-shocked than she should. The police would find her truck. Or, at worst, her insurance would mostly cover the cost of replacing it. The creepiest part was knowing that someone had been hiding not very far from where she parked. That somebody had been waiting for her, watching her.

"But?" he prompted her.

"Hugh and I were alone that morning. No one else saw him leave."

"Probably not," he said more slowly than she liked, as if he was seriously considering the possibility that somebody had been here that morning, too. "But you know how much talk there was. You repeated your story over and over. Hugh waving goodbye, driving away, turning out onto the highway."

"Not signalling."

His sharp eyes took in her expression and he gripped her elbow. "That," he said, "might have been coincidence. Kat…you need to sit down."

She shook herself. "I'm okay. Really."

"All right." He turned. "Someone's here."

"Joan," Kat said with relief. And then gasped "Oh, God, and Tess."

"Isn't Tess supposed to work today?"

She hadn't told him. "I'm going to fire her. You know those security cameras? One of them caught her stealing from me."

His fingers tightened on her arm. "Why didn't you call me?"

"She'd have thought of some excuse. Grabbed the figurine to be a last-minute gift, intended to pay for it the next day she worked. Forgot because she had two days off."

"And this is the end of her two days off."

"Yes."

"You going to give her a few minutes to remember to pay?"

"One hour. Starting right now."

Grant inclined his head. "Fair enough. If she

doesn't have a record for shoplifting, she wouldn't get more than a slap on the hand anyway. Will you let prospective employers know if they call for a reference?"

"Carefully." She grimaced. "I'll hint. These days, it's lawsuit city if she claims I'm slandering her."

"Save the footage."

"Oh, I will." Kat summoned a smile. "Joan."

Her friend hurried from her car with alarm on her face. "Not more bones?"

"No. My pickup truck was stolen."

Tess exclaimed, too, when she got within hearing distance.

Looking grim, Grant left with a murmured, "I'll keep you informed."

Kat didn't tell either Joan or Tess how unpleasantly reminded she'd been of Hugh's departure. She didn't suggest that this had been anything but common car theft, although Joan frowned and said, "Isn't your truck a 2003 or 2004? With a lot of miles on it? It has that big dent in the fender, too. Why would anyone want it?"

Good question. One Kat preferred not to think about. What she *wanted* was Grant to call and say, "The State Patrol pulled your truck over and arrested the kid driving it. Sounds like it was just a joyride."

Walking back to her office, she wondered whether kids knew how to hot-wire vehicles anymore. Weren't ignitions all electronic now? *Could* they be hot-wired?

Well, of course they could. Obviously. Because

she hadn't left the key in the ignition. It was in her purse where it belonged.

A cold lump settled in her stomach. What about the spare key?

Frantic suddenly, she dropped her purse on her desk and slid her hand into the small, inner, zippered pocket where she kept extra house and pickup keys. Neither was there.

Scared, she scrabbled through her whole purse, finally dumping the contents onto the desk. The only keys were the ones on her ring, still clipped to the strap. She groped the silky lining of the purse. If it had torn somewhere…but it hadn't.

Finally, hand shaking, she reached for her cell phone and called Grant again. The moment she heard his voice, she said, "My spare key is missing from my purse." She had to swallow. "So is my extra house key."

She'd never heard him use strong obscenities, but he did now.

"Kat, you need to call a locksmith. Now."

"Yes." She fumbled her way around her desk to the chair. "Okay."

"Get the locks on your house changed today. If you can't find someone to do it, call me."

"Yes," she said again.

"I don't suppose you know when you last saw those keys."

She shook her head, then realized he couldn't see her. "No. Months."

Grant was quiet for a moment. "Was your purse

in the office the day the bones were left in your desk drawer?"

"Yes." Her hand wasn't all that was shaking now; a tremor seemed to be running over her whole body. "I always keep it in the bottom drawer."

"A locked drawer?"

"No."

"Then that's probably when the keys were taken."

"This...person could have gotten into my house at any time."

"I've had patrol units driving by your house at least hourly every night," he told her.

"Thank you. It's not so much myself I've worried about as that I could be set up really easily. I keep thinking you'll get a tip about where to find the rest of Hugh."

The rest of Hugh. What a horrible way to think of it. Of him.

"That wouldn't have surprised me," Grant said. "I wouldn't have bought it, though. I'm not that stupid, Kat."

"Oh." Reassured, still she said, "Whoever this is took the house key, too, for a reason."

"I don't like that," he admitted. "Call me as soon as you know when the locksmith can come. I'll pick you up and take you home. I want to walk through your house."

"Yes. Okay." She hesitated. "Nobody has spotted my truck?"

"No." That was all he said, but she got a chill. It had disappeared.

Just like Hugh's.

She'd wait until nine to call locksmiths. Joan could cover for her today, so she didn't have to come back… No, Joan would be left shorthanded—*way* shorthanded—without Tess. All right. See who else could come in today.

James could, thank goodness. He promised to be there within an hour. By the time Kat spoke briefly to Joan, it was nine and she started calling locksmiths. The second one agreed to fit her in today, so she called Grant back.

"Three o'clock. Does that work for you? If not, I can have one of the employees run me home…"

"I'll be there in plenty of time to get you." He paused. "Tess's hour up yet?"

Kat looked at her watch. "Just about. Great. This has been a perfect day."

"And it's not over yet."

At ten, she checked in with Joan, who shook her head. Kat asked Tess to come to the office.

"You're fired," she said bluntly. "I'll pay you for the hours you've worked, even though I suspect you've made plenty off me in other ways." She had the check ready and extended it across the desk.

Tess widened her eyes in shock, but the reaction hadn't come quick enough. "What have I done wrong?"

Kat started the security camera feedback playing and swiveled the monitor so that Tess could see it. She stared.

"It was just the once."

"Sure it was."

She snatched up the check and left.

Kat realized her head was throbbing. There was a bottle of ibuprofen in the break room. Caffeine and drugs were what she needed. She'd give Tess five minutes to collect her things and be gone. Joan would watch to be sure she didn't take anything else on her way out.

She let the two other employees working today know that Tess had left, rearranged the staffing for the week and all but hugged James, who agreed to work another extra day. Then she called several of the people who'd sent résumés and arranged interviews. One came later that day and seemed adequate, if not exciting. A maybe.

Grant picked her up shortly after two-thirty. She was dismayed by how glad she was to see him. How could a man who wasn't handsome look better to her than anyone else ever had?

"Anything on my truck?"

"No," he said tersely.

It had disappeared into thin air, just like Hugh's had.

When she got in his official vehicle—in front, thank goodness, not in back behind the cage—Grant asked gruffly, "Did you have lunch?"

"No."

"There's a grilled chicken sandwich in that bag." He gestured at one that sat on the floor. She'd already smelled it and realized her mouth was watering.

"Your lunch?"

"No, yours."

She looked at him in perplexity. "You keep feeding me."

"You're losing weight before my eyes," he said bluntly. "Eat."

She gobbled the sandwich during the short drive. She and Grant had barely arrived at her house when the locksmith pulled in behind Grant's vehicle.

He and Grant consulted, and the guy went to work replacing the locks and adding dead bolts on both front and back doors as well as adding one to the side door of the detached garage that Kat rarely used. She was embarrassed not to have thought of that. She had a garage door opener, but parking in there wasn't a big advantage even when it rained because she'd still get wet between garage and house. Mostly it held the lawn mower, tools and clutter Hugh had never gotten rid of and she hadn't bothered investigating.

Grant started in there, poking around in random boxes, climbing a stepladder to see what was stowed on a couple of sagging sheets of plywood that spanned rafters.

"You won't lose anything if you burn the garage down," he reported finally.

"My mower..."

He booted the rusting machine with his foot. "Does it actually start?"

"*Yes.* What do you have, the shiniest, state-of-the-art ride-on?"

He grinned, a flash of merriment she had rarely seen. Good thing, too, because it almost stopped her heart.

"I have a reel mower. No engine. I get a workout,

it's quiet and ecological, and it doesn't need any care but an occasional sharpening of the blades."

"I did you an injustice," she said lightly. "I figured you for a guy who'd like his toys."

"I carry a Glock. I don't need any other toys."

He'd startled her into a laugh, something she would have sworn wasn't going to happen today of all days.

Grant smiled with what she thought was satisfaction.

They walked to the house together, and he began there by inspecting the window locks. When he started muttering about them, Kat rolled her eyes.

"What difference does it make, when someone could break a pane of glass and get in anyway?"

"Breaking glass makes noise. Neighbors hear." He frowned at her. "*You'd* hear, if you were home."

Oh, good. He'd given her another chill. Not that she hadn't already been lying awake nights listening for that exact sound, or for the creak the fourth stair always made under a footstep.

Grant's inspection of her house was slow and thorough. It reminded her unpleasantly of the search she'd agreed to four years ago after it became apparent that Hugh really had disappeared. She trailed behind Grant, glad she'd managed to get some housecleaning done Sunday. Even so, she found she was self-conscious about the shabbiness of the house and how little she'd succeeded in doing to make it feel like home. No surprise, there. She'd never decorated bedrooms the way most kids did, because they weren't really hers. They were just…a place to sleep. It was funny, because she hadn't put any stamp at all on the house when she lived here with Hugh, only on the yard. She hadn't known why then, but now she realized that the house hadn't felt like hers, any more than the foster homes had. It was Hugh's. She simply lived here. The nursery, strangely, was different. She'd taken almost immediate, fierce possession, as if it were her child. Hugh had indulged her, sometimes gotten annoyed with her ambition and impatience with him, but seemed overall relieved that she was willing to do the planning and work he couldn't be bothered with.

Kat let out a sigh more heartfelt than she'd intended. Hugh had only been using her. She'd known on one level, but...not let herself see quite how it was. Because of all she had to lose.

Holding open the door to the basement, Grant turned and looked at her, his eyebrows raised.

"I, uh, keep having these minor epiphanies." She made a face. "Ignore me."

"I'm...not very good at that," he said in a velvety deep voice. "In case you hadn't noticed."

She flushed.

He kept watching her, but didn't say anything. After a moment, he was the one to sigh and start down into the basement.

Kat sat on the bottom step and watched him explore, once again opening boxes, shaking his head over contents, brushing aside cobwebs to inspect dark corners and the space under the stairs.

"What is all this crap?" he asked at one point.

"Hugh inherited the house from his uncle. I think

he went through the stuff to see if there was anything valuable, but after that he lost interest. We talked about having a garage sale—"

"Ten garage sales," Grant muttered.

"See, that was the problem. Imagine hauling all this out, pricing it, taking half of it to the dump…" She shook her head. "I don't know whether all those old magazines are worth anything or should be recycled, for example. I don't have time to find out. The uncle worked on old cars. He collected parts, as far as I can see. I don't even know what they are. That's what's in most of the boxes in the garage."

"Yeah. I saw." Grant came toward her. Dust streaked one cheek, and a cobweb had caught in his dark hair. "Kat, I can't swear that a serious search wouldn't find a few bones tucked in some damn box or other, but I can't find anything."

"No. I've been looking, too," she admitted. "Telling myself I was paranoid, but—"

"You had reason." He braced a hand on the stair rail above her head and looked down at her. "You know how weird all this is."

She let out a huff that was almost a laugh. "You think?"

His eyes were dark, intent. "Kat…"

"Shouldn't we go see if the locksmith is done?"

Lashes veiled the heat in his eyes. "Probably." He gestured. "Ladies first."

The locksmith was done and waiting. She paid him, and after he left, said, "Thanks for coming, Grant."

He stood beside her in the foyer, making no move

to go. "It's almost five. Any chance you'd like to invite me to dinner?"

Stupefied, she said, "What would it look like to other people if…if…"

"We seemed to be friends?" He stood a step closer. "Or more than friends?"

She had to stand her ground. Had to, even if her heart was acting as if she'd run a half marathon. "Yes."

"I don't care." The words were underlaid by steel. "I've waited a long time for you, Kat. I won't ask for more than dinner right now. We do need to figure out what's going on. But I want to know you better. The other day, when I brought lunch out to the nursery, it occurred to me that I don't have any idea what you like to eat. Stupid little thing like that, and it bothered me." His voice softened. "Can we spend some time sharing the little stuff? Becoming friends?"

She closed her eyes on a tide of longing. Yes. *Yes.* She wanted to know his favorite food, too, his favorite color, his pet peeves. Whether he'd ever been tempted to return to the greater excitement of big city law enforcement. Whether he had sisters or brothers, whether his parents were alive, whether he was close to his family. She wanted to know *him.*

"All right," she said. "You're in luck. I froze spaghetti sauce the last time I made it. If you like Italian?"

"I like Italian." His voice sounded scratchy, and he had to clear his throat. Had he expected her to say, *"Thanks, but no thanks?"*

"I'll make a salad, too." She led the way to the

kitchen, where she had concentrated most of her re-
modeling efforts to date. She had stripped the old
cabinets—a horrible job—and had new vinyl laid
after discovering that the wood floor beneath the
ancient, peeling linoleum had been too damaged to
be refinished. She usually ate out here, too, at the
farm table set in front of a small-paned window with
a view to her back garden where early bulbs and a
fragrant *viburnum carlesii* were blooming.

She put him to work buttering a baguette and rubbing it with a crushed clove of garlic while she put
water on to boil for the pasta and gently heated the
sauce on the stove. Grant opened a bottle of wine
while she put together a salad.

Neither of them was a vegetarian; he was fonder
of red meat than she was, but they both agreed they
didn't like sushi. He admitted to a sweet tooth; Kat
didn't have much of one. He made a hell of a potato
salad, he said, and yeah, one of the few "toys" he did
enjoy was a fancy grill. His favorite color was green,
hers purple.

"That rich, reddish purple of some of the hybrid
lilacs," she said.

He nodded as if he had any idea at all what she
was talking about.

When Kat asked about family, he said, "One sister.
She's in Texas. My parents, too. I worked for the
Dallas P.D. before I came here."

The water was boiling. She dumped in the spaghetti. "You gave up being near your family so Rachel
could be near hers?"

"That's about the size of it."

"How did you meet?"

He gave her a glance in which she read wariness, but answered, "On the job. She worked for Macy's, had accepted a transfer there. Didn't know anyone. One of her coworkers was assaulted and Rachel was a witness. After we wrapped up the investigation, I gave her a call." He shrugged. "She was apparently a fan of television cop shows. She thought my job was sexier than it turned out to be, at least from a wife's standpoint."

Kat discovered she didn't like talking or even thinking about his ex-wife. And yet, she wanted to know what he'd felt, why the marriage had been troubled long before his eyes had met Kat's at that city council meeting all those years ago. He knew all about her problems with Hugh. In fact, Grant knew more about her than anyone else ever had, and that made her uncomfortable. She was entitled to ask some questions, wasn't she?

But…not that one, she decided. Not yet.

Instead, as they carried dishes to the table and sat, she said, "Did you think about moving back to Dallas after you and Rachel separated?"

"No."

The answer was so unexpansive, Kat looked up in the middle of reaching for a slice of the baguette. Grant was watching her.

"I'd taken the job here not that many months before. The department was understaffed and under-trained. I felt some responsibility to finish what I'd started." He paused. "And then there was you."

"Me." Her throat felt constricted. He meant it. He'd been waiting for her, all this time.

"You." He calmly dished up salad for himself. "This smells great."

"Grant…"

He smiled, a curiously tender curve of his mouth. "Why don't we put the big stuff on hold for now, and stick to the little stuff. That might be safer."

"Yes." Gulp. "You're right. Uh…are you close to your parents?"

"Reasonably. My dad and I have always butted heads. He's in construction, a contractor. Of course he wanted me to follow in his footsteps. Me, I signed up for the marines the minute I had a high school diploma in hand. Mom and Dad weren't thrilled."

Kat didn't blame them. They were probably scared to death.

"I served four years, decided it was time to come home. Law enforcement seemed a logical way for me to go. I haven't been sorry."

"What does your sister do?"

"She has a quilting shop. Babies, too." His grin deepened the lines on his cheeks, making them less grim. "Her husband works with Dad sometimes, but otherwise he's a professional bass fisherman. Go figure."

"I didn't know anyone was."

"Oh, yeah." Grant chuckled. "Did I mention that I not only don't like sushi, I don't like to eat fish? Leads to some spirited discussions at home."

Kat laughed, and felt the day's tension fall away. She liked the idea of being friends with Grant. She never had been with a man before, although she'd believed at first, with Hugh… No. She wouldn't think about Hugh tonight.

"How many babies?" she asked.

"Three to date. The youngest, Susie, is two. Won't shock me to hear Reggie is pregnant again."

"Reggie?"

"Regina."

"Oh." She had been twirling spaghetti on her fork, but didn't lift it to her mouth. "I always wished I'd had a sister or brother."

"There's something to be said for families." A couple of creases had formed between his dark eyebrows. He reached across the table and laid his big hand over hers. "Why didn't you and Hugh have children? Didn't you want any?"

"I suppose… We were putting it off. Until we were on better financial footing, we said. I don't think Hugh actually wanted kids. It took me a while to realize that." Kat smiled with difficulty. "He'd have had to be a lot less footloose, wouldn't he? And me…" She shrugged. "Like I said, part of me knew something was wrong. I was thinking earlier today that this house was always, in my mind, Hugh's. It's only been in the past couple of years I started to think of it as mine."

He nodded. She was too stoic to let the compassion in his eyes make her weepy, but there was a moment. Just a moment, when she came close.

"It didn't take Rachel six months to decide I should find a new career. She claimed she'd be doing all the work if we had a baby." He grimaced. "Probably she would have been. But I liked my job. I told myself she knew what I did going in. Making the move out here, that was my compromise." He took a swallow of wine. "It didn't work."

"You tried."

"Yeah." His face was unreadable now, his eyes turbulent. "But maybe not hard enough. Got to say, though, she didn't, either. Compromise is good, but there has to be acceptance, too. Of who the other person is."

Kat understood, although that hadn't been the issue for Hugh and her. It was the fact that whatever she'd labeled as love early on wasn't. Whatever needs each had met for the other had been unspoken. Love or real passion hadn't been among them.

With Grant, though… Her eyes were drawn to his. He wanted her, but did he love her? Could he?

Was that what this ache she had in her chest every time she saw him meant? How was she supposed to *know?*

It would be better, wouldn't it, to wait and see? To give each other time? To be able to bury Hugh, and be sure Grant didn't have to consider her seriously as a suspect in Hugh's death?

Of course it would be.

She couldn't look away from him. She wanted, oh, she wanted, to find out what it would be like to make love with this man. They had waited so long already. Would it be so bad, if she stood and took his hand, if she led him up the stairs to the bedroom where she'd moved after Hugh was gone?

Kat wasn't sure she was capable of saying a word.

The decision wasn't conscious. She knew that she was pushing back her chair, standing. That he was doing the same. One or the other of them groaned, and then, halfway around the table, their bodies collided and both reached to hold on tight.

CHAPTER TEN

THE MINUTE SHE STOOD, the minute he saw the decision she'd made in her eyes, Grant quit thinking. He only felt.

A groan tore from his throat. "Kat," he heard himself say hoarsely. "Kat."

Having her body hard against his, thigh to chest, her arms around his neck, her scent in his nostrils, staggered him. It was pure, sweet relief, if relief could be so powerful it hurt.

She was straining upward even as he bent his head. Their mouths met, open, hungry. He couldn't be tender or patient, he couldn't coax. All he could do was take, his tongue driving into the slippery depths of her mouth as his hips rocked and he squeezed her butt to drag her even tighter against him.

At last. Thank God. Thank God. At last.

He hadn't known it was possible to want so desperately. Four years, seeing her just often enough to keep the edge of his hunger honed, had been torture. And now she was in his arms, shaking. Or maybe that was him. Or both of them. She kissed him as fiercely as he kissed her. If his tongue retreated, hers followed. When he wrenched at her shirt, she yanked at his and he heard buttons pop.

The bedrooms were upstairs. They weren't going to make it that far. But he didn't want to take her on the hard floor like an animal. Living room. There was a sofa. Somehow even as they devoured each other's mouth and stripped each other, he also maneuvered her, a few feet at a time, in that direction.

Every so often he had to lift his head to stare at her face in disbelief and exultation. Kat, the way he'd dreamed of her. Passion had deepened her eyes to a color so rich, it defied words. The closest he could come was the twilight sky beyond the fiery reach of the setting sun. Her mouth was beautiful, lips parted and swollen and damp. That glorious, indescribable hair, tumbling loose from whatever knot she'd confined it to, fell over slim, bare shoulders and curled over breasts that were ripe and perfect. And then he'd have to kiss her again, lose himself in her taste and response to him.

He stumbled across the coffee table, vaguely surprised they'd gotten that far. He hoped like hell she'd never made love with Hugh here, but couldn't have stopped even if he knew the couch was their favorite place to do it.

He laid her down and peeled off her jeans and panties at the same time. Oh, damn; the V of curls at the juncture of her thighs wasn't a plain brown any more than the hair on her head. Chestnut, he decided. And he found the curls to be silky as, fascinated, he slid his fingers into them. He bent over her, one knee on the edge of the cushion, his own jeans unsnapped but as yet zipped. Momentarily dazed, he looked at her long legs and pale belly and breasts, curves, convex and concave, hollows beneath her collarbones and the sharp points of her pelvic bones. She was too thin, and yet his eye could find no fault. She could put on fifty pounds and he wouldn't then, either. It was her. Just her. Which made no more sense than it ever had.

"You have no idea…" he said rawly.

Her unblinking stare ate him up. Her fingers, splayed on his chest, kneaded as sinuously as a delighted cat.

"I do," she whispered. "I know."

Maybe she did. He'd seen her looking sometimes, too. It was those stolen, suspended moments when their eyes had met and held that had kept his hope alive. Foolishly, idiotically alive, he'd tried to tell himself a thousand times, but he hadn't been able to let go of it. He'd never wanted another woman like he did this one. Never would. It was that simple.

He kept kneeling there above her, stroking her slick flesh until her hips were rising and she threw her head back, whimpering. And then, all of a sudden, she jackknifed up and reached for his zipper. In an instant, she had him in her hands and was stroking with the same intent he had.

With a guttural sound, Grant pushed her down and followed her until he remembered that he had to protect her. Swearing, he found the packet in his wallet, tore it open and, with far from steady hands, got the damn thing on. He kicked off his boxers and jeans before he lowered himself on top of her.

Kat's legs wrapped his hips and she arched upward to meet him even as her lips sought his again. He pushed inside her. Slowly, slowly. She was a small woman. Tight, so tight. He'd never felt anything like this. He kept going until he was seated deep, and then he did it again. They were both making sounds, maybe words, maybe not. He held his weight off her on one elbow even as the other slid under her hips to lift them higher.

He made out words after all.

"Grant. Oh, Grant. Please. *Now*." And her body convulsed around him, nothing gentle about this climax, as if she'd been saving up not for four years but forever. He lunged, hard, deep, fast, following no more gently. The glory encompassed mind, body, heart. It washed out more slowly than it had come, ripples of sensation making his body jerk as he collapsed heavily, managing to come down with most of his weight between her and the couch back rather than crushing her.

He was breathing in harsh pants. His face was buried in her hair and he almost started to laugh, remembering that damn city council meeting when he'd lost forty-five minutes staring at her hair, trying to count the colors. It was as silky and vibrant as he'd imagined. Ticklish, too.

His chest must have vibrated, because she tilted her head back to try to see his face. "Are you laughing?"

He was. A rumble that wasn't amusement but something else altogether. Happiness, shaken until it fizzed.

"And they say anticipation is half the fun."

With a choked giggle, Kat wriggled her way out

from under him and onto her side so they were facing. Neither of them were laughing when they gazed solemnly into each other's eyes.

"I've never," she said, sounding stunned. "I didn't know…"

"I didn't, either." He thought for a minute. "No, that's not true. I suspected." His hand stroked her from nape to the curve of her ass. Her vertebrae were delicate, nothing like the knobs of his own. She was delicate, so finely made, and yet strong. It was the long, toned muscles that made her legs so amazing, that had let her wrap him with arms strong enough he'd thought she could hold on forever.

He kept thinking that word. *Forever.* Pretty stupid, when he doubted she was anywhere near as advanced in her thinking as he was.

Their eyes kept searching each other's. He wanted, in the worst way, to say, "I love you," but he thought that might scare her. Hell, it scared *him.* It always had. Being this vulnerable to another human being wasn't easy to take in stride.

She sighed at last. "This wasn't a good idea."

"Best one I've ever had."

"It's too soon."

He gave something close to another laugh over that. "Yeah, we really rushed into this, didn't we?"

"You know what I mean."

She meant that suspicion for Hugh's death could still fall on her. Grant knew that, but right this minute he didn't care. Maybe later he would; it was true that other people still wondered.

As if Kat were reading his mind, she said, "You don't know me that well."

He kissed her forehead, then nuzzled her hair. "Your favorite color is purple."

She made an indignant sound.

"Yes, I do," he whispered. "I know that much. I heard you tell old Mrs. Mallory the other day about how useful slugs are, the place they have in nature, and how you don't like to poison them. That in your own garden you trap them, and then dump them in a cow pasture on the way to work."

"Sometimes we poison them at the nursery. We have to. I can, you know."

He laughed gently. "The confession of a killer."

"Well, it's awful," she mumbled against his shoulder. "Especially when you get a banana slug. You know, the big ones? I really think they feel pain."

He laughed again, but silently. Did she think for a minute she was convincing him that she could have murdered Hugh if she were mad enough? He felt like an idiot for ever imagining she could have. But he knew he hadn't really believed it, not gut deep.

"I'm scared," she said suddenly.

Grant moved her away from him enough that he could see her face again. "What do you think's going to happen?"

"I don't know." She compressed her mouth. "But whoever is doing this keeps escalating. So…what's next?"

The same question had already been keeping him up nights, and that was before the theft of her pickup this morning. Returning the bones made one kind of statement, snatching the truck right out from her nose made another one altogether.

I can make you disappear, just like I did him.

"I'm going to drive you to work and take you home every day," he said.

Kat blinked at him. "It's a five-minute drive."

"But you get there first in the morning. And you're often last leaving, aren't you?"

"Yes, but…I don't have to be."

"For now," he said quietly. "It'll make me feel better."

"People will talk."

"Let them." He made his voice hard.

"No." Suddenly she was struggling. Caught by surprise, he didn't stop her in time. She'd scrambled off the couch and was wriggling into her jeans, lightning fast. "No. I can't afford to have people talking any more than they already are, and neither can you."

Grant sat up. "Kat, keeping you safe matters more than dodging some gossip."

As if self-conscious, she crossed her arms over her breasts. "You can't keep me safe by driving me to work, Grant. I'm alone at night, I'm alone in my office at the nursery, out in the greenhouses… I have to drive to the grocery store, to the library… You can't guard me around the clock."

She was right, but he didn't want to admit it.

Frowning, he said, "Will you quit arriving way before your first employees in the mornings?"

"Yes." Her throat worked. "I'll be careful. Okay? I promise."

Shit. He didn't see what he could do but concede.

God knows, she was right that he could do his job more effectively if no one knew they were involved romantically. He didn't like to think what Mortensen would say if he knew his police chief was screwing the wife of a man who'd died under suspicious circumstances. But it also didn't sit well with Grant to keep hiding how he felt about Kat. He'd been doing that for too long already.

"All right," he said reluctantly. "Why don't I pick you up in the morning and drive you to a car rental place?"

After a brief hesitation, Kat gave a choppy nod. She seemed to be working hard at keeping her gaze at the level of his face, which meant she was embarrassed now that he was still sitting here butt naked.

By the time he'd gotten his boxers and jeans on, Kat had retreated to the kitchen. When he got there, she'd already pulled on her shirt and had his in her hands. Cheeks pink, she said, "I think I pulled a couple of buttons off. I could sew them back on—"

"I can do that if we can find them."

They found one, but not the other. He shrugged and dropped the one in the breast pocket of his shirt. He had some stray buttons at home that were close enough. He kind of liked the idea of a mismatched one; every time he did it up, it would remind him that she'd wanted him enough to rip his shirt off his body.

"You're smiling," she said suspiciously.

"Yeah." Grant stepped forward and kissed her. Quick, keeping his tongue in his own mouth, but letting her know that he'd have liked to start all over again. "Just a thought."

She was looking shy again. It seemed a contradiction, for a feisty, spit-in-your-eye woman who'd been married and widowed, but he guessed she didn't have much practice in flirting and that her sexual experience was limited. Maybe to Hugh alone.

"There you go again," she snapped.

He wasn't only smiling this time, he was flat-out grinning. Because her experience was no longer limited to Hugh and whatever high school or college boyfriends she'd had; now it included him. And she'd liked it every bit as much as he'd liked making love with her. If that made him smug, Grant figured he was entitled. It had been a long time since he'd felt anywhere close to this good.

"Invite me to dinner tomorrow night," he suggested.

Her expression was reproving. "Two nights in a row? I don't think so."

The smile left him. "This wasn't a one time deal, you know."

"I hope it isn't," she whispered. "But…"

She didn't have to finish. *But*.

Find out what the hell happened to Hugh. Who'd hidden his bones, who was taunting Kat.

"I was thinking," he said. "Would you have noticed if your truck had turned off the highway right away? Say, onto Hazeltine Road?"

Kat blinked a couple of times. The change of subject, Grant realized, had been jarring.

"Yes," she started to say, then frowned and said

more slowly, "I think so. But there's that row of pop-
lars and the fence." She thought about it some more.
"It was definitely accelerating, though. I didn't see
brake lights."

"But it could have made the turn. Or gone a little
farther, turned around and come back."

Her mouth opened, closed. "Yes," she admitted.
"By then I was calling you."

"I wish it had occurred to me earlier that the best
way to make it disappear was to get off the road immediately. Aren't the Schultzes still in Arizona?"

"They don't usually come back until May."

"I'm going to drive out there," he said. "Poke
around a little."

"You think it was stashed there temporarily."

"I don't know, but it would have been smart,
wouldn't it? Could've been parked behind the barn,
or even in it."

"It's probably locked. They still have a tractor and
some farm equipment."

"Okay, how about the RV garage? It'd be empty.
Would they bother locking it?"

She shook her head to indicate she didn't know.

He pulled her into his arms for the pleasure of
feeling her close, kissed her again and said, "I'll see
you in the morning."

On the drive out to the nursery and the Schultz
farm, which lay behind it, Grant metaphorically
kicked himself a few times. Chances were, Hugh
had driven to his fate. But whoever took the pickup
had a problem. The whole point was to steal it right in
front of Kat's eyes; to mimic the last time she saw her

husband. That meant she'd be reaching right for the phone, though, and there might have happened to be a patrol car close by. So the pickup had to disappear immediately. What would be quicker than to turn off on the road that ran alongside the nursery and stash the truck on the farm until dark? Any local would know it was deserted this time of year.

The logistics puzzled him some because it seemed unlikely that there were two people involved in Hugh's death and the current campaign to terrify Kat. Getting here this morning might have been a problem.

Or maybe not, he reflected. The river curved from town past several farms, including the Schultzes'. Walking along the riverbank from town was doable. He or she could have walked back, too. Or not. He—for convenience Grant decided to make it a *he*—might have taken a good book and spent the day at the farm, waiting for the cloak of darkness to drive away again.

Darkness which, unfortunately, had fallen a good two hours ago. If he'd used his damned head, Grant would have thought of this possibility midmorning, not at eight at night.

He didn't find a thing at the farm. The long, hard-packed gravel driveway that ultimately circled in front of the barn, garage and big metal RV garage wouldn't have held tire tracks even if the ground had been wet. A padlock secured the barn doors, but he managed to aim his flashlight in a small window and saw the tractor and a whole lot of empty space. Definitely no pickup. The rolling doors of both the

garages slid up to show him more emptiness. Will and
Martha towed their car behind their RV to Arizona
every winter. After looking around, Grant thought
that if he'd wanted to hide a pickup out here all day,
he'd have used the RV garage. The other one had
windows. But the tall metal building didn't, only a
side door that locked. A person could drive into the
garage, come out the side door and padlock the big
door on the outside, then go back in, lock and be snug
as a bug all day long.

He shined his flashlight on the hasp and saw
scratches, some newer looking than others, but no
surprise there; Will probably kept the building locked
when his fancy $100,000 plus RV was inside it.

There was nothing to find inside. No convenient
cigarette butt, no half-empty pop can, carelessly left
sitting there. But the hairs on the back of Grant's neck
prickled, and he *knew*.

Sure as hell, Kat's pickup had been concealed here
today.

GRANT DIDN'T HAVE A LOT to say in the morning
when he drove her to the rental car office, and Kat
was grateful. It was hard enough exchanging the few
words they did, when every time she looked at him
she remembered him naked.

She'd have said she didn't like hairy chests, but his
was different. The dark, curling hair over hard muscles had struck her as intensely masculine, just the
way he was. Thinking about the thin line of downier
hair that led down below his navel was enough to
make her shiver. A few dark hairs curled on the backs

of his fingers, too. Her eyes kept being drawn that way, to where those big, competent hands gripped the steering wheel. She remembered looking down at his hand on her breast, seeing her own milky pale skin between his dark fingers, loving the rasp of his palm over her nipple.

Oh, *damn.* She turned her head to look out the passenger window. This wasn't going to be easy, dealing with him in a businesslike way. She'd known better, but some foolishness had overcome her.

Four years of longing had slammed through the dam she'd erected so carefully.

"Did you find anything last night?" she asked.

He shot her a glance. Cheeks warm, Kat knew he had to be remembering, too.

"I'd have called if I had," he said. "But it would have been a good place to hide temporarily. Both garages were unlocked."

"We're not going to find my truck, are we?"

"We'll find it." Unexpectedly he removed one hand from the wheel to squeeze hers, knotted on her lap. "I'm betting it's parked right next to Hugh's now."

After a pause, during which he took his hand back, she flexed hers. "We could be wrong. It might turn up abandoned in Everett."

"It might." He glanced at her again. She didn't meet his eyes. "Where to?" he asked.

The closest place to rent a car was in Marysville. She directed him there.

He made a couple of other remarks. She replied, although by the time he dropped her off she didn't have the slightest idea what either of them had said.

"Don't stay at the nursery by yourself," he told her as she slid out.

"I promised I wouldn't."

He gave a terse nod.

"Thank you for the lift."

"Call if you have any problems."

She agreed then closed the door, walking into the rental place without looking back.

She rented a compact car. Joan drove a pickup, if something absolutely had to be hauled. If her own pickup was recovered, fine; otherwise, she'd get by until the insurance company deemed enough time had passed to reasonably assume it wouldn't be recovered and paid out.

She got to the nursery by ten-thirty, in time to interview another applicant. This was the one with so much experience, she ought to be running her own plant nursery.

When Kat said something to that effect, if more tactfully, Helen Kitts grinned.

"But I don't want to." She sighed. "Here's where I'm going to say something that isn't exactly music to employers' ears. The thing is, I started a family. You notice a big gap in my résumé."

Kat had.

"I'm starting to get bored, and we can use some extra income. But I have three kids—four, five and seven years old. I don't really want full-time, and you have to understand that kids get sick. Sometimes I'll want to rearrange my schedule so I can go on a field trip. I'll be a good employee, but right now I can't give any job my all."

"In return for my being flexible," Kat said thoughtfully, "I'd be getting a walking, talking horticultural encyclopedia and someone who might even have ideas about what we can do better."

A small but stocky woman with a cheerful face and a few threads of gray in her curly dark hair, Helen said, "Which I'll keep to myself unless you want them."

Kat laughed. "Oh, I want them." She pushed away from her desk. "Let's take a walk through the nursery."

They took their time, talking about favorite plants and the difference between growing conditions locally compared to central Oregon, where Helen had lived last. She was as knowledgeable as her résumé had claimed her to be, and likable besides. Kat promised to check out her references, and didn't doubt they'd be good.

They were. The two people she reached raved, and only a few hours after the interview, Kat called and offered her the job. Helen was ready and eager to start immediately. Hallelujah.

One problem down.

The nursery was busy. Mike Hedin caught Kat in an unwary moment to ask about the rumors he'd heard that Hugh's remains had been discovered. He whipped out a small spiral notebook and held it with a pen poised.

She froze for an awful moment, but knew she couldn't dodge the question entirely. "It's true," she said finally. "I can't tell you any more than that, though. You'll need to talk to Chief Haller for details."

"He said he can't compromise an investigation by giving out details." Mike's disgruntlement was obvious.

"Your deadline's not for a couple of days, isn't it? He might be able to tell you more by then." She hoped. Prayed.

Or did she? Because if Grant learned more, it would probably be because something else happened. And she didn't *want* anything else to happen.

Except, if it didn't, she'd be caught in this state of suspension forever. Purgatory. And she didn't know if she could bear that.

"Any chance you'd like to have dinner tonight, if I promise not to grill you?" Mike asked, ultracasually.

Was he asking her on a *date?* Oh, God, he was, Kat realized in dismay. For a wild moment, she thought about accepting. Being seen publicly with another man would divert any interest in her relationship with Grant.

But she couldn't do that. Not to Mike, who was a nice man, and not to Grant, who would be livid and hurt both. And…she didn't want to make conversation with Mike, however nice. If she couldn't spend the evening with Grant, she didn't want anyone.

"I'm sorry," she said. "I'm afraid I can't, Mike."

He nodded, glum but accepting. Making conversation after that was hard going, but they both made the effort to dissipate the awkwardness.

At the end of the day, Kat and Joan left together.

"I can't believe Mike finally asked you out," Joan was saying, shaking her head as she unlocked her pickup. "He's been thinking about it forever." She shot a wicked grin over her shoulder. "George Slagle, too."

"Oh, ick." Kat grimaced. "I didn't say that."

Joan clapped both hands over her ears. "Can't hear anything."

Kat grinned. "I'll see you in the morning. You can meet the new hire then."

"Good."

Kat drove home, and, despite the shiny new locks, walked through the house to make sure everything looked untouched. It did. She had soup from a can and a bagel with cream cheese, probably not nutritious but easy. She couldn't concentrate on a book, and the TV sitcom she turned on wasn't any better. At eight-thirty, her cell phone rang. She picked it up to see Grant's number.

"Hey," he said, when she answered. "I just wanted to hear your voice."

Warmth percolated through her. She hadn't known it, but she had wanted to hear his, too.

"I'm glad you called," she admitted.

"Okay day?"

"Yeah. I hired someone to replace Tess." She told him about Helen. "Business was good. No surprises."

"I half wish there had been."

"Bite your tongue."

"I've never liked sitting on hold."

Kat's fingers tightened on the phone. "That's

what we're doing, isn't it?" After a moment, she said, "What I'm doing."

He didn't like that. "We're in this together."

She opened her mouth to argue then closed it. It scared her, how much she wanted that to be true, but she did. Last night had been…wondrous. Revelatory. She'd thought sex with Hugh was the way it was. That her whole relationship with Hugh, sometimes tepid, sometimes frustrating, sometimes hurtful, was also the way it was. But now she knew. It didn't have to be. She wanted—oh, she wanted—to believe that Grant would be her future, but fear blossomed in her chest again. Wanting something so much was dangerous. She'd never gotten what she wanted.

Except the satisfaction and growing self-esteem the nursery had given her. Which made it all the more frightening that her foolish assumptions about her marriage weren't the only thing under assault—it was her business that might be in the most danger.

Or her. But she didn't want to think about that.

"Kat?" Grant prompted. "You're not alone."

She closed her eyes and said softly, "Okay."

"Don't shut me out."

"No."

"Swear."

She remembered his rumble of laughter last night, and found herself, despite everything, smiling.

"Cross my heart."

"Poor choice of words," he said gruffly, "but I'll take it in the spirit it was meant."

Poor choice…? Oh, Lord. *Cross my heart and hope to die.*

"You're right," she said hastily. "I'm glad you called, Grant. Today, I kept wishing…"

"Me, too." His voice had lowered so it was deep, tender. "Good night, Kat. Sleep tight."

"Good night," she whispered, ending the call. Weirdly enough, she was smiling again even as her eyes prickled with tears.

CHAPTER ELEVEN

KAT PULLED A SWEATSHIRT over her head and let herself out the rear door of the main building.

She was grateful to have a little time before they had to open. Joan, bless her heart, had volunteered to start arriving at eight-fifteen.

"You shouldn't be here alone," she'd said in her stalwart way.

So she was currently opening the cash register, and Kat began the walk-through that had always been her habit, but now had a different purpose than it used to. She still saw the plants, the gaps in rows, still thrust her fingers at random into the soil in pots to be sure nothing had gotten too dry, still made mental notes about low inventory or how a particular impatiens on the annual table or a new hybrid of spirea didn't seem to be selling. But really, of course, she was looking for bones. Human bones.

Hugh's bones.

She walked through all of the greenhouses, annoyed with herself at how uneasy she was made by how closed in she felt, how heavy the humid air was. Finally she circled by the toolshed. Part of her morning routine was to unlock it... But, frowning, she saw that the padlock hung open. Hadn't she checked it last night? She wasn't positive.

Kat unhooked the padlock so she could turn the hasp, then opened the door and recoiled. Good Lord, what smelled so bad?

A dead animal. It had to be. At least, thank goodness, it must be inside the shed and not underneath, where they might not have been able to get to it. Breathing through her mouth, she reached for the cord and turned on the bare, overhead bulb. Ugh, there it was, a dead…something. Rabbit, she thought, but whatever creature it was didn't have a head. How could it have gotten in here…?

And then she forgot the dead rabbit. Because right there on the floor, beneath rakes and shovels hanging on the wall, were what she momentarily took for a jumble of bones.

Breath coming fast, she crouched over them, her back to the door.

Which closed with a bang, followed by a scraping sound.

She jerked in surprise and almost fell over, then swiveled on her heels. What…? Had Joan not seen her in here? There hadn't been any wind…

She hurried to the door and pushed on it. It didn't give at all. Oh, God. She'd left the padlock hanging, as they always did, on the open hasp. Had somebody locked her in? Kat hated the feeling of panic. There wasn't any reason to be scared, for goodness sake. The other employees would be arriving soon. She'd hammer on the door until someone heard her. At worst… She gave a queasy look over her shoulder. At worst, she'd be stuck in here with her only company a beheaded rabbit and more of Hugh's bones.

Bile rose in her throat and she laid a hand on her stomach to quell the nearly irresistible need to retch. With the door closed and with no windows, the stench was almost unbearable.

The rabbit had been bait, she realized. She might not have stepped in otherwise. She might not have discovered the bones until later. Gagging, she tried to figure out why that mattered. Somebody would have needed a tool out of here in the next hour or two, and seen the bones.

She battered on the door with her fists for several minutes, yelling, "Let me out!" There was no answer. She couldn't hear anyone or anything at all.

Her stomach did heave. She clapped a hand over her mouth. Maybe if she put a terracotta pot over the rabbit, upside down. And plugged the hole with gunnysacks or something. She followed through quickly, but the whole space was permeated with that awful stink of decomposing flesh.

She hammered again. Yelled some more. Her hands were getting sore.

Then, gulping, she went to the bones and crouched again.

It wasn't a jumble, as she'd first thought. That was…it was a pelvis. It had to be. Those cupped sort of wings were hipbones, she thought. But it was butted up to *another* pelvis. And no human had two.

Nose plugged, sobbing for breath beneath the hand she'd clapped over her face, she stared at the two pelvises, and thought, *Dear, God, if two people were having sex, their hips would press together almost like that.*

The taste in her mouth suddenly wasn't just stomach bile, wasn't that unholy stench. She went still, some primal instinct screaming an alarm. Kat let go of her nose and smelled it. Wood smoke.

When she turned, she saw the smoke, too. Seeping in from the back corner, dark and somehow oily.

She flew at the door and began hammering again. The first curls and drifts of smoke were thickening, and a lick of flame ate through the wall.

"Help!" she screamed. "Help!"

GRANT WAS GETTING OUT of the shower when his cell phone rang. While he let hot water beat down on his bent head, he'd been mulling over a meeting he'd had the previous afternoon with half a dozen owners of downtown businesses. They were concerned about the increase of shoplifting they were seeing, and linked it to the numbers of teenagers loitering along the main street. The high school, unfortunately, was within easy walking distance, and school let out early for those not staying to play a sport. Grant wasn't a fan of closed campuses; damn it, these kids were on the cusp of adulthood and should be eased into responsibility, not locked down as if the school had the dual function of educating and jailing them. But he was having trouble thinking of a better fix. If he had the budget to add officers—at least one bicycle officer who did nothing but cruise downtown during the peak afternoon hours, pop in and out of stores…

He snorted. *If* he had the budget. He didn't.

The sound of the phone ringing made him go rigid. It couldn't be later than 8:45. Either dispatch or one of his officers was letting him know about a major crime, or…it was Kat.

He grabbed for a towel and walked, wet, into his bedroom where he'd left the cell phone on the bedside stand. The number on the screen was local, but not Kat's cell phone he saw, with a rush of relief. He answered, "Haller."

"Chief Haller?" The woman's voice was familiar. "This is Joan Stover at the nursery. I thought you'd want to know. Kat was locked into the shed and it was set on fire. One of our employees saw the smoke as she was pulling in. Thank the Lord, she ran out back and heard Kat yelling for help."

He felt like his heart had just stopped. Throat dry, he said, "She's all right?"

"I called for an ambulance. I think she's suffering from some smoke inhalation. She can't quit coughing and retching." She was quiet for a moment. "Chief Haller, there's some more bones in there. We're still pouring water on the shed, but I shut the door."

"I'm on my way," he said tersely.

He'd never gotten dressed so fast in his life. He didn't bother drying himself first; the cotton of his uniform shirt clung clammily to his back and the trousers to his legs. He grabbed keys, weapon, badge, and ran for the garage.

Camera. Hell. He went back for it.

He wanted to go to the hospital, not the nursery. He didn't like to think of Kat there alone, hacking up black phlegm, scared. But his obligation was to go to the crime scene, and that's how he could help Kat best.

Maybe somebody from the nursery had gone with her. He wished that was a comfort. Grant couldn't help thinking the nursery employees were in the best position to be behind this crap. The trouble was, he hadn't been able to find anything on any of them. Most of them hadn't even worked there when Hugh was alive.

The closed sign still hung on the front door when he tore in, even though it was now 9:05. The front door was unlocked, though, and a white-faced woman he didn't know was waiting for him inside.

"Um…Joan followed the ambulance to the hospital. I'm new here. Today. She asked me to meet you."

"Good," he said, holding out his hand. "Chief Grant Haller."

"Chief Haller." She shook his hand. "Helen Kitts. Kat just hired me. This isn't quite how I expected my first day to go."

"Hell of a thing," he agreed. "I need to go take a look."

"I'm assuming it would be better if I didn't open."

"Please don't," he told her. "If any customers show up, tell them there's been a fire and you're not certain whether the nursery will be open today or not."

She nodded. "Okay."

Out back, he found James Cheung holding a hose, the stream of water directed over the roof of the red-painted toolshed. Acrid smoke still rose from the charred back. Grant knew the smell immediately. The fire had been fueled by gasoline. He'd have to get the fire marshal out here.

After greeting Cheung, Grant inspected the pattern blackened on the shed wall opposite the main nursery building, saw footprints that weren't adequately defined in the squishy—and now wet—sawdust to even let him venture a guess as to size, and finally circled to the front.

"It looks like it's out," he told James. "And I need to go in. Why don't you turn that off, but I'd appreciate it if you'd hang around in case the fire flares up again."

"Yes, sir."

Grant put on latex gloves before he reached to turn the metal hasp. He was careful not to touch the padlock itself. They hadn't gotten a print yet, but everyone got careless eventually.

The minute he opened the door, a foul stench fairly boiled out. Cheung choked and backed up. Swearing, Grant looked immediately for the source of the smell. The overhead bulb was on despite the fire. Kat would have turned it on when she stepped in. It wasn't hard to guess that she'd gone in to see what the hell stank so bad.

He didn't see anything immediately, although he couldn't miss the bones. Pelvis… Hell. He stared for a minute. Two of them. Pressed together in a way that was damned suggestive. Somebody had to be making a comment on Hugh's sexual mores.

The question was, if one of those pelvises was

Hugh's, who did the other one belong to? He was no expert, but even he could see that they were different. One was female, one male. Had to be.

The large, upside-down terracotta pot was oddly placed. Especially with a couple of gunnysacks bundled atop. Grant gingerly lifted it and came closer to puking than he would have wanted any of his subordinates to see. He let the pot drop, although he wasn't sure that helped the smell any.

He stood very still, closed his eyes for a minute, then, breathing through his mouth, studied the interior of the shed. He turned slowly, doing his damnedest not to miss any small thing. Once he'd looked carefully, he started moving piles of plastic plant pots, the couple of other larger terracotta pots, the gunnysacks, a metal toolbox that held only the usual assortment of screwdrivers, hammer, wrench. Nothing caught his eye; nothing seemed out of place.

Except, of course, for the small, headless corpse and the pair of human pelvises. And, oh, yeah, the charred, steaming wall of the shed.

He snapped a couple dozen digital photos from every angle: bones, rabbit sans pot, blackened wall and some wide-angle shots of the interior. Then he used one of the sacks to gather up the two pelvises.

When he walked outside, he tried not to gulp fresh air too obviously. His stomach chose that moment to heave in protest, but he ignored it. God knows, he'd seen and smelled worse. He'd had to crouch over floaters pulled in after days in salt water, the burned remains of arson victims, insect-infested bodies unearthed from shallow graves. This was nothing, and he wouldn't succumb to the weakness of nausea.

He went straight to the security camera pointed toward the shed, and was pissed but not surprised to find a brown plastic grocery bag wrapped over the lens. An adirondack chair had been pulled over to serve as a step stool. He'd look at the footage, but someone who knew the camera was there could have approached from the side without ever appearing in front of it.

So much for the crisscross cedar slats that almost disguised its presence.

Disgusted, Grant pulled out his cell phone and called Jed Beier, the arson investigator, who agreed to come out. After a brief conversation, Grant asked Cheung to continue to keep an eye on the shed for now, went into the main building to tell the new woman not to open the nursery yet, then left for the hospital.

Kat was in a curtained cubicle in the emergency room. He heard her hacking long before he saw her.

Somehow he wasn't surprised, though, to walk in as she slid from the bed, hospital gown discarded and her already dressed again in one of those damned sweatshirts he knew had been Hugh's. "I'm ready, Joan," she was saying.

"The hell you are." His gaze dropped to her hands, both wrapped in gauze.

Kat turned. "Grant." That set her off. She coughed for a good minute, Joan wrapping an arm around her in support.

"The doctor is releasing you?" he asked incredulously.

Joan shot him a look of sympathy. "They think she's okay. She's just going to have to get all the junk up."

"I can do that at home," Kat said, in a gruff, whispery voice.

"Damn." He wanted nothing more than to haul her into his arms. The fact that it wouldn't be politic to do so where someone might see them only increased his frustration and anger.

Her eyes latched on to him as if she didn't want to let him go. "You…saw?"

He unclenched his jaw. "I saw."

"Who…?"

He knew what she was asking. "We'll find out," he said grimly.

Human bones could be purchased online. It was possible a female pelvis had been bought to stage this scene, that it was merely a symbol. But somehow Grant didn't think so. His gut told him the woman, whoever she was, had died with Hugh. That she'd had something to do with his death, was maybe even the reason for it. What this looked like to him was jealousy.

Somebody besides Kat had expected something Hugh apparently wasn't capable of giving: fidelity. Maybe even love. What Grant couldn't figure out was how it all tied in to Kat. If one of Hugh's lovers had killed him because she found out she wasn't exclusive…why hadn't she acted on it by attacking Kat back then? And if she thought she'd won and Kat was on the way out…why had she clung to this obsessive hatred?

He pulled himself up short. No, *clung* wasn't the right word. *Developed* was maybe a better one. Whoever this was had been okay with Kat for a long time. Maybe didn't see her as a rival. But she'd finally done something to set this off. Grant was thinking, more and more, that the whoever-this-was had to be another woman.

He also had a bad feeling that he knew who that other pelvis would turn out to belong to. Proving it, though, was another story.

"Joan," he said, "would you go home with Kat? Stay with her? I've got to get back to the nursery and meet the fire marshal. I don't think you should open today. Can one of the employees lock up?"

Kat in her croaky voice started to protest. Joan overrode her. "Yes. Tell James to stay until you're done and then make sure everything is locked." Under her breath she muttered, "As if the horses haven't escaped already." A sentiment with which Grant sympathized.

He walked the two women out, watching as Joan settled Kat into the passenger seat of a pickup with a brusque kind of tenderness. He was still standing there when the truck pulled out of the parking lot. This was one of those times when merely looking at Kat had left him feeling as if he'd been pummeled. The resultant deep bruises might not be visible, but they did hurt. He looked down to see that he was actually rubbing the heel of his hand over his breastbone, as if that would help. A brief, humorless bark of laughter escaped him as he climbed into his patrol car. Would it ever quit hurting, loving her the way he did?

He called in to let dispatch know where he was. Jed Beier was waiting for him out front of the nursery. The two men shook hands and he said, "Gasoline."

"Good nose."

"I'm like a vintner. My nose is a connoisseur of smoke."

This laugh felt a little better. Grant liked Jed.

Jed took his own photos, whipped out a measuring tape and scribbled indecipherably with a blunt-tipped pencil in a breast pocket-sized notebook. He used the pencil, Grant knew, because so many fire scenes were also saturated with water, fire retardant foam and the like. Ink ran.

"Not much I can tell you that you don't already know," he said finally. "I take it this didn't happen out of the blue?"

"No." Grant encapsulated events to date.

Jed meditated. "This setup seems to be more of an attention grabber than a murder attempt." He glanced at Grant. "Not saying Ms. Riley couldn't have died. But employees were due to arrive momentarily. Of course they'd rush out to see what was on fire."

Staring at the charred, dripping side of the shed, Grant imagined Kat trapped inside as fire ate its way through to her, hammering on the door until her hands were raw. And he said, in a voice that sounded feral even to his own ears, "But whoever did this didn't much care if Kat died."

"No," Jed said quietly. "Most fires I see are set either for profit or for fun. This one's different."

"That's because the fire wasn't the point. Like you said, it was an attention getter."

Grant saw Jed off, then told Helen and James Cheung to close up. He waited while they did so, and drove out behind them.

He paused before turning onto the highway to call Kat. Joan answered.

"She just got out of the shower. The coughing seems to be letting up."

"Okay. Tell her the place is locked up. Your new employee seems to be sharp. She put a sandwich board out front that says the nursery will be closed today because of a fire."

"Good. We usually use that to mark specials."

"I figured."

"Are you…coming to talk to Kat?" She sounded hesitant.

"Not yet," he told her. "I'm going to take the bones to Dr. Erdahl at the hospital first, and then do a little research. I have an idea." He paused. "Why don't you see if you can get her to take a nap."

She snorted. "Fat chance. But I'll try."

He got lucky and the doctor squeezed him in between two autopsies. She confirmed that the second pelvis was indeed female. "A young woman," she said. "Not an adolescent. Probably hadn't borne a child yet. Say, eighteen to twenty-five. I'm sorry not to be of more help."

Grant shook his head. "I keep hoping we'll discover a cause of death."

"We might get lucky if you find the full skeleton. A bullet passing through the body does damage that would be recognizable. A knife blade often nicks bone."

He thanked her and took the two pelvises to the funeral home to be stored with the other bones. Then he went to his office and pulled out his own notes about what he'd learned so far about Hugh's life and death.

Angela Jo Hiatt. He had already gotten far enough to get a copy of her original application of employment from the school district office, but the information it contained hadn't given him an easy way to trace her. In Next of Kin she'd written *None, grew up in foster homes.*

She'd been vulnerable, he thought now, as he had when he'd first read that. Just like all Hugh Riley's victims. And despite their foolish decisions to sleep with a married man, that's what they were: victims. He'd worn a lazy, charming disguise, but beneath it he was a sexual predator.

Grant had tried at the time calling the names Angie Hiatt had given as references, but neither of the numbers had been in service anymore. Now he went online and got the phone number for the alumni office of Pacific Lutheran University, where she'd graduated. They hadn't received any updates from her since graduation, and had no current address; the alumni magazine had become undeliverable. They confirmed that the last known address they had for her was the one here in Fern Bluff.

He checked motor vehicle records for the names

she'd given as references and found both. When he called the first one, he got a chirpy message followed by a blast of heavy metal music that made him wince. He explained who he was and asked her to call. The second woman, whose name was Margaret Proctor, answered.

"Meg here."

Once again he explained that he was attempting to track down Angela Hiatt. "May I ask how you knew her?"

"She worked for me part-time most of the way through college. I have a day care center." Meg's voice was warm; the fact that she'd liked Angie Hiatt rang through in it. "She was great with the kids."

"And have you stayed in touch with her, Ms. Proctor?"

"I did for a while. She was working for the school district up in…" She stopped, apparently connecting the dots. He'd told her he was the police chief of Fern Bluff. "I guess you knew that."

"Yes."

"Well, as far as I know, she finished out the school year there, but then she dropped off the map. I was surprised to quit hearing from her. But you know how it is. I figured she'd met a guy. Moved to Florida." She sounded resigned but also regretful. "Did something happen to Angie?"

"It would be premature for me to suggest that," he said carefully. "I may find her in Florida. At this point, I'm pursuing a hunch. That's all."

Silent for a moment, she said finally, "Will you let me know?"

"I will," he promised. "Please do call me if you hear from her unexpectedly. And thank you for your help, Ms. Proctor."

He leaned back in his chair and laced his fingers behind his head. His hunch was hardening into near-certainty. Angie, he was now convinced, had not sent that email letting the school district know that she'd had a family emergency and wouldn't be able to finish out the year. Whoever had sent it hadn't known that the young teacher's aide had no family. Nor had Angie packed up the contents of her own apartment.

Two hours later her other reference returned his call. Siobhan Seton hadn't heard from Angie in four years, either. Her feelings were hurt; they'd been roommates their junior and senior years at PLU. Siobhan had married a guy they'd both known in college, and had wanted Angie to be her maid of honor. But she never got a reply to her email, and the phone number was disconnected. She'd wondered if Angie had secretly liked the guy, too, and that's why she'd cut ties.

Siobhan became hysterical despite Grant's repeated assurances that he was merely attempting to locate her friend to get some information. "Oh, God!" she kept saying. "Something happened to her, and I didn't even try to find her!"

"Did she tell you about a man she was seeing here in Fern Bluff?" he asked.

Siobhan sniffed. "Kind of. I didn't meet him or anything. I wasn't even sure she hadn't made him up. You know. Like, see, I have a boyfriend, too." Angie, she said, had told her he was older, and really hot, and he was getting a divorce because his wife was such a bitch.

Grant wondered how often the son of a bitch had described Kat that way and to how many people.

He already knew that the apartment manager hadn't seen Angie moving out. Odds weren't good that other residents were still around four years later, or would remember someone they'd seen carrying boxes out to a car. Why would they? It wasn't the kind of place you became best friends with your neighbor.

He did some searches online in law enforcement databases as well as Google and Facebook and anything else he could think of. He found what he'd expected to: nothing.

Angie Hiatt had had a car, too. An older Chevy Geo. She'd sold it the same day she quit her job and moved. It had changed hands one more time and then been scrapped.

He'd butted up hard against a dead end, and Grant didn't like it. Prickles of unease raised the hair on the back of his neck and skittered over his body. The possibilities for further escalation of this campaign of terror were now limited.

Kat hadn't died today, but she would soon if he couldn't manage to protect her.

CHAPTER TWELVE

SINCE NAPS TENDED TO make Kat feel groggy and grumpy afterward, she hardly ever let herself take one. But after her shower, she lay down on her bed, for a minute. The next thing she knew, she surfaced to find herself curled on her side, her mouth hanging open and dry with a disgusting taste, and her brain in a fog. Ugh. Obviously, she'd fallen asleep.

She worked her mouth and jaw, managed a swallow and groaned. She opened her eyes to find herself alone. She'd half expected to find Joan perched like a vigilant guardian angel at her bedside.

Kat stumbled into the bathroom, used the toilet and then took an unhappy look at herself in the mirror. More ugh. Her hair, wet when she lay down, was flattened on one side and tangled on the other. Her cheek was decorated with creases. Her eyes were puffy.

With water splashed on the brush, she repaired the damage to her hair, although she was clumsy with her hands wrapped. The gauze was probably overkill, but she'd wait until tomorrow to take it off. Her knuckles had been bloody, she knew, when Helen had opened the shed door and Kat had fallen out.

After brushing her teeth to get rid of the icky taste,

she inspected herself again and decided there wasn't anything else she could do.

Grant was standing in the bedroom when she came out of the bathroom. His gaze moved swiftly over her, taking in her long, bare legs. She'd gone to bed in her T-shirt and panties.

"How are you?" he asked, in a voice made gritty by emotion.

"I'm…" Fine. She tried to say it, even though she wasn't. The word stuck in her throat.

"Oh, damn," he said explosively. "Come here."

In an instant, he'd yanked her into his arms. She wrapped hers around his waist and pressed even closer. She felt his cheek against her hair, or maybe his lips.

"You scared the hell out of me," he muttered. "I don't know if I can take any more."

A giggle welled up from somewhere. "*You* can't?"

He tried to laugh, she knew he did, but it didn't quite come off. "I swear, you're not getting out of my sight again."

Kat sighed and reveled in the slam of his heartbeat and the strength of his arms. It was a while before she murmured, "That's not very practical."

He was gently rocking her. "Doesn't matter."

"Of course it does." But she was smiling anyway, even if her lips wobbled, because he meant it. Feeling ridiculously happy, scared to death and wanting to bawl all at the same time was weird. It was like teetering on a tightrope stretched over an abyss. She never wanted Grant to let her go.

"Is Joan still here?" she finally asked.

"No." His big hands skated up and down her body, as if he had to feel for himself that she was there and safe. "I sent her home."

"Oh."

He eased back finally. "I put some soup on to heat when I heard the toilet flushing. It's probably boiling by now."

"Okay." She swiped at her eyes—the thick gauze was good for something, it turned out—and made herself step away from Grant. "I'm hungry, now that you mention the subject of food."

"Good."

He waited while she pulled on jeans, and didn't say anything else as they went downstairs, although she felt his gaze resting on her. The way he looked at her had unnerved her from the beginning, in a whole lot of ways. One was the intensity of his gaze. She'd have sworn he saw all the way through her. The sensation was especially unsettling for someone like her, who had been very, very careful all her life to keep the essence of herself buried deep inside. He was giving her that look now, as if he knew how tangled her feelings were. It was a relief when he had to turn his attention to dishing up the soup and making sandwiches while she waited with her hands folded docilely on the table.

Only after he'd poured them both milk and sat did she clear her throat and ask, "Did you learn anything?"

"Not as much as I'd have liked." He frowned. "You knew those were pelvises?"

Kat nodded.

"One male, one female."

She felt sick and set down her spoon. "I… guessed."

"Eat," he said gently.

After a moment, Kat picked up the spoon again. Eating his own lunch, Grant watched her, too.

"Here's what I think," he said finally, when she'd finished half of the turkey sandwich and most of her soup. "It's possible Hugh messed with the wrong guy's wife. But I doubt it."

"Wait." Kat stared at him. "Were any of the women he…he was seeing married?"

"One that I've discovered." He hesitated, his dark eyebrows drawing together again. "No, actually two of them, I guess. In both cases, their marriages were breaking up. That doesn't mean an almost-ex-husband isn't going to resent his wife taking up with another man right away."

It took Kat a moment to identify her acute discomfort with the topic. Okay, she didn't like thinking about Hugh screwing around on her. But there was more, she recognized, and the more was what she and Grant had felt for each other when they were both already married. She'd been carrying around that guilt for a long time.

His eyes narrowed, and she wondered if he'd read her mind, but if so he didn't comment. He was a good man who took his vows seriously, she knew now. He'd have felt guilty, too.

"Why do you doubt it?" Kat asked, backtracking.

"I mean, that Hugh was killed by some woman's husband."

"There are a couple of things wrong with the theory. One, why the other pelvis?"

"Maybe he killed his wife, too."

He moved his shoulders in a not-quite-shrug. "Conceivable, but the two women I know of who were getting out of marriages are both alive and well." He paused. "The one woman I know he was seeing that last spring who may have disappeared was single. I haven't found even a hint that there was a boyfriend."

Kat felt as if the air had been squeezed out of her chest. "Oh."

"To all appearances, she quit her job abruptly and moved away. The day after Hugh disappeared."

"How could somebody not notice if she'd died?"

His expression was compassionate. "She grew up in foster homes. The couple of friends I've found were surprised when she dropped off their radar, but they hadn't seen much of her in the previous year, and friends do drift apart."

"I see," she said. She lowered her gaze to the table-top. There was a spot of something crusted on the blue-checked tablecloth. She needed to wash it.

"Usually, it takes family to refuse to *let* someone disappear." His voice was deep and deliberate. "Even then... Take me, for instance. I call my sister and Mom and Dad every month or so, but it would be at least a couple of months before they got worried about not hearing from me."

Would anyone worry about her? She couldn't help wondering.

Well, all of her employees, of course. As a business owner, she couldn't disappear so easily. But on a personal level…Joan. Joan would. And just about nobody else. She felt hollow until she thought, Grant would, too. Grant was scared for her. Maybe as scared for her as she was for herself.

He hadn't said anything about loving her, or marrying her, or about the future at all, but Kat thought that already he cared more about her than anyone else ever had. She didn't understand why. Why her? But maybe it didn't matter. It just was, and the knowledge warmed her deep inside.

"Okay." She moistened her lips. "You said a couple of things were wrong with the theory that an ex-husband or boyfriend killed Hugh."

Grant nodded. Without exactly moving, he gave the impression of relaxing just a little. No, he didn't like talking about married men running around on their wives, and he hadn't liked any better reminding her that she had precious few people to care if she vanished from the face of the earth. He wanted to move on.

"Why fixate on you?" he said bluntly. "If anything, this hypothetical husband would sympathize with you. See you as another wronged party."

"That makes sense," she admitted. "All right. You obviously have a theory."

"It's one of Hugh's lovers." He turned his empty milk glass in his hand without ever taking his eyes from her. "A woman who thought she meant more to Hugh than she really did."

"Join the club," Kat muttered.

"Hugh had a way of ending relationships when he lost interest. But what if he hadn't done that yet? Or this woman wouldn't accept it? And what if she caught him with someone else?"

"And killed both of them?"

"Right. Since she hadn't planned it in advance, she had to hustle, then, and make sure nobody missed the other woman. Hugh, though, was another story. He *was* missed, and there wasn't anything she could do about that."

Kat thought about it. "Wouldn't she have hated me, too?"

"Maybe. But maybe not, if she believed Hugh was leaving you for her. You weren't the enemy. She was the winner, right? She might have even felt sorry for you."

A shudder ran through Kat. "Well, she doesn't anymore. So…why's this happening?"

"I'm still working on that part. What changed?"

She'd thought about this, too. "The award," she said. "I got it the week before the first bones showed up. It brought a lot of attention to me and the nursery."

"I keep going back to that award," Grant agreed. "The only thing is, it didn't change anything."

Slowly, Kat said, "But what it did do is highlight how much more successful the nursery has gotten since Hugh disappeared. I mentioned him in my thank you, remember? But…I've gotten funny vibes from some people. As if they think it's not fair I've gotten recognition that should have been Hugh's. The business was his."

"That's occurred to me," Grant said. "So, okay. All was fine as long as you were the meek little woman not sure whether you'd been widowed or abandoned, but suddenly you came across as a superconfident businesswoman instead. Maybe all that fanfare was an unpleasant reminder that you had actually profited from Hugh's death."

"And that didn't seem fair to her, not if she'd believed he loved her and was going to marry her." Kat felt weird having this discussion while they ate lunch. It was as if they were players in some murder weekend at a bed-and-breakfast, not two people talking about real murder.

Grant let out a sigh and stretched his arms above his head. Joints cracked. "It hangs together, but, hell, I'm being charitable to call it a theory."

Kat nerved herself. "How many of his women have you identified?"

He didn't try to look away. "Four."

"But you don't suspect any of them."

"No. I could be wrong, but the three I've talked to all seemed resigned to the fact that Hugh had lied to them. He used, uh, similar terminology when he cut each of them loose. So none of the three would have been surprised to see him with someone else."

She bit her lip and nodded.

"I haven't looked further back. I figure it had to be someone he was seeing that last year. Probably the last few months."

That made sense.

"I've got a gap of a few months in there. Either there wasn't anybody, or…"

Talking about Hugh's infidelity, thinking about it, was getting easier, as if it didn't really relate to her at all, Kat thought. He didn't *deserve* any grief or misery from her. She realized she resented the amount she'd already expended on him.

"Tell me your timetable."

He did, with her thinking back to that spring before he disappeared.

"There was definitely someone else in there," she said. "When we were first married, he'd stay focused on me for longer periods. But by that time, I was lucky to get a few weeks before I could feel him sort of drifting away."

It made her feel stupid, in retrospect, to see so clearly now what she hadn't then. But she also recognized that she just hadn't *wanted* to see. So—not stupid. What she'd been was willfully blind.

"Let's think about how he met these women," Grant suggested. "One of them cleaned his teeth."

She went to the same dentist Hugh had. Faces of various dental technicians, dimly remembered, flickered through her memory. It horrified her to think that the woman who cleaned her teeth had been one of Hugh's past lovers.

"One met him when he was briefly shopping for a second mortgage."

Kat remembered that. She'd talked him out of it.

"One, at least, met him at the nursery. I gather she hired him to do some landscaping."

A customer. Maybe a woman who was still a customer. Kat worked to keep her breathing steady. Was it a surprise to find that he'd cheated on her with women he'd met at the nursery? Where had she thought he'd found them?

"Hugh did that sometimes," she said. "I think he'd have liked to be a landscape designer, but that's a really hard way to make a living."

"So where else did he go? How else could he meet women?"

They talked, but the truth was Hugh could have taken up with a clerk at the grocery store or pharmacy, a neighbor, someone who worked at one of the wholesale nurseries or other suppliers he'd dealt with…. The possibilities were almost endless.

"Not the doctor's office." She shook her head when Grant threw that idea out. "I don't remember Hugh ever going."

"Was he involved in the garden club?"

"Are you kidding? It's mostly women. He loved it, they loved him." Kat heard herself and felt a chill. It was true. She'd gone to meetings with him sometimes, but had felt the next thing to invisible. It was uncomfortable enough that mostly she hadn't gone, until she had to take his place if she was to maintain the ties between the club and the nursery.

"Can you give me a list of members?"

She nodded numbly. "A whole bunch of them were on the lists Joan and I made up of people who'd been at the nursery when I found those first bones. A lot of them are good customers."

He pushed back from the table, as though suddenly restless. "I'll check out those first, then."

Kat found she'd crossed her arms and was squeezing them tight to herself. Until this moment, the possibility that someone she knew well might have killed Hugh hadn't seemed real. The lists she and Joan had made had been an academic exercise to take their minds off the horrific possibility that the finger bones might be Hugh's.

She couldn't help remembering the last garden club meeting and trying to imagine who among the group hated her this much. She shivered slightly, wondering how many women in the club Hugh might have slept with.

Comforting herself, she thought, not Dorothy Glenn, who was in her sixties. Or Andi Barrick, a scrawny, leathery woman in her late fifties. But there were two many genuine possibilities.

Amanda Hinds, who'd snubbed Kat at that last meeting? Bridget Moretti was pretty, and about the right age, and she hadn't been very friendly, either. Fay Cabot was…maybe thirty-five, but homely; Kat didn't know if she could bear to ask Grant whether Hugh had chosen only beautiful women. There must be eight or ten women, now that she considered it, who were at least reasonably attractive, in an age range that might have appealed to Hugh, and who had been around in those days.

Annika Lindstrom, for one, and she'd been on both lists Joan and Kat had made. Wasn't Becca Montgomery, too? But both of them had continued to be friendly.

Carol Scammell? Lisa Llewellyn?

She couldn't help a shudder, and suddenly Grant tugged her out of her chair and into his arms again.

"Don't," he said, voice low and harsh. "I can tell what you're thinking. It's not going to do any good."

"I have to think about it," Kat cried. Her hands balled into fists. "I know them all better than you do. I see them all the time."

"I know you do," he said. "I know. But wait until you've calmed down a little. My guess is your gut will tell you how unlikely some of them are."

He was massaging her neck to comfort her. Focusing on the gentle kneading helped. Gradually her own hands relaxed, and finally she found the strength to straighten away from him. Her eyes burned, as if she hadn't blinked in too long a time, but she was all right. She was.

"You need to go to work," she said. "I'll be fine. I wasn't really hurt. Mostly scared. Nobody is going to attack me here at the house in the middle of the afternoon."

He frowned at her. "Maybe Joan will come back."

"Don't be silly. I'll take a baseball bat to bed with me tonight. How's that? Hugh had a couple, you know. They're still in the hall closet."

"I'm not worried about tonight. I intend to be here. No, damn it." He reached out and gave her a little shake. "Don't argue. I don't care what anyone thinks. I'll sleep on the damn couch."

She swallowed. "You...don't have to do that."

A muscle spasmed on his jaw. The flare of emotion in his eyes sent a shiver of awareness through Kat.

"You mean that?"

She nodded and whispered, "Yes."

The air in here was even harder to breathe than it had been in the enclosed, smoky space of the shed.

Grant closed his eyes briefly, said, "Thank God," and kissed her. It was quick, but potent. As if he was staking a claim. "I'll be back for dinner," he said, in that rough voice she knew meant he was aroused or deeply moved. Maybe both. "Do you want me to pick something up?"

Kat gave a tremulous smile. "No, I need to stay busy. Cooking will be good for me."

"Lock behind me."

"Yes."

She walked him to the front door. He stepped out on the front porch, turned and came back in. One thorough kiss later, he finally left, although he waited until she shut the door and he heard the dead bolt snick closed.

TWO DAYS LATER, GRANT WASN'T sure whether he'd gotten anywhere. He'd started his inquiries with garden club members he knew well and had good reason to believe were unlikely to have been Hugh Riley groupies. One was Carol Scammell, a school board member and parent of four kids ranging in age from six or seven to sixteen. Carol's husband Rod was a plumbing contractor and a hell of a guy. Grant had seen them together enough to find it hard to imagine either of them fooling around on the side.

Carol had been willing to be frank. She admitted she'd heard gossip about Hugh and had even wondered about a couple of fellow garden club members.

"Bridget Moretti," she said. "Do you know her? She works at In Full Bloom."

He knew Randy Nyland, who owned the florist shop, but hadn't had reason himself to go in.

"I, um, saw them together once." Color had risen in Carol's cheeks. "Maybe a year after he married Kat. I couldn't be sure about what I saw, but… You know what a dead giveaway people's body language can be sometimes."

He knew.

"Bridget dropped out of the garden club a month or two after that. She didn't come back for, oh, ages." Carol looked reflective. "Maybe after Hugh was gone."

Bridget, he learned, had been and still was married. When he stopped by the florist to talk to her, she fiercely denied ever being unfaithful to her husband or thinking that way about Hugh. She was lying. Grant could tell, and she knew he could. She was vibrating with fear when he said, "Thank you for talking to me, Ms. Moretti," and left.

Turned out the other woman Carol had named, a Nicole Flood, had moved the year before. Only up to Bellingham, which was just over an hour's drive from Fern Bluff, but when he made a few calls he found she worked in the Whatcom County assessor's office and hadn't missed a day since she started there nine months before. That didn't make her impossible as a suspect, but she was pretty damn unlikely.

He'd talked to Greg Buckmeier, too, something of a character, and one of the only men who were dedicated garden club members. Turned out Greg was more observant than you'd expect. He hadn't much liked Hugh. He suggested a couple more names, and both made more likely prospects than either Nicole or Bridget, who'd stayed married despite having succumbed to temptation at one point.

Lisa Llewellyn was one. She was a real estate agent, which meant that tying down her whereabouts for any particular time and day was next to impossible. Who'd know whether she had been showing houses or not? Lisa was married, Grant knew, but her husband was a long-haul trucker. She might easily have been lonely enough to be vulnerable to Hugh's appeal. And maybe she'd started imagining having a man who wasn't gone more than he was home.

Annika Lindstrom was the other possibility Greg cited. "Hugh was working with her on her garden not that long before he disappeared, you know." His mouth puckered. "She let everyone think she designed it and maintained it all by herself, but I overheard them a couple of times. He redesigned some flowerbeds, sketched an arbor she had built. Oh, yes. She'd deny it, but Hugh had something to do with her getting her garden in the *Seattle Times*. You can't tell me he didn't."

Annika, Grant knew, didn't work at all. She'd reputedly been left well-off by her long-deceased husband. Which meant she didn't have to account for her time or whereabouts to anyone at all.

Of course, it was also possible that Buckmeier

had let envy get the better of him. *His* garden had never been featured even in the more local Everett *Herald*, never mind the *Times*. Plainly, he resented the fact that Ms. Lindstrom might have taken advantage of Hugh's professional advice while pretending her garden was entirely an amateur achievement.

When Grant's phone rang, he answered absently while scowling at his notes, spread on the desk before him. "Haller here."

"Mortensen," the city manager said brusquely. "I need you to come to my office."

Grant didn't much like being summoned as if he were a schoolboy being called over the intercom to the principal's office, but he kept his voice even. "I can make time."

Jeffrey Mortensen was six feet four or five and painfully thin, giving him a peculiarly storklike appearance. He had his priorities: dollars and cents first, and the wishes of the city council members second. Any needs the citizens of his town might have came in a distant third. He and Grant had clashed more than once. Unfortunately, although he'd have to get council backing to fire his police chief, he was technically Grant's boss.

Grant knocked on the glass inset of his office door and entered without waiting for a "come in." Mortensen sat behind his desk, the lenses of his wire-rimmed glasses glinting.

His mouth tightened. "Haller."

"Jeffrey." Grant knew he didn't like to be called by his first name. He, therefore, always used it.

With no suggestion that Grant get comfortable, he

snapped, "Explain what in hell you're thinking of, spending nights at Kathryn Riley's."

Having had a bad feeling this was going to be the topic, Grant had braced himself not to give away his wariness or the anger that simmered just below it. Uninvited, he pulled up a chair, sat and stretched out his legs as if he was completely at his ease.

"You heard about the fire at the nursery?"

"Of course I heard about it."

"Ms. Riley is being terrorized," Grant said flatly. "I believe she's in danger. I doubt you'd agree to extend the city budget to provide around-the-clock protection to her. I'm making damn sure she doesn't get killed before I can figure out who's after her."

Lips thinning, Mortensen contemplated him. "She could have set up that fire herself. Given the time of day, she wasn't in any real danger."

Resisting the temptation to lunge across the desk and slug the son of a bitch, Grant took a moment to get a grip on himself before he said, "She was treated for smoke inhalation. Another couple of minutes, and she'd have died. Yeah, there was a real possibility she would be rescued. There was an equal possibility the rescue wouldn't have come in time." He gave that a minute to sink in. "Want to explain how she locked herself in with a hasp that closes on the outside?"

The city manager made an impatient gesture. "She must have friends. For God's sake, use your head. Who else would have any reason to kill Hugh?"

"Plenty of people." Grant summarized the investigation to date. "I trust you'll keep this to yourself," he added.

An irritated flush mottled Mortensen's cheeks. "I don't chatter about city business. I also don't display my bias to any and all eyes when I'm conducting an inquiry. Your conduct is indefensible."

Too pissed now to be politic, Grant rose to his feet. "Take it up with the city council," he suggested in a hard voice. "In the meantime, I'll be doing my job."

He stalked out, shutting the door behind him with enough force to make the glass shiver although he hadn't quite slammed it. Damn it. He didn't really think he'd lose his job over this, but it was conceivable. He'd had a suspicion for a while that Mortensen would like nothing better than to find an excuse to get rid of him.

"To hell with him," he muttered, earning a startled look from a middle-aged woman exiting the women's restroom. Grant didn't apologize. He kept going. Thanks to Mortensen, he'd already wasted fifteen minutes. He had barely another hour to work on a background check of Annika Lindstrom and Lisa Llewellyn before he had to leave.

There was no way he was letting Kat go home to an empty house.

CHAPTER THIRTEEN

As the week went on, Kat got quieter and quieter. Grant could see the strain wearing on her.

Tonight, over dinner, she told him that she'd bought a window at a secondhand store. "James is going to install it in the shed."

Grant doubted anyone would ever be trapped in the toolshed again before it was set on fire, but he didn't blame her for planning an escape route nonetheless. James, he knew, had already torn out the burned portions of the walls and rebuilt them. The guy was apparently handy.

"Sounds like a good idea," he said.

With her fork, she poked at her asparagus without actually impaling a spear. After a minute, she said, "People are talking."

Pretending to be unconcerned, he raised his eyebrows. "About?"

She lifted her gaze to his. "Us."

He tensed. "I know."

"Grant, at the best of times there'd be plenty of people who would frown about their police chief openly living with a woman he's not married to. This is a conservative community, you know."

"I have noticed that," he said drily. "Although

you've got to admit, it's ridiculous that we're having this discussion at all in this day and time."

"We wouldn't be if you weren't a public official. But you know what? You can't tell me the citizens of Dallas or Seattle or, heck, San Francisco, would like it any better. Your private life is supposed to be aboveboard and by the book. Or at least out of sight."

He didn't like where she was going with this. "That may be true," he conceded, "but these circumstances are a little out of the ordinary, you have to admit. I'm not leaving you alone any more than I can help."

Kat quit pretending to eat and set down her fork. "Grant, you could get in trouble over this. You know darn well half the people in this town think I had something to do with Hugh's death. You're supposed to be investigating. Instead, you're sleeping with me."

Despite everything, he grinned at her. "And enjoying it."

Kat let out a frustrated huff. "What if you lose your job over me?"

He shrugged. "Then I find a new one."

She stared at him with seeming despair. "You're not going to back down, are you?"

Deadly serious now, he said, "Nope."

He could see the worries churning in her, and God knows he shared them. The city manager had gone ahead and started talking to council members. One who didn't much like Mortensen had told Grant privately, and added that he'd better clean up his act.

Meanwhile, he felt as if he was spinning his wheels on the investigation.

Lisa Llewellyn was looking less viable as a suspect, if only because he hadn't been able to figure out where she would have stashed the two missing trucks and two sets of skeletal remains. She and her husband had a smallish house in town and owned no other property that he could find. Turned out she had a fifteen-year-old stepson who lived with them, too, which limited her movements and privacy. She had no family nearby; her parents had a ranch near Cheyenne, Wyoming, and her one brother lived in Montana.

Meanwhile, Grant had come up with another possibility, a woman named Crystal Sanderson. He'd been more than interested to see that she had appeared on the list of customers at the nursery on the second day when the first bones had appeared. In recent years, she'd been only an occasional attendee of garden club meetings, but she had apparently been way more gung ho back when Hugh was the central attraction at them. She was a good-looking woman whose marriage broke up the year after Hugh's death. That alone had caught Grant's attention. Since the divorce, she'd lived with a wheelchair-bound, elderly father in the family home on what had once been a dairy farm—which meant there were half a dozen barns and outbuildings, long abandoned. Grant had taken an illicit scouting expedition and been able to see into a couple of the barns and a loafing shed, but had noticed a concrete structure with a tin roof and no windows as well as a large detached garage with two small windows covered by roll-down shades. He'd loitered in a side road a quarter of a mile away and seen that Crystal did not park her wheelchair-friendly van in the garage.

He'd checked out Annika Lindstrom's place, too, waiting until he saw her drive away in her shiny black Land Rover. He'd been all too conscious of how much trouble he would be in if he got caught trespassing and peering into windows, but he was getting edgier with every day that passed, more certain that time was running out. It wasn't as if he had even a shadow of a justification for search warrants. "I've got a bad feeling" wasn't going to cut it. He couldn't take anything he learned in illicit searches to court, but all he was looking for was a reason to focus his suspicion.

He was no gardener, but even he could tell that Annika's would be spectacular in another month, when more was in bloom. Flower beds were sharply edged and gracefully curved within a meandering, emerald green lawn that didn't look anything like the one he reluctantly mowed once a week front and back of his place. Vines clambered up trellises and the pillared porch of an elegant, Colonial-style house. More were expertly trained on half a dozen arbors, painted white and deep green to echo the colors on the house clapboards and shutters. Small, weeping trees and sculptural shrubs suggested skillful pruning. Stone statues and huge terracotta pots peeked out here and there. He could hear the trickle of a small waterfall coming from somewhere. Brick and cobblestone walkways led to hidden alcoves.

The potting shed was a work of art, the greenhouse handsome and integrated into the garden design.

This landscape had required a massive infusion of cash and labor. Grant didn't blame Greg Buckmeier for his bitterness. If you were any normal human being, there was no way you could realistically compete with Annika's garden.

A tall, perfectly trimmed hedge disguised the garage. The windows sparkled and, looking in, Grant saw a second vehicle, this one a beige sedan of some kind. A Camry, he thought; a nice enough car that no one would be surprised to see her driving it, but innocuous enough not to draw attention, either.

An even taller hedge and a cedar fence nearly buried in honeysuckle would keep visitors to the garden from even noticing the two big metal buildings on the back of the property. Annika's husband, Grant had been told, had been a car collector. Nobody knew whether she'd kept the cars or sold them. Clearly, money wasn't much of an issue, so she might have held on to them for sentimental reasons.

Unfortunately, neither building had a window, and the rolling, garage-style doors and smaller side doors were all locked. Frustrated, he finally gave up.

Kat had been asking questions about the investigation, but Grant was torn about how much to tell her. He had an obligation to keep what he learned confidential. He'd already said a hell of a lot more to her than he should have. Besides, these women might be friends of hers. He knew all three were good customers. She had to be uncomfortable already around anyone who could conceivably have been one of her husband's lovers.

He sure as hell didn't want her to get in a car to go anywhere with one of them, though.

Why limit it to those three? Grant reflected. He didn't want her alone with anyone right now.

But when he said as much, she jumped up from the table.

"Not Joan? What about my other employees? How do you expect me to run a business?"

He knew she was getting mad to cover her fear. "Damn it, Kat. I'm just asking you to be careful. Is that unreasonable?"

Hugging herself, she paced to the window, looked out for a minute, then swung back to face him. "I hate this. I hate everything about it."

He would have been afraid she was including having him in her bed at night if it weren't for the way she responded to his touch. What he felt when they made love bore only a distant relationship to anything he'd ever experienced before. He knew it was the same for her.

"Yeah," he said quietly. "I don't blame you. Just… be patient. That's all I'm asking."

She pressed her lips together and for a minute he thought she might cry. But he wasn't surprised when she did battle with herself and won. Her jaw firmed. "I'm going to clean up the kitchen and then take a hot bath."

"Leave the dirty dishes to me," he said. "You cooked. Go take your bath."

"Fine." She wheeled and left the kitchen. Her footsteps sounded on the stairs.

Grant didn't follow her for quite a while. Plainly, she needed some time alone. She was under a lot of stress right now. It occurred to him, too, that she'd lived alone for four years now. All of a sudden a man had, for all practical purposes, moved in with her and taken over her life. It had to be unsettling.

He realized he was frowning as he climbed the stairs. He'd lived alone for the past four years, too. He would have expected living so intimately with another person to require an adjustment. It had with Rachel. He wasn't sure he ever really had adjusted. She'd flown home without him to visit her family a few times, when he and she were still in Dallas, and he'd been ashamed to be intensely grateful for a week or two of solitude.

With Kat, though, it was different. This morning he'd woken up before she did, and found her draped over him. Her head was nestled on his shoulder, her arm stretched across his chest and her hand tucked cozily in his armpit. One of her legs, silky smooth, lay across his.

He'd rolled his head slightly so he could see her face, her lips softly parted, her eyes flickering behind delicate, blue-veined lids. Her hair, that glorious, indescribable hair, tumbled over his shoulder and arm. He could feel her breasts pressed against his side and chest. He'd all but held his breath, not wanting to wake her, and was struck by the damnedest feeling. He could hardly contain whatever it was, as if he was a bottle of champagne, or maybe pop, that had been given a good shake and was near to exploding with thousands of tiny, lighter-than-air bubbles.

He was happier than he ever remembered being in his life. He'd wanted to stay there in that bed forever. To hell with the needs of his bladder or his stomach's demands. He'd lain there smiling, probably looking like some kind of besotted fool, and thought, *This is all I ask. To wake up every morning with Kat in my bed. In my arms.* He wouldn't have called himself a praying man, but he thought maybe that's what he was doing.

Inevitably, she'd woken up. She nuzzled him sleepily and his body hardened, but then she gave a little squeak at her first sight of the clock and leaped from bed, grumbling that she'd forgotten to set the alarm.

So much for staying there forever.

Tonight, he finished cleaning the kitchen and then watched the ten o'clock news before he went up. He hoped she had succeeded in contending with whatever mood had been gripping her this evening.

The bedroom was dark but for the bedside lamp. Kat had a couple of pillows piled behind her and was reading. He'd glanced at the book that morning. It seemed to be a compilation of essays on the peculiar joys of digging in the dirt and watching things grow.

When he came out of the bathroom, she'd set the book aside and restored one of the pillows to his side. She watched as he stripped his clothes off. He went around to his side and got in under the covers, unable to hide his arousal.

Kat rolled to face him. "I'm sorry," she whispered.

He stroked her cheek. "For what?"

"Being difficult."

"You're not difficult." He brushed his lips over her forehead, her temples, her cheeks. "You're scared and mad. That's not the same thing."

He felt her stillness. After a moment, she said, "I guess I am."

"I am, too," he murmured. "I want you safe, Kat."

"But I am when I'm with you."

He lifted his head enough to give her a half smile. "You sure about that? I feel a little bit dangerous right now."

Her mouth was curved, too, when it met his. One deep, drugging kiss later, she whispered, "Oh, I think I can handle some risks."

He laughed. "I like the way you handle me, babe. Keep right on doing it."

Her hand slid down his body and found its target. "As if I needed permission."

Grant pretty well ran out of words after that, and if her sighs and moans were any indication, she did, too.

Half an hour later, as he edged toward sleep, he realized he was smiling again. Broadly. Idiotically.

GRANT HADN'T BEEN CRAZY about her going on her own, but Kat ignored him and drove to Skagit County the next day to visit RoozenGaarde, Tulip Town and a couple of smaller bulb farms. She liked to see for herself some of the new hybrids when they were in bloom. She was less inclined to carry ones that didn't hold up to the incessant Northwest rain, for example.

She walked through display gardens, making notes in her catalogs. There was a new grape hyacinth with snow-white edging the traditional deep purple. She was seeing the late season daffodils now and the early tulips. She made a mental note to come again in a few weeks for the later tulips.

The colors were spectacular, and not only in the display gardens. Driving here, she'd passed acres and acres of tulips in glorious bloom—fields of yellow and deep rose and scarlet. Even on a weekday like this, traffic on the narrow, two-lane country roads was slow, with so many cars pulled onto the shoulder so that the tourists could snap pictures. You couldn't pay her enough to come up here on a weekend.

Usually, she'd feel refreshed by an outing like this. Today, Kat brooded.

Grant didn't want to talk about the flack he had to be taking for planting himself so solidly and publicly at her side. He might shrug off the threat to his job, but she couldn't. Not when it was her fault. It was *her* life that was a mess, not his. She couldn't help thinking that none of this would be happening if she hadn't stuck her head in the sand and refused to see that Hugh had the moral code and habits of a tomcat. She'd gambled so much on him when she married him, and for her, trusting someone was hard. Really hard. Then, she hadn't been able to admit to herself how badly she'd screwed up. If she had…

She'd have left him. Somebody might still have killed him, but she wouldn't be tangled up in it. Grant wouldn't be stuck feeling he had to protect her whatever the cost to him.

It scared her, to think of him paying such a big price for her.

Everything she felt for him scared her. It was so huge, so out of her control. If she trusted him completely, one of two things would happen: either he'd let her down the way Hugh had, or he'd suffer on her behalf. Kat hated both ideas. Panic kept pressing on her rib cage. She'd realized she'd been staring at a bed of mixed tulips and hyacinths for several minutes without seeing it at all or even noticing the heady scent of the hyacinths.

What if she found somewhere else to stay? Someplace she'd be safe, so Grant didn't have to worry?

Not Joan's—she was married and her thirty-year-old daughter was home with two young children after a divorce. Kat ran through the few other possibilities, but really none of them were good enough friends she felt like she could ask such a huge favor. She could go to a hotel and change rooms every night like a spy on the run…but a determined enemy could follow her from the nursery.

If it wasn't spring, she'd think about going to Hawaii for a couple of weeks, leaving the nursery in Joan's competent hands. But it was spring, and she couldn't possibly leave. They were getting busier by the day.

After several hours, she decided she'd made enough notes about the hybrids to be able to come to decisions later on which ones to order. She liked to change out which bulbs she carried every year. Of course, the gardeners like Annika who put in hundreds of bulbs every fall would shop at Roozen-Gaarde or Tulip Town themselves. Kat catered to the ones who put in a couple of dozen, or decided to add bulbs to a planter, or to buy a handsomely packaged dozen for a Christmas gift.

She arrived at the nursery to find it hopping. James was loading flats of perennials and flower baskets into the trunk of someone's car. Joan was behind the register with three people in line. Helen seemed to be helping someone choose a rhododendron, while Melinda was deep in conversation with a couple of women looking at the hybrid maples.

Kat plunged into work, persuading an eager new gardener to scale back the scope of her plans and dip her toe in the water first, so to speak.

"Autumn is a great time to plant, too," she said. "Why don't you start with the one bed and find out how much work it is. Get it just right, then once the weather cools off in September you can start digging out the second one. You'll want to be putting in bulbs then, too," she added. "Plus, that's a good time to look at the shrubs with great fall color and take a look at fall-blooming perennials. Too many gardens end up spectacular in the spring and dull the rest of the year."

The young woman nodded and said, "That's probably good advice. I'm a little bit prone to going overboard when I get excited about something. It's just, with a new house…"

Kat smiled. "Believe me, I understand. The wonderful thing about gardening is that it's a perfect, lifelong hobby. You can scale back when your life gets busy, expand when you have time. Start modestly, and who knows what your yard will look like five years from now?"

She left the customer happily choosing perennials and went on to help someone else pick out a floribunda rose for Mom on Mother's Day. Pete Timmons, one of Grant's deputies, was hovering then, wanting her advice on which flowering basket he should choose for his wife's birthday. Kat stayed so busy, she didn't have time to worry, or let the panic swell until it left her breathless.

She'd save that for when she got home.

"GODDAMN IT, GRANT! USE your head, man." Otto Crawford scowled at Grant from the other side of his desk. The senior member of the city council, both in longevity of service and in years, Otto was a broad-shouldered, once athletic man whose muscles had gone stringy with age. Over a brown-spotted pate, his white hair bristled; he'd never let it grow an eighth of an inch longer than it had been when he was a U.S. marine fifty years ago. The old coot was hard to get along with. He thought men weren't men unless they'd served their country in uniform, which meant he tended to throw his support behind Grant rather than Mortensen, who'd never put on a uniform in his life.

Otto's faded blue eyes now sparkled with outrage. His politics had solidified during the Cold War. He frequently lectured bored audiences about waning modern morals.

Otto liked to use physical intimidation. Right now, he was leaning forward over Grant's desk, both hands planted on the surface. A couple of times, Grant had felt the cool spray of Otto's spittle. Out of respect for the old guy, he'd refrained from showing his distaste.

Abruptly losing patience, though, he interrupted. "Have you been satisfied with the job I've done for this city?"

Otto's glower didn't diminish. "You know I have. Until your brain sank below your belt."

Grant's hands flexed on his thighs. "Watch it, Otto. You might want to do your own thinking instead of buying into Mortensen's story. You know he hopes to get rid of me."

"And I'm telling you, if your car's parked in that woman's driveway one more night, he may get his way."

"No matter why I'm there."

"People in this town don't want to see their police chief shacked up with some woman. Especially a woman under suspicion of murdering her husband."

Grant pushed back his chair and slowly rose to his feet. "This police department doesn't consider Kathryn Riley a suspect."

"Can you prove she didn't have anything to do with it?"

"The burden is on law enforcement and the courts to prove a suspect *did* do it. Not to prove someone's innocence. You know that, Otto."

The old man snorted and straightened. "You mean, the answer is no."

What the hell did he think? Of course the answer was no. Everyone knew Kat alone had watched Hugh drive away. Hell, even if somebody had been with her that morning, she'd have had to have another person with her 24/7 for weeks thereafter to be able to claim an unshakable alibi.

Cursing himself for even the briefest hesitation, Grant said expressionlessly, "I have a couple of viable suspects. Ms. Riley isn't one of them."

"You've been warned," Otto said. "I'm usually behind you. This time I'm not."

He walked out of the office.

Shit, Grant thought. Things were moving faster than he'd expected. He'd counted on having another two weeks until the next scheduled council meeting. If Mortensen or someone else called for an emergency session, Grant could be in trouble.

He would be to the point where he didn't give a good goddamn about the job, except that he knew Kat wouldn't want to pull up stakes and move. The nursery was too important to her. She didn't just take pride in it, she was fiercely invested in every acre and plant and bag of potting mix. He wasn't sure she would know how to separate herself from her business. He wasn't about to make her choose between it and him. The possibility that her choice wouldn't be him was unthinkable.

He had every intention of marrying Kat. Sitting again, he leaned back and pondered. What if he asked her now? How would opponents like Otto Crawford react if Kat was Grant's fiancée? Would it still be considered *shacking up* when his 4Runner was seen in her driveway?

He didn't know, but the rest of the day he was conscious of a restless sense of dissatisfaction. It bothered him not to be sure where he stood with Kat. He'd intended to put off confronting the issue, but, damn it, he wanted to have her pinned down. It was stupid, maybe, to feel insecure when she came so sweetly into his arms every night, but four years of waiting not-so-patiently for her had taken their toll.

He suddenly wasn't sure he could wait another day.

GRANT'S MOOD SEEMED GRIM all through dinner. Kat would look up to catch him watching her oddly, as if he was searching even deeper below the surface than usual.

She stood to clear the table, then let her plate clatter on the surface. She sat again. "All right. Are you going to tell me what's wrong? Your mood stinks."

He raised his eyebrows and she flushed. Okay, so she'd been the one in a bad mood last night. He was entitled. Except, he wasn't brooding or foul-tempered. It was more as if he had been biding his time before taking on an unpleasant task.

"No," he said. "I was wanting to talk to you, that's all."

"We *have* been talking. All through dinner. I told you about the tulip fields and Pete Timmons's present for his wife. You complained about the bridal shower for a dispatcher. That's talking."

Even though Grant was really good at hiding what he was thinking, she could see that he was holding some kind of internal debate.

Alarm jolted her. He'd learned something he didn't want to tell her.

"What is it?" She heard her voice rising.

He made up his mind. The muscles in his jaw bunched, then relaxed, and he stood and held out a hand to her. "Come here."

Kat stared up at him and that outstretched hand. "Why?"

He waggled his fingers.

She was both tempted and worried. Was it so bad, whatever he had to tell her, that he wanted to offer comfort in advance? What could *be* that bad? Her eyebrows drew together. He couldn't suspect *Joan*...

"Damn it, Kat." Patience evaporating, he grabbed her and lifted her from the chair. "What do you think I'm going to do, apply thumbscrews?"

"I don't know." She eyed his deep frown warily. "You're the one making a mystery out of this."

He expelled air with what might have been a growl. "It's lucky I didn't go for candlelight and bended knee. You'd probably think I was planning to slit your throat."

She gaped at him. Her mouth moved a couple of times before she managed to say, "Candlelight?" *Bended knee?*

His fingers tightened on her arms. His voice took on a rough timbre. "I'm trying to ask you to marry me, Kat."

CHAPTER FOURTEEN

"MARRY YOU?" KAT EXCLAIMED. "Are you crazy?"

The minute the words were out, Kat wished she could pull them back. Grant's face went blank, expression wiped clean as if it had never been. After a long pause, he said, "You know how I feel about you. We're sleeping together. I wouldn't call asking the question crazy."

"Grant." She searched his face, feature by feature. Why did that nose, a little too big in context, those broad, blunt cheekbones, that permanently furrowed brow, make her heart drum every time she looked at him? Her ever-present panic fluttered again. What if he was fired and went away, so that she never saw him again? Would she survive?

She swallowed, although her throat was dry. It had never once, in all her life, occurred to her that she needed one person so much she might not be able to get by without him. She wanted to say, "Yes." She wanted to say it so much, she bit her lip to keep herself from opening her mouth at all.

He *was* crazy. Getting engaged to her, in the middle of this mess? Political suicide. What was he thinking?

Do I know how he feels about me?

"Why are you asking right now?" she asked slowly. "Think about how few people would say 'Wow! Isn't that great! Our police chief is marrying Fern Bluff's very own Black Widow.'"

"Don't say that."

"Why not?" she challenged. "You know that's what everyone thinks about me."

"You have more friends in town than you believe you do."

Did she? "Maybe," she conceded. "Business hasn't fallen off as much as I expected when all this started."

"There are plenty of people who'd congratulate us."

"And a few important ones who'd decide you didn't have enough judgment to continue on as police chief."

A muscle in his cheek spasmed. "I don't care, as long as I don't get fired before I find this nut who's threatening you."

"Would finding another job really be that easy if you left this one in disgrace?"

She saw the answer on his face. The answer she already knew.

"I'd find something."

"Grant, this is a silly thing for us even to be talking about right now." She tried to sound…breezy. Probably came closer to wretched.

His eyes bored into hers. "What about later?"

She was afraid to tell him. Afraid he'd take it as a promise, afraid he'd commit even more obviously to her. Afraid he'd make a sacrifice for her that he shouldn't make.

Wasn't this supposed to be the pinnacle of any woman's dreams? That the man she loved was willing to sacrifice everything for her? So why did his offer make her feel as if she were locked in that shed again? Kat wondered.

"I can't give you an answer now," she managed to say. "It wouldn't be fair." *To you.* But she didn't say that part.

His hands dropped from her arms. He took a step back and stared at her, his eyes very dark. "It's not such a good sign, is it, when you can't say a simple yes or no."

"Grant." Her fingernails bit into her palms. "What if I did kill Hugh?"

He didn't move. Didn't react in any way that she could see. Just looked hard at her. "That's ridiculous," he said finally.

"No. It's not. You've asked me before whether I did." She had to do this. She had to. For him. "You don't *want* to think I could have murdered Hugh. But you don't know. Not for sure. Do you?"

"Of course I know!" he snapped.

"Do you?" She put her hands on her hips. "Search your heart. I think you'll find a kernel of doubt in there. You've buried it deep, but it's still aggravating you, isn't it? Giving you a twinge every now and then. Because, whoa, what a mistake you're making if I'm not who you want to think I am."

He swore. "Why are you doing this, Kat?"

She was getting to him. She should be glad.

Pushing him away was the idea. It was the right thing to do.

"Because I think we need to be really, really honest." Suddenly she was yelling. "I don't want to marry a man who has those kinds of doubts. I deserve better than that!"

"What in hell…?" Looking both furious and baffled, Grant took a step closer to her.

Kat backed up, stumbled against her chair. She edged behind it and gripped the back with both hands. The singed feeling around her heart made her realize this wasn't all pretense. She hated, *hated,* knowing he must still wonder about her for all his protestations to the contrary. She knew she was a complicated person, that she'd never bared herself completely to anyone, including Grant. But if he loved her, really loved her, shouldn't he see her clearly?

"Say it!" she all but shrieked at him. "Say it. I could have killed Hugh." Very, very quietly, she said, "I could have."

"I'm not so sure the son of a bitch didn't deserve to get knocked off."

Kat flinched. She couldn't help it. So there it was. He was acknowledging that she had all the reason in the world to have murdered her philandering husband. After all, she'd come out of it smelling like roses, hadn't she? No, she'd come out of it *owning* the roses she sold.

"Wow." Suddenly she had a lump in her throat. "I'm glad we got that in the open. You know, Grant, I think I'd like it if you left now. Somehow the idea of going to bed with you doesn't really appeal to me tonight."

He looked dazed. Shell-shocked. His hands dangled at his sides as if he didn't know what to do with them. "Why are you doing this?"

"Because you brought up the idea of marriage, and there was too much we hadn't said."

He let out an incredulous huff of air. Bent his head. After a minute he reached up and pinched the bridge of his nose. It had to be a full minute before he lifted his head again and looked at her with bleak eyes. "I'll sleep on the couch."

"No."

He turned, just like that, and left the kitchen. Kat stood without moving. She heard him going upstairs. A few minutes later, he came down. When he reappeared in the doorway, he carried his packed duffel bag.

"I love you," he said quietly. "I've been so goddamned in love with you for four years, I'm sick with it. Think about that, Kat."

Then he left. The front door opened and shut behind him. She listened to the sound of the engine as he backed out of her driveway and left her alone.

Which was exactly what she'd wanted.

Except, it wasn't at all.

HE'D BEEN SO STUNNED, he had gone home last night. It wasn't until hours later that he realized he should have parked where he could see her house, or even bedded down on her back porch. Because of his hurt feelings, he had left Kat unprotected.

Grant drove by on his way to work and saw that her rental car was still there. His foot lifted from the gas and he stared at the house, wanting to see her passing in front of a window. A light go on or off. Something to tell him she was in there and okay. But there was nothing.

He could just imagine the reception he'd get if he knocked on her door and said, "Just checking."

All right. He'd call the nursery when it opened. Make sure she'd gotten there safely.

He did. A woman answered. Not Kat or Joan. Maybe the new one? When he asked for Kat, she said, "I think she's back in one of the greenhouses. Can I help you?"

Grant thanked her and lied, saying he'd stop by later.

Midmorning, the clerk at the Shop 'N Gas in town was held up at gunpoint. A local farmer, coming in to pay for his gas, saw what was happening and tried to tackle the robber. He got shot—not fatally, thank God for small favors—but bled all over the shiny linoleum floor. The clerk had hysterics and fainted. The strung-out idiot with the gun panicked and fled in his souped-up Mazda, slamming into a passing car. Radiator steaming, he tried to keep going, but didn't make it three blocks. By that time, Grant himself was there to wrestle him out of the car and facedown on the ground.

Grant studied the face of a boy who couldn't be more than sixteen. Swearing as he applied handcuffs, Grant then helped himself to the kid's wallet and walked back to his unit with the boy's driver's license in hand. Gosh, his estimate was off; the boy was no longer sixteen, he'd turned seventeen three weeks ago. He was a chronic runaway with an already lengthy rap sheet who'd left the last group home right before his birthday. Now he was hooked on meth, if Grant was any judge, and in serious trouble.

The whole thing pretty well ate up Grant's day. It reminded him why he'd settled more happily than he had expected into small town law enforcement versus the big city version. He didn't miss a nonstop diet of random shootings, drug-addicted kids and stores that had to have barred windows and employ security guards.

He did break free in time to watch Kat leave the nursery and make her way to the grocery store. He loitered on the street where he could just see one of the fenders of her car. Eventually, she pushed a laden cart out and, after putting her groceries in her trunk and restoring the cart to the front of the store, drove straight home. He parked a block away and saw her carry everything into her house.

Now what?

Neighbors were coming home. A girl rode her pink bicycle past. A fat tuxedo cat sauntered down the sidewalk. Down the block, a man cranked up his lawn mower.

Kat would be safe enough for now. Hell, Grant thought, he'd starve to death if he did nothing but follow her around. He'd missed lunch as it was. Since he couldn't remember the last time he'd shopped for groceries for his own kitchen, that meant eating out. And, unfortunately, *that* meant making nice with the citizens of his town, unless he wanted to waste the time to drive somewhere else.

He chose a downtown café that had good burgers and fries, exchanged a few greetings and ate quickly, trying to keep his head down.

Of course, he couldn't get lucky enough to have dodged the entire city council. Eugene Gedstad came in with his wife, who was still walking slowly after hip replacement surgery. Eugene was the next oldest council member after Otto, which meant he was probably seventy. His gaze zeroed in on Grant right away.

With a hand on his wife's arm, he stopped here in front of Grant's table. "See you took Otto's advice," he said.

Grant ground his teeth. *Don't be stupid. Don't be stupid.* "Busy day," he said, as though he hadn't understood what Eugene was saying.

"So I hear. Good thing you were there to take the guy down, instead of one of those kids you've hired trying to do it."

"Did you also hear that the guy was a kid himself?"

Eugene hadn't. Shirley expressed shock and regret. They talked about it for a minute before they went on to their table and Grant decided to skip the slice of key lime pie he'd been considering in favor of a quick getaway.

He went home, where he noticed that the shrub he'd bought all those weeks ago at the nursery had dried up from neglect. Well, damn, he thought, gazing at it. So much for the tender, loving care he'd meant to give it. What had Kat said it was called? A girl's name. Dinah or Dahlia or…Daphne. That was it. What Grant knew was that he'd spent a ridiculous amount of money on it, and now it was dead.

Feeling morose, he went into his house, which had a closed-up, musty feel, as if it had been long-abandoned. It was in his imagination, of course. He'd only been staying at Kat's for a few days. Not even quite a week.

He tried to think what he'd usually do when he got home, and came up empty. He didn't want to be here. Didn't like the house, which he'd stayed in when Rachel moved out. In four years, he hadn't bothered to replace the furniture she'd taken except for the bed. The dining room was empty; he ate at the breakfast bar in the kitchen. No sofa in the living room; his big recliner, a sturdy if ugly table where he could set the remote control and a beer, and a plasma TV were all he needed.

Man, his life was pathetic, he thought. Maybe Kat was right. Maybe he had gone a little crazy sometime in the past four years. Had he really believed that someday she'd fall into his arms and say, "I've loved you all this time, too?" Just because he could tell she felt some spark, too?

After a long time, he sank into his recliner and gazed at the blank television screen.

Was she right, too, that he had been harboring some doubt about whether she could be a killer?

Most people could kill under the right—or wrong—circumstances. He did believe that. Kat held a lot of hurt inside, but was a strong woman. Strong and ruthless weren't the same thing, though.

Killing in a fit of fury was one thing; hiding the body, lying to the police and coolly going on with your life was another altogether.

There were those who thought *cool* described Kat perfectly. And he couldn't deny that she had a talent for planning. Marketing, too. Did that translate to selling herself to the cops—specifically, to him?

No. His every instinct revolted. No. He didn't believe it. Her eyes gave too much away. She could be calm and utterly in control, while those blue eyes teemed with emotion. If you looked closely, she gave away what she was feeling. And when had he ever not looked closely at Kat Riley?

So what was that scene last night about? He mulled it over, considering what he knew and guessed about her. She was undeniably vulnerable, like all the women who had been conned by Hugh. Despite her fears, Kat had had the guts to take a chance on him. She was also strong enough to have accomplished more than Hugh had been able to with the business. Despite having to live with unanswered questions and nasty gossip after his disappearance, she'd maintained her grace and dignity. The one person she'd chosen to trust had let her down big-time.

Wouldn't that leave her unlikely to want to trust anyone else?

Grant laid his head back and groaned. Was that what happened? Had she chickened out about him?

Yeah, but why then had he had the sense that there was something calculated about every word she'd said, at least until the end when she'd seemed genuinely upset?

Maybe he'd blown it by introducing the subject of marriage too soon. She'd cautiously, bit by bit, let him into her life and then her bed. Maybe she could cope with sex but not commitment. He'd pushed too hard, and triggered a fight-or-flight reflex. Kat being Kat, she'd acted on both instincts.

After a moment, Grant gave a harsh laugh and scrubbed his hands over his face. Hell, it could be that *his* behavior was off, not hers. It sure didn't make sense that he hadn't given up and moved on years ago.

And maybe he should get realistic. Once he knew she was safe, he could do what he should have long ago. Make a clean break. Go back to Texas, maybe. He wouldn't mind being closer to his family.

But the emotion crowding his chest told him he wouldn't be doing any such thing. Leaving was even more unthinkable now that he'd made love with Kat, seen her face when she climaxed, felt her somehow tentative yet wondering touch. Heard her awed whisper, "I've never… I didn't know…"

Damn it, he couldn't be alone in what he felt. He couldn't. She was panicking and feeling she had to push him away, but she loved him. Her eyes hadn't lied to him.

She loved him. Grant sat up. She'd thought he was crazy to want to marry her. Was it even remotely possible that she was trying to save him from what she saw as his own idiocy?

He heard himself laugh, a low, hollow sound. He

was trying to save her, and she was trying just as hard to save him. Now, that made sense.

Well, damn.

AUTOMATICALLY NOTING the nearly empty parking lot, Kat said, "Helen, I'll be out back if you need me. I want to get that compost shifted before it starts to rain. Can you keep an eye on the cash register?"

Her new employee was out front in the covered area, rearranging the annuals which had begun to look rather picked over and disorganized. Shoppers were prone to picking up a sweet william, say, then deciding to go with an orange and yellow color scheme instead and plopping down the discarded choice among the zinnias. With rain threatening, business was slow today and Helen had volunteered for the task.

Helen turned, a black plastic flat in her gloved hands. "Sure. Unless you'd rather I shovel compost?"

"No." Kat made a face. "I feel like doing something strenuous and mindless."

Helen laughed. "Right."

Kat grabbed her own gardening gloves and made her way to the back, where the bins of compost, bark and shavings were hidden from browsers. Wallinger's was to deliver a truckload of compost later this afternoon. She wanted to consolidate what was left in one bin before the new load was dumped.

She slowed to glance into one of the greenhouses. The door had been hooked open, and Chad was in there, watering baskets of begonias. Kat didn't stop to say hi.

Instead, she located a wheelbarrow, pushed it into the nearly empty bin at the back of the last greenhouse, and began shoveling. Within minutes, she had to stop and take off her vest. A few minutes later, her sweatshirt joined the vest on top of the sidewall built of railroad ties. She got the first bin scraped down to hardpan and started on the second one. She distantly heard car doors slam and then voices; a few dedicated gardeners must have come shopping despite the gathering clouds.

At one point she glanced at her watch and decided to open the side gate in case the guy from Wallinger's came early. She unlocked the padlock and carefully pulled the chain-link gate open and anchored it, then went back to heaving one shovelful of compost after another into the wheelbarrow.

The muscles in her arms and shoulders began to burn. She welcomed the feeling. With spring, she spent most of her time helping customers, doing ordering or other administrative stuff and not enough of the hard physical labor that kept a plant nursery going. She missed it.

After dumping a load, she tackled the last corner. Ten more minutes and she'd be done.

She'd just plunged the shovel in to the loamy, dark compost when she thought she heard movement behind her. She started to turn. "Helen…?"

Something slammed into her head, bringing an explosion of pain. Her vision went dark. She crumpled to her knees, and felt herself toppling forward onto her face.

GRANT LEANED AGAINST the scarred wooden counter. "Ms. Sanderson, I do understand your reluctance to discuss any relationship you might have had with Hugh Riley. I'd appreciate any help you can give me, though. I can keep confidential anything you tell me."

Crystal Sanderson didn't look as if she had any intention of helping him. He couldn't even blame her. He'd driven by half a dozen times today, until he saw that the paneled truck with the logo of the home decor company was gone, presumably out delivering flooring. He'd parked and sauntered in to catch Ms. Sanderson alone in the front office. She was one of the partners in a business that sold and installed flooring, tile and window blinds. The fact that part of her job was to go to customers' homes and measure their floors and windows and show them samples had caught his attention. Her time couldn't be pinned down, any more than a real estate agent's could.

"I suppose it's my ex-husband who's claiming I had an affair." Her voice was sharp enough to cut glass. "I thought he'd gotten over it."

Interested, Grant said, "It?"

She glared at him. "Me."

"So your husband believed you did have a romantic or sexual relationship with Mr. Riley."

"Lee thought I had a relationship with the postman, the animal control officer, my father's male nurse…" She flung up her hands. "He was jealous of anybody male between the ages of fifteen and sixty. Do you get the picture?"

"Yes, ma'am. I apologize for raking all this up."

"Then why are you?"

Because I think you might have killed Hugh Riley.

"You misunderstand. I'm interested only in what you can tell me about Hugh Riley."

"*Did* you talk to Lee?"

"I have had no contact with your ex-husband, Ms. Sanderson."

"Then how…?" She broke off, her eyes filling with tears. "Oh, what difference does it make?"

Were her tears calculated or genuine? They were making him uncomfortable either way, but he wasn't going to let a little weeping stop him from prying open her past. He'd gotten as far as he could without actually talking to her and Annika Lindstrom, or breaking into their respective outbuildings to search for the rest of Hugh's remains. Since his second option was illegal, he'd settled on interviews as a next step.

Crystal was thirty-four years old, a brunette with hazel eyes and a centerfold figure that she seemed to be trying to play down with loose-fitting clothing. She wore tiny gold hoops in her ears and a minimum of makeup. Mascara, obviously, because it was starting to run.

She'd have appealed to Hugh, no question, Grant thought. By most men's standards, she was prettier than Kat, with a body that was lush instead of slender and strong. He could imagine an insecure husband being convinced that every other man lusted after her. Grant didn't feel even a twinge of sexual attraction, but then he couldn't remember the last time he'd taken a second look at any woman except Kat.

He waited while Ms. Sanderson blew her nose and dabbed at her eyes. At last she said in a hopeless voice, "What do you want to know? Whether I slept with Hugh? Why? That was years ago."

"So you did," he said gently.

She wrapped her arms around herself. "Yes! Yes! Okay? Once. I was so tired of being accused of cheating on Lee, I did it. And then I felt like crap. But I did do it. Are you satisfied?"

"Ms. Sanderson, I'm not here to make a moral judgment or to—" His cell phone rang, and he took a look at the number. Local, but he didn't recognize it. "Excuse me a moment," he said, and turned away, cursing the interruption. "Haller here," he said into the phone.

"Chief Haller, this is Joan Stover." She sounded upset. "I'm off today, but Helen just called me from the nursery. She can't find Kat."

"Is her car still there?"

"Yes. She was working out back, and…and she seems to have disappeared."

His stomach clenched with fear. "I'm on my way," he said hoarsely.

KAT MOANED. GOD, HER HEAD HURT. It hurt so bad another helpless groan escaped her. She fumbled a hand up to feel the back of her head, where she thought the pain started. Her hand didn't want to cooperate. Or her brain didn't know how to direct it. But finally she touched a huge lump up there and felt the sticky mat of her hair. At sluglike speed, she figured out what that meant.

Blood. It had to be blood.

Had she fallen? She didn't want to open her eyes. They hurt, too. Maybe she was in the hospital. But if she was, wouldn't they have cleaned up the blood? And…and this didn't *smell* like a hospital. It didn't smell like anything in particular.

What's the last thing I remember?

Digging. She'd been digging.

She felt like the shovel had connected with her head. Ugh. She had a vision of herself collapsing. Going to her knees, then falling forward. So maybe she was still lying there.

Except…she didn't smell compost, pungent and easily recognizable. And she wasn't lying down. She knew that much. She was sitting up. Oh, God. She *had* to open her eyes.

She was scared to open her eyes.

She heard herself breathing hard. Panting. She couldn't hear anyone else breathing. In fact, the silence was absolute, except for the smallest rustle when she moved, and her every exhalation.

Slowly, so slowly, Kat opened her eyelids. She was sitting in a car or truck, looking straight ahead through the windshield. Only, she was looking at a wall. No—not a wall, a tall garage door. She turned her head painfully to the right and saw through the side window what must be another vehicle, shrouded in a dustcover. And beyond that was a black pickup.

Her pickup.

Her heart jumped, began pumping hard. Oh, dear God. She was sitting in another truck, and she knew suddenly that it was familiar. She was in the passenger seat, where she'd always ridden. More scared than she could ever remember being, Kat turned her head the other way…and saw the crumpled heap of bones in the driver's seat.

Hugh's truck. Hugh.

She screamed and reached frantically for the door handle.

CHAPTER FIFTEEN

BEEP, BEEP, BEEP. THE TRUCK from Wallinger's backed in the side gate of the nursery, the driver's face visible in his side mirror.

Beyond one swift glance, Grant was impervious. He stood in the midst of one of the bins staring at the half-full wheelbarrow and the shovel that lay on the hard-packed ground where it had likely fallen from Kat's hands. A single heavy canvas glove lay beside it. The other was missing. He'd already seen her vest and sweatshirt draped over the sidewall of the bin.

A dark splotch on the ground caught his eye. *Shit, shit.* He crouched and touched the spot. His fingertips came away red with blood. It hadn't had time to dry.

"Is—is that blood?" The striken voice was that of the new employee, Helen.

"Yes." He couldn't have gotten another word out to save his life.

Kat's blood. She'd been hurt. Snatched.

She might already be dead.

"Send the truck back to Wallinger's," he said brusquely. "They can't unload. This is a crime scene."

"Yes. Okay." After a moment, the woman moved toward the truck, which had stopped.

Don't just react, Grant told himself. *Think.*

Crystal couldn't have snatched Kat. He'd been keeping an eye on her store. This had happened in the past hour, and he knew she'd been there.

Schultz farm. He'd go there first. But despite the sense of urgency that drove him, Grant grabbed his phone first and called the real estate office where Lisa Llewellyn worked. He knew the guy who'd established the office, got him on the line and asked if Ms. Llewellyn was in today.

"Yeah, sure," Bob Standish said. "Is this something I should know about?"

"Is she there right now? Has she left the office in the last couple of hours?"

"No," he said without hesitation. "Things are slow today. Weather puts people off, you know. Her door's open. I've gone by several times. She's making calls, trying to drum up some listings."

"You're sure."

"I'm sure."

"Then no, I was given some misinformation. Don't even tell her about this call."

"All right," Bob said, puzzled but cooperative. "Is there anything else I can do for you?"

"No. Thanks."

The truck from Wallinger's had rumbled into motion and was slowly pulling out through the gate. Helen stood waiting for further instructions.

"Here's what I want you to do," Grant said, not caring how curt he sounded. "Close the nursery again. Ask any customers that are here now to stay.

A couple of officers will be here soon to talk to them, and to the other employees."

She nodded.

"We need to find out if anyone saw anything. Noticed a vehicle out here on Hazeltine Road."

"I didn't," she said.

"All right. Find out who was last to see Kat. When. I've got a couple of ideas, and I'm going to follow up on them."

"This has something to do with the bones and the fire, doesn't it?"

"That's safe to assume."

He left her his phone number and kept going when she stopped to talk to a man who was working in one of the greenhouses. There were only three cars in the parking lot besides his and Kat's. All belonging to employees? He hadn't seen anyone else around.

He drove out of the nursery, waited for an opening in traffic and then turned immediately onto Hazeltine. Calling into dispatch, giving clipped instructions, he drove faster than he should have. Once he reached the end of the pavement, a cloud of dust rose behind him.

Nothing looked any different at the farm. He peered in windows of the house and barn, and rolled up the doors of the two garages. Nothing. He felt the first drizzle on his face as he got back in his car.

He was going to Annika Lindstrom's next. By God, he was going to look inside every outbuilding on her property no matter how many laws he was violating. He'd put bolt cutters in the trunk of his car a few days ago, so he would be ready.

What scared the crap out of him was to think that his whole theory about Hugh's death was way off base. If he was wrong, if Annika had never been one of Hugh's lovers, then Kat was dead.

Simple as that. They'd never find her in time.

"No." The word ripped out of his throat, leaving it raw.

He put his squad car in gear, swung in a wide circle and jammed his foot down hard on the gas.

KAT LANDED HARD ON THE concrete floor of the garage. Hard enough that she felt her brain wobble and her vision faded again. *No, no, please,* she thought desperately. *Don't let me lose consciousness.*

She knelt there for a minute, two minutes, the heels of her hands and her knees hurting fiercely, before her vision gradually cleared. She scrambled behind the shrouded car as if she were an animal diving for a burrow.

She was in one of those big metal garages. There were two double garage doors, both closed, and a side door beyond Hugh's truck. She didn't see anyone else. Her head turning, she made her cautious way to her own truck. The key was in the ignition. She could drive away, if the garage doors weren't locked.

What were the chances of that?

She tugged, trying to lift one. It creaked but wouldn't lift. She rushed to the other and tried, with no more success. There were rails above, but no automatic opener.

She tried the side door next. The handle turned,

but there seemed to be a dead bolt just above that could only be opened with a key.

Kat heard herself whimpering. This was worse than being trapped in the shed. Whoever had brought her here couldn't let her leave, not now that she'd seen Hugh's truck and bones. It must have been here all this time, she realized, his body slowly decomposing. The seat cover had rotted beneath the bones. Kat shuddered at the idea of what the body had done, just propped there, staring sightlessly forward until it crumpled in on itself.

She imagined herself sitting for eternity next to Hugh in his old pickup, her own body melting into the upholstery of the seat, until eventually there was only crusted stuffing and rusting springs and bones.

Every breath shuddered in and out.

Don't panic. Find something to use as a weapon.

She didn't see any racks of tools. The garage was spotless and remarkably empty but for the row of vehicles.

There was a second covered vehicle beyond her pickup. Who covered their cars, inside a garage? Kat hurried over and lifted the heavy canvas. She saw a running board and a gleaming burgundy finish. The car was an antique, the kind an owner would take out once or twice a year to display at a show or drive in the Fourth of July parade. It had beautiful leather upholstery and was completely empty. She tiptoed back and lifted the other cover. Another antique. Something about the style made her think gangsters. Late 1920s or early 1930s then.

She'd never been especially interested in old cars,

but hadn't she heard that someone she knew collected them? With her head pounding, it was hard to think.

There was a tire iron in her truck. That was the closest thing to a weapon she could think of. When she took it out of the well that hid the spare tire, she banged it against the metal body of the truck and cringed. When she froze and listened, she heard nothing.

What about Hugh's truck? He often left tools in it. There were sure to be things like a rake and a shovel and who knew what else. Frightened as she'd never been in her life, she crossed the short open space back to his truck and looked into the bed.

A skull leered up at her.

With a cry, she leaped back. *Oh God, oh God.* She stared at the truck, hating the little gasps that she couldn't seem to stop making.

You knew there was another body. Remember? Two pelvises?

Okay. Nobody long dead could hurt her. She crept back and looked again. An entire human skeleton lay there.

No—not entire. The pelvis was definitely missing. Okay. This was a woman. There was a hole in her skull that didn't belong there. If Hugh had been shot, it wasn't in the head.

Kat saw a bundle of clothing. She reached in gingerly and separated one piece from another. She recognized the shirt as Hugh's, the one he'd been wearing that morning. And—God—those were his boxer shorts. His work boots lay there, a woman's athletic shoe atop them, another a few feet away. None of the clothes seemed to be bloody. Which meant… It meant Hugh and the woman had already been naked when they died. Surely they hadn't been having sex in the back of the pickup? It was dirty and the ribbed metal bed would be horribly uncomfortable. Hugh had never bought a rubber lining.

Does it matter? Kat thought semihysterically. They were dead. *She'd* be dead if she couldn't escape from this garage before the killer returned.

Or would anybody return at all? Maybe she'd be left to die in her own good time. No, no, no! That didn't make any sense. Starving must take forever. She could make an awful racket if no one came. Maybe even batter her way through the garage door with her truck.

Maybe, she thought, she should try to do that now. *Before* anyone came.

But she was too late. She heard the snick of a lock, and then the side door swung open.

GRANT TURNED ON LIGHTS and siren before he reached the highway. As he roared into town, cars scattered to get out of his way. He switched off both lights and siren a quarter of a mile before he reached Annika Lindstrom's place. He didn't want to alert her if she was holding Kat there.

He skidded to a stop on the shoulder of the road in front of the neighbor's place. Her hedge still blocked the sight of her house from him. Then he got out, grabbed the bolt cutters and unholstered his weapon. Moving fast, he rounded the hedge.

No vehicles were in the circular drive. The windows of the house were blank. Bending low, he ran to the garage. The Land Rover was in there, the Camry was missing.

Had she not brought Kat here?

It's not Annika Lindstrom at all. Why the hell did you think it was? You've completely screwed up. Some nut has Kat while you're chasing the thinnest of possibilities.

Damn it, he had to keep his cool. She wouldn't have Kat at the house or garage. He knew that. If she'd taken her anywhere, it would be one of those metal buildings in back.

He started that way, and the cell phone on his belt rang.

"HELLO, KAT." ANNIKA Lindstrom walked in, as calm as if she'd just arrived at the nursery to shop for the newest *Papaver orientale* hybrid. Her chinos held a crisp crease, and the striped shirt that she wore tucked in had the silky sheen of expensive cotton. Her blond hair was, as always, sleekly styled. Without looking away from Kat, Annika locked the door behind her, then pocketed the keys.

Kat backed away, her eyes fixed on the handgun Annika held.

"I'm so glad you've woken up. I thought you deserved to know why I have to kill you. I was getting a little bit impatient, though. You were unconscious longer than I expected."

And to think I accused Grant of being crazy, Kat

thought. *I didn't know what crazy was.* Mouth dry, gripping the tire iron with a hand that was trembling, she edged around the rear bumper of one of the shrouded cars. She had to try to keep a car between her and Annika.

"Nothing to say?" The other woman's mouth twisted, making her, at that moment, ugly. "Did you always wonder whether Hugh might be alive? Or did you know?"

"I didn't know."

"He took that little slut to the same place we always met. I thought we were meeting, you see." Annika passed Hugh's truck, keeping pace with Kat's retreat. "When I got home, I found a phone message. He'd cancelled. He blamed you. You were making a scene, he said. He couldn't get away."

Could she reason with Annika? Kat put one hand on the hood of her truck as she circled it. "He lied to both of us."

"Why wouldn't you let him go?" Annika asked, as if this was a reasonable conversation. "You knew he didn't love you. Why try to hold on to a man who doesn't want you?"

"He never asked for a divorce. I didn't know—" Her voice cracked. "I wondered if he was seeing other women, but I didn't know."

Annika took a couple of shockingly quick steps to keep Kat in sight. "He fell in love with me. Me!"

Kat banged her shin on a bumper in her own hurried retreat. The pain barely registered. "No. He had affairs. Lots of affairs. You weren't any different from the rest."

"That's not true. We were going to get married. As soon as you agreed to the divorce."

"He lied," Kat repeated.

Annika visibly calmed herself. "I felt sorry for you. After I found him with *her*. I felt sorry for both of us. But lately I realized that you didn't love him at all. I mourned him, and you were glad he was gone."

"No." Could she throw the tire iron and have any hope of connecting with Annika's head? This had to be the world's most bizarre slow-motion chase, with the two of them doing figure eights around the garaged vehicles. "I wasn't glad. I was never glad."

"You liked being in charge of the nursery. Doing everything he dreamed of doing and taking credit for it."

What if she dropped and shimmied underneath the truck? She could scramble fast and try to grab one of Annika's legs. Kat edged around behind the truck as Annika circled the front.

"I finally knew at that awards banquet that you weren't sorry at all about what you did to him. There you were, glorying in all that attention and exchanging significant looks with our police chief. You had an affair with him, didn't you? And all the time you pretended your heart was breaking because Hugh wanted a divorce."

"He never asked for one. I didn't know."

"You're lying!" Annika shrieked, and lunged around the fender.

GRANT BARELY PAUSED TO TALK to one of his officers, Ernie Butler, who informed him that unfortunately Helen had been the last to actually see Kat. They couldn't narrow down the time of her abduction any more closely. Hoping like hell Annika, if she was nearby, hadn't heard his phone ring, Grant stowed it and ran. A narrow, paved drive passed behind the greenhouse and disappeared into an opening in the tall back hedge. When he rounded the hedge and the two metal garages came in sight, Grant saw the Camry parked in front of one. The hard kick of satisfaction he felt was followed by fear.

Let Kat be here. Let her be alive.

The Camry was empty. Unlocked. He popped the trunk and found it empty, too, but for a single canvas gardening glove. He stared at it for a long, shattering moment. Then he saw the smear of blood on the custom-fitted rubber mat that covered the carpeted interior.

And he heard a woman's voice. His head came up sharply. Was it coming from within the metal building?

A shot rang out. The bullet pinged on metal. He shouted, and heard an answering shout from inside.

KAT HAD SEEN THE INTENT in Annika's eyes and thrown herself behind one of the shrouded cars just before the gun barked. The car vibrated when the bullet struck it.

Annika would be coming. Around the front or back? Kat made a decision and scrambled toward the front of the car.

Did she hear a shout outside? How could that be? But she yelled, "Help!" and kept going.

The rush of footsteps came behind her. Kat turned and swung the tire iron as the gun went off again. She didn't feel anything. She wasn't sure she would even if she'd been shot. The tire iron connected with Annika's shoulder and she lurched and dropped the gun. It skidded on the concrete floor. Kat thought of diving for it, but Annika was closer and already leaping toward it.

Kat took the chance and ran, yelling. Please let there be someone outside the garage, someone who'd heard the shots. But whoever it was wouldn't be able to get in, she realized with despair.

She leaped into her truck, turned the key in the ignition and heard the engine roar to life. Emergency brake. Had to release it. The side window glass exploded and something smacked the seat inches from her head. She flung herself sideways and down at the same time as she pressed her foot hard on the accelerator. The truck leaped forward and slammed into metal.

IT TOOK BOTH HANDS TO OPERATE the bolt cutters. Grant had to set his Glock down. He didn't quite have the padlock cut through when a vehicle inside started up and collided hard with the door.

Bang! Another shot. He was cursing as he applied all his strength.

The garage door shuddered as the vehicle hit it again. *There.* The padlock fell loose. He pulled it off and lifted the garage door. As he did he grabbed his gun and threw himself to the side.

A black pickup truck exploded through the opening. From this angle, he couldn't see anyone behind the wheel. Behind it ran a woman brandishing a handgun. She pulled the trigger and the bullet pinged on metal again. The rear window of the cab had already been shot out. Hell, the windshield, too. Had Kat fallen, dead or badly injured, her foot still jammed on the accelerator?

But just as he yelled, "Police! Drop the gun!" in his peripheral vision he saw taillights flash red.

Annika Lindstrom swung toward him, the gun pointing at him and her eyes insane.

Grant's finger tightened, and he shot with deadly accuracy.

In the wake of the deep bark of gunfire, the truck came to a stop, its nose buried in a yew hedge. Shaking, Kat crawled across the seat. If Annika was still coming after her, she should get out the far side. She wrestled the door open as the driver's side one opened. Making animal sounds of panic, she tumbled out seconds after her eyes sent to her brain the message that it was Grant who had opened that door, not Annika.

Grant. He had found her. Saved her.

He circled the truck so fast he was lifting her in

his arms almost as soon as she hit the asphalt. At first all he seemed able to do was swear, but finally, as he held her so tightly she couldn't breathe, he said roughly, "Kat! Oh, God, Kat. Where are you hurt? I didn't think I'd get here in time. I've never been so damned scared in my life. Tell me you're all right." He gave her a little shake.

"Annika. Where's Annika?"

"Dead," he said grimly. "I had to shoot her."

She heard a siren in the distance. Then another joining it, like the howl of a coyote answering the first. She burrowed against his broad, strong body. "You came."

A tremor ran through him. "Are you hurt?"

"No. I don't think so."

"You don't think…?" He laid her down and knelt above her. Tears were running down her face. She couldn't seem to help herself. "So damned scared," he said again, his hands moving over her, astonishingly gentle. But the tremor hadn't left him, and she saw the look in his eyes.

"I love you," she said, and suddenly a siren blasted so close her whole body jerked. Then she and Grant were surrounded by a swarm of other police officers and emergency medical personnel.

Grant backed away and let the EMTs take his place at her side, but his gaze never left hers.

IT WAS EVENING BEFORE THEY had a chance to be alone. The doctor who saw Kat decided she was concussed and should spend the night at the hospital for observation. She had her various scrapes and bruises treated. A bullet had grazed her upper arm and left an ugly gash.

Because he had been involved in the shooting, Grant called in county law enforcement. Kat told her story several times to various detectives.

Grant had followed her to the hospital and stayed with her until he was sure she was all right. He'd walked beside her wheelchair when they transported her upstairs to a room, and bent over to give her a quick kiss once she was settled into bed.

"I'll be back as soon as I can," he said. At the door he had stopped and taken another, long look at her. Her heart skipped a couple of beats at the expression on his face. She'd have sworn he'd aged years today. He'd torn the shoulder of his uniform shirt and skinned the back of one hand. But mostly it was the look in his eyes.

Kat stared helplessly back until he groaned, squeezed the back of his neck and departed.

Joan came and hovered, sitting with Kat and watching as she poked at the dinner an orderly brought. Helen and James both visited. Mike Hedin came by, but Joan drove him out of the room in short order.

"The nerve," she muttered, coming back to plop herself again into the chair beside the bed.

"Come on," Kat chided her. "How can you blame him? He's a journalist, even if he will get scooped by all the dailies. Plus, he's in the garden club."

"I'll bet the phone lines are burning up tonight."

"Yes." Kat pushed away the rolling table that held her meal. She wasn't very hungry.

She'd been given a couple of pain pills earlier. She didn't know what they were, but they had worked. They'd also left her feeling not-quite numb, but close. Wrapped in cotton batting.

Annika Lindstrom. The only passion she'd ever displayed was for her garden and the acquisition of a new perennial or rose that wasn't yet widely available. Otherwise, she'd never been anything but poised and pleasant. Except now Kat knew; underneath, Annika had simmered with hurt and rage.

"I'm glad I didn't kid myself that we were really friends," Kat said aloud.

Joan grunted agreement. "I wonder if anybody really knew her."

"Hugh sure didn't," Kat said wryly.

Of course, *she* hadn't known Hugh as well as she'd thought she did, either.

She eventually persuaded Joan to go home, and agreed that she'd take a day or two off work. "I'm not feeling too sharp," she admitted. "Besides, who knows whether the police are done with me?"

"What's a shame is that I don't suppose whoever buys Annika's house will want to keep her garden up." Joan shook her head and said, "I'll call in the morning."

Kat must have dozed, because when she opened her eyes Grant sat in the chair Joan had earlier occupied. He'd tugged his tie loose and rolled the cuffs of his shirt to expose hard muscle and sinew. He looked weary, but he was watching her.

"How are you?"

"I'm not too bad." She tried to smile. "Considering."

"Yeah." He squeezed his eyes shut momentarily. "Damn. I'm going to have nightmares about today for a long time."

"I never dreamed that you'd find me."

"You knew I was focusing on a couple of possibilities. Ms. Lindstrom was one of them."

He told her about the past couple of hours. "I'm on administrative leave for now," he said. When he saw her indignation, he raised one hand. "Calm down. It's routine. Nobody is arguing that I shouldn't have pulled that trigger."

"I should hope," Kat muttered, and subsided.

He smiled and stood so that he could gently run his knuckles over her cheek. "Head hurt?"

"Yes." She rested her face against his hand.

He traced her lips with the broad pad of his thumb. "You called me crazy."

Kat gave a small laugh, and winced at the way it jolted her head. "That's funny, because one of the first things I thought when Annika started talking is that now I knew what crazy really looked like."

He kept looking at her, his eyes dark and serious. "Did you mean it?"

"That you shouldn't throw your career away for me? Of course I meant it."

His hand had slid around to the back of her neck and was kneading. It felt unbelievably good.

"I've wondered if I wasn't crazy," he murmured. "Taking one look at you all those years ago and going down for the count. Waiting, when I had no idea whether you'd ever feel the same."

"I think," she said with difficulty, "I always did. You must have suspected."

"Yeah, once in a while our eyes would meet and I'd see something." He paused. "Kat, you said 'I love you.'"

"Yes," she whispered. "Of course I do."

"I know taking a chance on me can't be easy for you."

She felt her mouth curving. An absurdly giddy feeling swelled inside her. "Don't be silly. I'm not so dumb I don't recognize steadfast and faithful when I see it."

He grinned, but ruefully. "You make me sound about as exciting as a Saint Bernard."

"You are very sexy, and you know it." She reached for his free hand, which came between the bars of the railing and clasped hers, strong and warm and reassuring. "But I've got to tell you, steadfast and faithful really, really work for me."

Grant nodded. "I can see why that might be."

"Are you, um, planning to stay in Fern Bluff?"

"Yeah," he said, his voice deep and slow. "I like it here. You're here, and you have a business." He paused. "Unless you're disgusted with the gossip and want to move. Your call, honey."

"I love my nursery and…I guess I have more friends than I realized. You said that, didn't you? Carol Scammell called to tell me how many people are worried about me. I think she meant it." She took a deep breath and said in a rush, "But I'll sell the nursery and move with you if that's what you'd prefer."

Grant stared at her for the longest time, unblinking. Finally he released her hand and fiddled with the bed rail until he managed to lower it. Then he sat on the edge of the mattress and bent down until his lips brushed hers. It was the softest kiss she'd ever experienced. She lifted upward, wanting to deepen it.

"Thank you," he said, in a voice that sounded shaken. He lifted his head again. "I need you to know that I never believed you could have killed Hugh." A smile touched his mouth. "Even if it is in you to murder slugs."

"I wouldn't really blame you if you did wonder," Kat admitted. "I don't like to think it, but you almost had to. That isn't why I sent you away, you know."

"Yeah." He kissed her again. "I finally figured that out. You hurt me, though, Kat. You're going to have to learn to trust me."

The knowledge welled up in her. She had to try twice before she could say "I do." Her voice shook. "I do, Grant. And I love you."

"You'll marry me?"

"Yes. Oh, yes!"

He made a rough, growly sound and abruptly kissed her with serious purpose. His teeth found her lower lip and his tongue plunged deep in her mouth once, twice. But he was the one to ease back. "You don't need this. You've already got the headache of the century." He only smiled at her squeak of protest. "We've got plenty of time, love. I'm going to sit right here tonight. I'm not going to leave you. And tomorrow we're going to think about putting both our houses on the market and buying one that'll be ours. We'll get a wedding license."

Suddenly, she wanted to laugh. "Are you in a hurry?"

His answering grin wiped the exhaustion and tension from his face. "Seems to me," he said, "that I've waited long enough. What do you think?"

"I think," she said softly, "that you've been very, very patient. And I love you." The laugh bubbling inside her began to transmute into tears. Abruptly she flung her arms around his neck and held on hard. "Just…don't ever leave me, Grant."

"Never," he murmured. "Never." And he kissed her again.

* * * * *

COMING NEXT MONTH

Available April 12, 2011

#1698 RETURN TO THE BLACK HILLS
Spotlight on Sentinel Pass
Debra Salonen

#1699 THEN THERE WERE THREE
Count on a Cop
Jeanie London

#1700 A CHANCE IN THE NIGHT
Mama Jo's Boys
Kimberly Van Meter

#1701 A SCORE TO SETTLE
Project Justice
Kara Lennox

#1702 BURNING AMBITION
The Texas Firefighters
Amy Knupp

#1703 DESERVING OF LUKE
Going Back
Tracy Wolff

You can find more information on upcoming
Harlequin® titles, free excerpts and more at
www.HarlequinInsideRomance.com.

REQUEST YOUR FREE BOOKS!
2 FREE NOVELS PLUS 2 FREE GIFTS!

Harlequin

Super Romance®

Exciting, emotional, unexpected!

YES! Please send me 2 FREE Harlequin® Superromance® novels and my 2 FREE gifts (gifts are worth about $10). After receiving them, if I don't wish to receive any more books, I can return the shipping statement marked "cancel." If I don't cancel, I will receive 6 brand-new novels every month and be billed just $4.69 per book in the U.S. or $5.24 per book in Canada. That's a saving of at least 15% off the cover price! It's quite a bargain! Shipping and handling is just 50¢ per book in the U.S. and 75¢ per book in Canada.* I understand that accepting the 2 free books and gifts places me under no obligation to buy anything. I can always return a shipment and cancel at any time. Even if I never buy another book, the two free books and gifts are mine to keep forever.

135/336 HDN FC6T

Name _____ (PLEASE PRINT)

Address _____ Apt. #

City _____ State/Prov. _____ Zip/Postal Code

Signature (if under 18, a parent or guardian must sign)

Mail to the **Reader Service:**
IN U.S.A.: P.O. Box 1867, Buffalo, NY 14240-1867
IN CANADA: P.O. Box 609, Fort Erie, Ontario L2A 5X3

Not valid for current subscribers to Harlequin Superromance books.

**Are you a current subscriber to Harlequin Superromance books
and want to receive the larger-print edition?
Call 1-800-873-8635 or visit www.ReaderService.com.**

* Terms and prices subject to change without notice. Prices do not include applicable taxes. Sales tax applicable in N.Y. Canadian residents will be charged applicable taxes. Offer not valid in Quebec. This offer is limited to one order per household. All orders subject to credit approval. Credit or debit balances in a customer's account(s) may be offset by any other outstanding balance owed by or to the customer. Please allow 4 to 6 weeks for delivery. Offer available while quantities last.

Your Privacy—The Reader Service is committed to protecting your privacy. Our Privacy Policy is available online at www.ReaderService.com or upon request from the Reader Service.

We make a portion of our mailing list available to reputable third parties that offer products we believe may interest you. If you prefer that we not exchange your name with third parties, or if you wish to clarify or modify your communication preferences, please visit us at www.ReaderService.com/consumerschoice or write to us at Reader Service Preference Service, P.O. Box 9062, Buffalo, NY 14269. Include your complete name and address.

HSR11

*Selene wanted nothing to do with the father of her son,
Alex; but Aristedes had other plans...that included them.*

*Read on for an sneak peek from
THE SARANTOS SECRET BABY by Olivia Gates,
available April 2011, only from Harlequin Desire.*

"You were right to turn my marriage offer down," Aristedes said.

And Selene found her voice at last, found the words that
would not betray the blow he'd dealt her. "Thanks for letting me know. You didn't have to come all the way here,
though. You could have just let it go. I left yesterday with
the understanding that this case is closed."

Before the hot needles behind her eyes could dissolve
into an unforgivable display of stupidity and weakness, she
began to close the door.

The door stopped against an immovable object. His flat palm.

"I can't accept that." His voice was low, leashed.

What did her tormentor mean now? Was he ending one
game only to start another?

She raised eyes as bruised as her self-respect to his,
found nothing there but solemnity and determination.

Before she could voice her confusion, he elaborated. "I
never let anything go unless I'm certain it's unworkable. I
realize I made you an unworkable offer, and that's why I'm
withdrawing it. I'm here to offer something else. A work-
ability study."

She leaned against the door, thankful for its support and
partial shield. "Your son and I are not a business venture
you can test for feasibility."

His gaze grew deeper, made her feel as if he was trying
to delve into her mind, take control of it. "It's actually the

other way around. I'm the one who would be tested."

She shook her head. "Why bother? I know—and *you* know—you're not workable. Not with me."

His spectacular eyebrows lowered over eyes she felt were emitting silver hypnosis. "You're right again. Neither you nor I have any reason to believe that isn't the truth. The only truth. It might be best for both you and Alex to never hear from me again, to forget I exist. But then again, maybe not. I'm only asking for the chance for both of us to find out for certain. You believe I'm unworkable in any personal relationship. I've lived my life based on that belief about myself. I never really had reason to question it. But I have one now. In fact, I have two."

Find out what happens in
THE SARANTOS SECRET BABY by Olivia Gates,
available April 2011, only from Harlequin Desire.

SPECIAL EDITION

Life, Love, Family and Top Authors!

In April, Harlequin Special Edition features
four *USA TODAY* bestselling authors!

FORTUNE'S JUST DESSERTS
by *MARIE FERRARELLA*
Follow the latest drama featuring the ever-powerful
and passionate Fortune family.

YOURS, MINE & OURS
by *JENNIFER GREEN*
Life can't get any more chaotic for Amanda Scott.
Divorced and a single mom, Amanda had given up on
the knight-in-shining-armor fairy tale until a friendship
with Mike becomes something a little more....

THE BRIDE PLAN (*SECOND-CHANCE BRIDAL* MINISERIES)
by *KASEY MICHAELS*
Finding love and second chances for others is
second nature for bridal-shop owner Chessie.
But will *she* finally get her second chance?

THE RANCHER'S DANCE
by *ALLISON LEIGH*
Return to the Double C Ranch this month—where love, loss
and new beginnings set the stage for Allison Leigh's latest title.

*Look for these titles and others in April 2011
from Harlequin Special Edition, wherever books are sold.*

Harlequin®

A *Romance* FOR EVERY MOOD™

www.eHarlequin.com

SEUSA0411